ESCAPE TO THE COUNTRY

KIM NASH

Boldwood

First published in 2020 as *Escape to Giddywell Grange*. This edition first published in Great Britain in 2024 by Boldwood Books Ltd.

Cover Design by Head Design Ltd

Cover illustration: Shutterstock

A CIP catalogue record for this book is available from the British Library.

Paperback ISBN 978-1-83603-602-9

Large Print ISBN 978-1-83603-601-2

Hardback ISBN 978-1-83603-600-5

Ebook ISBN 978-1-83603-603-6

Kindle ISBN 978-1-83603-604-3

Audio CD ISBN 978-1-83603-595-4

MP3 CD ISBN 978-1-83603-596-1

Digital audio download ISBN 978-1-83603-598-5

Boldwood Books Ltd
23 Bowerdean Street
London SW6 3TN
www.boldwoodbooks.com

To Ollie

My world!

You fill every day with sunshine.

You are handsome, brave, funny, kind and just wonderful and are growing up into the most amazing young man that your papa would be so very proud of. I know I am.

Dream big, my darling, you can achieve anything that you put your mind to, but don't ever change!

Thank you for being my son.

Love you

Xxx

1

Anticipation and nervous energy were making me feel sick to the stomach right now. I was trying to hold it all together while I pottered around the kitchen at work, laying out cups and saucers and a plate of chocolate biscuits ready for the meeting.

It was soooo exciting. I'd been like a cat on a hot tin roof all weekend. Instead of making the most of the gorgeous July weather, I'd been inside brushing up on my presentation skills and making sure I could go in there and promote my backside off.

There'd been so much talk around the office for the last couple of weeks. There was definitely something big going down. I'd worked for Ronington's PR and Marketing for twelve years and I could tell there was something on the cards because of all the secrecy that had been going on. There had been lots of meetings recently with the accountants and solicitors and, before she left the office on Friday lunchtime, Celine, the managing director, said she wanted to see me first thing on Monday. Celine was my idol. She was elegant, dramatic, stunning and just amazing. She took no crap from anyone. She was a badass. If I could have been anyone in life, I'd wanted to be her.

Everyone in the office had heard what she'd said to me.

'First thing Monday morning, Madison, I need to see you. It's very important.'

They'd all been saying that it was my time; that after all these years, the company had recognised my hard work and commitment. All the early mornings and late nights were going to finally pay off. All those miles of driving my company car up and down the country meeting clients. All the times I'd had to cancel going along to things that my friends were going to, the times I'd had to cancel seeing my mum because I'd had to work. The arrangements I'd had to cancel. The relationships I'd jeopardised. They were all heading to this exact place and time. This was what it was all for!

It was my time.

Melissa, the MD's operations director and right-hand woman who had worked at the company for about a million years, was about to go on maternity leave. Everyone had been buzzing around me, saying that there was absolutely no shadow of a doubt that I'd be formally promoted from my role as senior sales executive to operations director. After all, I'd been practically doing the job for the last couple of years, working alongside her. I was pretty damn sure I was going to be made a director.

I was so ready for this; so ready to fill her boots and make that job mine. It was what I'd always dreamed of and I'd been thinking about it all weekend. On Saturday I'd bought myself a new promotion-worthy power suit. I had a ton of other work suits, but for this meeting today I wanted something special so I opted for a navy-blue trouser suit and a light flowery camisole top to soften the look. I'd had my highlights touched up and nails polished this weekend, and if I said so myself, with my hair scraped back in a tight bun, bright red lippy for a bit of extra confidence and a pair of red high heels to finish it off, I looked immaculate.

Even though I was feeling apprehensive, I wasn't going to let anyone see that. I'd built up a persona over the years of being really cool, calm and ultra professional, and I'd never let the people I work with think anything else. I put on a bloody good show, I can tell you. Inside, there were times when I was totally lacking in confidence, my nerves in tatters, and I'd be shaking like a leaf, but I would never let on to anyone – I didn't let people get close enough to me.

I just wanted to show Celine that I was the perfect person to take the company forward and ensure it ran smoothly and efficiently.

* * *

I was in a world of my own while making the tea and I thought about the lady I saw every morning, when I drank my first coffee of the day while overlooking the lake from my lounge window. I wasn't sure why she'd just popped into my mind. She fascinated me, and I wondered about her life. She always looked glamorous, immaculately dressed even when walking her dog, and she ambled along in a leisurely way as if she had not a care in the world. So very different to me. I might have looked like I was in control, but most of the time I felt completely stressed out, always someone to call, to email or to have a meeting with. Today she was meandering along in flowery navy Joules wellies (that looked like they'd never been through a puddle in their life), figure-hugging jeans, a cashmere jumper (which she seemed to have in a million different colours – today's was powder-blue) and what looked like a Gucci scarf tied air-hostess-style around her slim neck, and a fake fur gilet (at least I hoped it was fake!). I wished I was less stressed. I loved my job completely but it was so full on. This promotion should have meant a more office-based role, so I could cut down on the travelling. That should definitely take away some of the pressure I seemed to currently work under.

You never knew what went on in someone's life, did you? I wondered how she filled her day. Did she work? If she did, what job did she do? If she didn't, what did she do with herself all day? Did she have children? Grandchildren, even? Did she have a husband? A lover? What was her story? I was totally intrigued by her.

Watching them walking together, her dog tucked closely into her leg, tugged at my heartstrings, and they were still preying on my mind now; the way he looked up at her from time to time for her approval and the way she smiled back at him, chattering away to him. He sat for a treat along the way and she laughed and said something to him before she handed him one. I wondered now what she'd said. They seemed to have a really special relationship and there was a tiny bit of me that was a tad envious. The connection they had made me yearn for a dog. I'd always wanted one but it had never been the right time.

I'd have loved a true companion to share my life with. Someone to go home to at night after a hard day, to babble away to and who loved you unconditionally. Someone who didn't care if you a had a spot on your chin, or if you were in your jimjams, or didn't have your lippy on. Most people would have said that should be a person, but after what happened with Jamie, I thought I'd be better off with a dog than a human. However, with all the white furnishings in my apartment, I didn't suppose my landlord would even consider me having a dog, and with my hectic career, it wouldn't have been fair on a dog either. It was too much of a commitment right now, especially as this promotion was in the bag, so I'd parked the idea for way into the future.

* * *

The kettle boiled, breaking me from my daydream. I poured the water over the teabags in the pot and took a deep breath before picking up the tray and making my way across the main office, trying to balance everything as I knocked on the door to Celine's office and opened the door with my hip. She was the first one in the office every morning. Goodness knew what time she got up but I knew she didn't see her kids before she came to work as she was in the office by 7 a.m. every day and it took her an hour to get here. They must have been in bed before she got home at the other end of the day too, as she was normally the last one in the office apart from on a Friday when she finished at two. It must have been great to have a live-in nanny, but surely her children must have spent more time with her than they did with their parents.

I gulped and felt melancholy as I thought that if I was ever lucky enough to have children, that wasn't the way I'd want to bring them up. I'd want to be the one who walked their children to school, holding hands and chattering as we walked up the street. Couldn't think about that right now, though. And the hours that she kept wouldn't bother me. For the last few years, it wasn't as if I'd had anyone waiting at home for me, even though it might have been nice if there was, so perhaps it would have taken some of the pressure off her a little too. It was just a great solution for everyone.

Celine looked up from her desk as I walked in, and I noticed that a frown crossed her brow then disappeared as quickly as it arrived, before she stood to greet me with what appeared to be a nervous smile, not her normal cheery composure. Perhaps she'd had a bad night's sleep.

'Madison, dahling, good morning. Come, come. Let me take that tray from you.'

She placed the tray on the coffee table and invited me to sit while she poured the tea.

'Madison, you've worked here now for many, many years?' She sat on the sofa directly opposite me and sipped her tea.

'Just over twelve actually, Celine.'

'Wow, doesn't time fly.' She smiled at me and I realised that she was beginning to look old, with the start of wrinkles around her eyes and frown lines that I hadn't noticed before. 'You've shown such a sterling commitment to the company over the years and we couldn't have asked for a better ambassador for the business. You've brought in millions of pounds of revenue over that time.'

I smiled at her, so happy that she'd recognised everything I'd been working towards.

'You've also been one of the most loyal members of staff we've ever had. People have come and gone over the years, yet you've remained here by my side, doing a job that is incredibly important to the company and to me personally and going over and above what was asked of you, taking on any task you were asked to do.'

'Thank you so much, Celine. Working here is not just a job to me, it's my way of life. I love it here.' I felt a million dollars, so proud of her words and so glad that she understood how hard I had worked over the years and that she was finally recognising it.

At that exact point, her mobile phone rang and she excused herself as she moved over to the window and explained briefly in hushed tones, that I could only just hear, to someone that she couldn't talk now, as she was in a very important meeting. That was me! She was in a very important meeting with *me*! I couldn't have been more pleased. I grinned from ear to ear.

I looked across at the other desk in the room where Melissa had sat before she'd left on Friday and imagined placing my new gorgeous planner there. I could put my pen pot on the right-hand side of the desk, and my rack of trays on the left.

Celine came back to the couch, sighed deeply and breathed in. 'I'm so sorry Madison, but I'm going to have to let you go.'

I smiled. 'Oh OK, no problem. Shall I come back in a little while when you are less busy? How long do you think you'll need?' I was disappointed of course, but it could wait until later. This was way too important to not make the most of.

'Madison.' She sighed loudly. 'I'm not sure you understand me. There are lots of changes taking place, and with the boom in the online marketplace, the company isn't doing anywhere near as well as it used to. There's no easy way to say this. I'm going to have to let you go. I have to make you and some of the other staff redundant. I'm so very sorry and it breaks my heart to do this to you but I have no other option. Either I make a few people redundant or we close completely. We're so sorry but we have to do this to give the business one last chance.'

Time stood still as I looked at her in disbelief.

'Let me go? Make me redundant?' I questioned. Was I hearing her correctly? Numbness set into my body. I couldn't move.

'Yes, dear, that's right. I really am sorry. It's not what I wanted but we've explored every option. The HR department will be in touch with you and I think you'll find that we've been most generous with your redundancy payout to show our thanks for your support over the years. I'm so sorry, Madison, but I have no alternative. As you know, we've had accountants and solicitors in over the last few weeks and we really have explored every option, but there is nothing else we can do.'

A tear plopped into the cup of tea I was holding and my hands began to shake.

'Now now, dahling, please don't cry. Let's not make this any worse than it already is.' She came across, took the cup from me and placed it on the table. Putting her arm around my shoulders, she tried to comfort me.

'Sometimes these things work out for the best. You'll have enough money to see you through for a good few months, while you look around. And you will find something else, something wonderful – just like you – and I shall give you a personal glowing reference. And if ever I need a right-hand woman in the future, you're the first person I'll call. I promise you that.'

She stood to indicate that our chat had come to an end and steered me towards the door. 'I think that under the circumstances, you should just pack up your things and leave now, before the others come into work and you have to face them. Less upsetting for everyone. I'll leave you to gather your things together. There should be a letter in the next day or so from the HR department, detailing your settlement. Your company car will need to be returned at the end of the month and if you could leave your company mobile phone on your desk, that would be good. I really am so sorry, Madison. I wish things could have been different.' Her voice broke and the strain on her face told me that this was hard for her too. 'Goodbye and thank you for everything. Good luck for the future.' She leaned into me and pecked my cheek nervously, blinking away tears before walking back to her desk.

And just like that, after twelve years of working at Ronington's PR and Marketing, I was dismissed.

* * *

In a daze, I stumbled to the kitchen and found an empty box and took it over to my desk. I packed away the mug that I had used every day for the last two years; the mug I was presented with, along with an engraved paperweight and an Amazon voucher, on my ten-year anniversary of working here. I packed away my pens and my note pads, my calculator and my ruler. I opened my desk and removed the emergency pair of natural-coloured tights and the headache tablets that I always had close at hand in case anyone needed them. The packet soups and the bars of chocolate that I kept handy for the late-night shifts got thrown into the box. There was nothing left. That was it. My drawers and my desk were empty.

Twelve years of hard work, dedication and a working life were packed away in a small box within a minute or two at the most. I did a small calculation in my head and worked out that I'd spent more time here in this office than I had at home awake. How very sad was that! I was officially redundant. I didn't have a job. My job was my life. What was I going to do? And more than that, what would people think? I'd told so many people that I had the best job and the best life, and that I was going to get promoted. They'd all be laughing at me now. My heart started to pound. I couldn't let it happen again. I couldn't go back to the point I'd been at before. My breathing started to become erratic and my head was banging. I thought I was going to have a panic attack.

Trying to remember all the mechanisms that I'd been taught to cope with this feeling, I tried to stay focused and leave the office by the stairs, to avoid bumping into anyone when I was coming out of the lift. I went through reception and out of the revolving doors, looking back only once. I walked around the corner from the entrance and took a seat on a nearby wall and started to inhale slowly and deeply through my nose, imagining my lungs filling with good air. Then I breathed out through my mouth, pushing all the bad thoughts away. I closed my eyes and concentrated on nothing else but my breathing until eventually it started to steady and I felt better, calmer, more grounded. Stumbling a little but taking it really slowly, I made my way over to the car park, where my black Mercedes C Class, my pride and joy, awaited me. As I sank into the driver's seat, I leant back into the headrest and did those breathing exercises. And I made my way home.

2

I drove home in a bit of a daze to my rented lakeside apartment. As I walked through the door and looked at its sparseness, something hit me. Because I was always at work or working away, I never spent much time there, but I saw it this morning through new eyes and as I looked around me trying to gain some comfort from the one place that you are supposed to feel safe and content, I realised that my home actually had no soul.

This was the place that Jamie and I had picked eight years ago, to spend what I thought would be the next chapter of our lives together. We chose the gorgeous Staffordshire lakeside setting as it was quite a trendy location, not too far from Stafford town centre where we both worked, and there were a few bars close by too. It was also the place that held so many memories; some great and some that I couldn't bear to think about.

Out of habit, I picked up my phone to see whether I had any missed calls and realised that actually no one was going to call me. This was my personal phone and all my work calls would be going to the phone I'd left at the office. I felt like I'd lost my purpose. It was a really strange feeling. Normally I would walk through the door and set up my Mac on the dining room table, and it was always there in the background. But now, I had no computer to turn on. There was no pinging of emails, or dinging of our automated work communication system. Just silence. Even when I took time off, which was very rare for me, I always checked in every day, just in case anything important came through. But now there was nothing to check. I supposed at the agency I liked to feel like I was indispensable but now I thought about it, was anyone, ever? Was anyone at work even thinking about me now and how I felt? I'd thought some of them may have phoned me, to be honest, after they'd been told the news, but I had heard not a sausage from a soul that I had spent every day of my life with. It was weird and deathly quiet. And I hated it.

I had some serious thinking to do. What did I do now? What would the time ahead hold for me? Ronington's PR and Marketing was everything to me; I'd thrown my heart and soul into that company for the last twelve years.

I really didn't know what I was going to do with myself going forward and it was hugely worrying. What was I going to do with the rest of my life? How was I going to cope? What was I going to do for money? Would I have to go back to live with Mum and give up this flat? How did I actually feel about that? So many questions were running through my mind and it was overwhelming.

When I heard of other people losing their jobs in this way, I always wondered what sort of person it happened to. But now I'd been made redundant myself, I realised that anyone could be affected like this. How life could change in a heartbeat. And right now the overriding feeling I had was that I clearly must be totally useless and they didn't want or need me.

I always thought I'd be settled in life by now, with a family of my own, juggling work and home life effectively, but at the grand old age of thirty-seven, I was single and childless. I'd always been the successful one, the one who left Giddywell to make a fantastic life for herself elsewhere. But now? I felt like such a loser. What would people think?

My heart began to beat faster once more as I focused again on what had happened to me. It had come as such a shock. This morning I was going to work thinking I was going to be promoted, and *bang*! Not only did I not get the promotion that I'd been expecting, but I also now didn't have a job at all.

As I started to feel nauseous again, I grabbed the back of the sofa for support. A wooziness took over my body and I had so much stuff going through my head, I felt like it was going to explode. So many questions to answer. I hadn't felt this discombobulated since everything happened with Jamie.

This wasn't me. My life was sorted. I was busy from early on a Monday morning to late on a Friday night and I worked most weekends too from home. Living alone and rushing around all the time meant that most days I didn't bother with breakfast, grabbing a sandwich from a petrol station which I ate while driving and dining on ready meals each night, which probably weren't all that good for my health or my weight. Which was probably why my backside wasn't getting any smaller these days.

I wasn't one for wasting time, even if it was just a few seconds. When I got up in the morning, I had my little routine where I filled the kettle and flicked it on while I went to the loo, so that the kettle was boiled when I got back, saving me valuable minutes of standing around doing nothing. While filling the sink with water to do the washing up, I'd be wiping the already sterile sides down. It was almost like I had to fill every second of my life with doing something.

I'm not sure when I started to do that. Probably when my thoughts began to overtake everything and I filled every second of my time with activity of some sort to stop me thinking. It struck me now though that I didn't know how to relax. And right now, I felt like I didn't even know what my purpose in life was. My breath started to speed up once more and I recognised the feeling that I hated. I was going to have to revert to my failsafe coping strategy which always calmed me down. I was going to have to make a list.

What did I need to do next? What steps did I need to take to move my life forward?

- *Buy a computer*
- *Buy an iPad*
- *Buy a car (in a month my company car will go back)*
- *Find a job*
- *Invest my redundancy money*
- *Write a CV (blimey, haven't done one of those for years!)*
- *Fill my time (that was a list on its own)*

The phone rang and Mum's name flashed up.

'Maddy, darling, it's me. Mum.' Normally I got quite annoyed when I received a call from Mum because a) she always called at the most inconvenient times and b) she always told me who it was despite the fact that her name flashed up in blooming big letters on the screen.

'I'm sorry to bother you. I know you must be busy, but do you have one minute for me to ask you a very quick question? I know I'm a pain and I won't keep you long. I promise. I just can't think of anyone else to ask.'

I realised that for the first time in a very long while, I had all the time in the world to chat to Mum and she sounded delighted when I offered to pop round early afternoon instead of chatting on the phone. She said she'd make me lunch. I tried to remember when I last saw her and thought it must have been a good couple of months ago. What sort of a daughter must I have been to not see my mum for that long, when she only lived twenty minutes away and for her to start the conversation with 'sorry to bother you'?

Looking at the clock, I realised that there were still three hours before I was due to see her. What had happened this morning was only just over an hour and a half ago, yet it seemed like hours had passed. My head was thumping, but I realised that I didn't have to find the answers right this very minute, so I tumbled into bed, pulled the covers up over my shoulders as I felt a little cold and shivery, and surprisingly, slept.

* * *

When I woke, it took a couple of minutes for me to remember why I was in bed when it was light outside. Looking at the bedside clock, and realising that it was 12.24, reality came flooding back and hit me like a ton of bricks. *Breathe, Maddy. Breathe!* I told myself.

While I really wanted to wallow in bed and feel sorry for myself, I realised that could only be the start of a very slippery slope, so I dragged myself out of bed and over to my walk-in wardrobe, where I saw that my cleaner must have been in at some point early this morning as it was filled with my ironed clothes.

I supposed that was something I would have to start doing for myself if I didn't have a job. How was I going to afford a cleaner? And did I really need one when I was at home all day? I hadn't done my own cleaning for years.

Instinctively, I went to grab a suit and blouse, then realised I was going to Mum's so I chose a pair of jeans and a casual shirt that was right at the back and that I hadn't worn for ages, because I was always working. Even when I was at home, I always wore something reasonably smart, just in case I had to go into work at the drop of a hat.

Catching sight of myself in the bathroom mirror, I realised that I should probably sort my face out before I scared any small children that may be around. Not sure the Alice Cooper look was really me!

I used a little concealer under my eyes in an effort to hide the dark circles and red rims, brushed a little blusher over my cheeks, gave my lashes a lick of mascara and finished off with a little rosy-pink lip gloss. I normally wore my hair in an efficient bun, but I really couldn't be bothered right then, so just ran my fingers through it and gave it a shake so it fell in natural waves around my shoulders. I was sure Mum wouldn't mind and to be honest right now I didn't have the energy to even worry about it. Jamie would never have wanted to see me like this and I'd never go to work in this dishevelled state.

Work! All of a sudden, it hit me that I wouldn't be going back to Ronington's. Ever. I had put my heart and soul into a job which I thought defined me, where I had thought I was valuable and part of something amazing. I knew it was my choice, to put my own life on hold, but it was only now that I realised that I had given far more out than I ever got back and that when the chips were down, a company had to do what they had to do, and if that meant that you were a casualty then that was just the way it was. Sometimes life seemed very unfair.

3

As I walked up the front path of my childhood home, a path I'd walked up a million times before, the door flung open. Mum had clearly been waiting for me to arrive. 'Oh Madison, it is so lovely to see you.' She hugged me tightly, then pulled away and looked me up and down.

'Your hair looks so pretty like that, darling; you should wear it like that more often. It really suits you.' She stood back and studied my face closely.

'Your eyes are red. And what are you doing here in the middle of the day? Are you ill, darling?'

Mum being so lovely overwhelmed me. I had been determined to hold it together but I couldn't help bursting into tears. 'Oh, Mum. I've... I've been made redundant.'

'Oh, darling, what a shock for you. But don't worry. We've always been able to get through anything life throws at us, haven't we? And this won't be any different. Come here.' She wrapped me in her arms and I suddenly felt safe, realising that the one person I'd been pushing away for so long was the person I really needed to be close to right now, because she made me feel protected. I thought back to my childhood, a really happy time, with just Mum and me against the world. We were such a close-knit little family and I loved her more than I imagined any other child loved their mum because mine was really special. I'd never had a father in my life, so she was my mum and dad rolled into one and she spent her whole life doing everything she could to make me happy, even if it meant working lots of jobs all at the same time, to bring the money in to keep a roof over our heads.

When had I stopped feeling that way about her? When had I started to feel like she was a nuisance in my life? I'd grown into someone who was so work-orientated, I'd forgotten about the person who had brought me into this world and loved me unconditionally, who had put her life on hold to concentrate on me. *God,* I thought, *I must be an awful person.* Why did it take something like this to make me realise?

'Let's go and have a cuppa and you can tell me all about what happened.' Normally, when Mum said that to me, I got irritated and told her I didn't have time, but time was probably the only thing that I did have now and I wanted her to help me. I wanted her to make everything feel better like only my mum could.

As we walked towards the kitchen, she opened the cupboard under the stairs and hung my coat on the pegs behind the door and I sighed as I breathed in the familiar smell of the home I'd grown up in. The home that Mum had poured her heart and soul into and lovingly made for us. The walls seemed to be ingrained with the mixture of aromas of baking bread, coffee and lilies; all the things an estate agent tells you that you should have around when you are trying to sell your house.

Home was a 1920s honey-coloured stone cottage in the village of Giddywell, Staffordshire, where the small population of just over one thousand people all knew each other's business. The village consisted of one pub, The Dog and Duck, a small supermarket which somehow managed to stock everything you ever needed, St Saviour's Church, a Chinese take-away, and a specialist bike shop, which was quite handy when you lived near the colossal forest of Cannock Chase, which was stunningly beautiful and full of dog-walkers and bikers. Our cottage overlooked the village green and a pretty little duck pond and probably had one of the best spots in the village.

After I'd left school, I didn't appreciate it at all and couldn't wait to get away, but right now it felt like it was just where I needed to be.

I told her about my awful morning and she held me in her arms while I cried again. 'Come on, my darling, you have a good old cry now. Better out than in.' This was a phrase I'd heard many times over the years.

'Do you know, Madison, sometimes things happen in our lives that are a blessing to us eventually, but we don't realise it at the time. Perhaps this has happened because you need a change. This could be an opportunity for you to do something different. Change sometimes is good, even if it comes about because it has to, rather than because it's your choice.'

Maybe Mum was right, but I just couldn't get my head around it. I had worked my whole adult life, never having any time off. Except the sickness absence I'd needed to get over what had happened with Jamie.

Now was not the time to be thinking of that, though. I had enough to worry about.

'Perhaps it's time to rethink your life and consider other options. Maybe there's something you've always had a burning desire to do. Set up on your own; you are clearly good at what you do or they wouldn't have kept you for twelve years.'

'But now I'm wondering if I ever was that good, Mum. If I was, why would they get rid of me?'

'Sometimes, companies have to make sacrifices, darling. I know it's hard and I know it's all you've ever known, but it could be a godsend too. Maybe time will tell.'

I just couldn't see that right now though. All I felt was hurt and sad and disappointed and my pride had been severely dented. I felt like a fool.

Mum served us both up a dish of homemade chicken and vegetable soup and crusty bread and butter. It surprised me how hungry I was, although I hadn't grabbed any breakfast that morning, and I devoured the whole dishful.

After lunch she took me through to the lounge and made me lie on the settee while she tucked me up under the cashmere throw that I'd bought for her last Christmas. I felt like a little girl again being looked after by her mum and it felt good. Really good. We watched a couple of programmes on TV about antiques and their value and a programme about people who wanted to relocate abroad that didn't take any concentration but just got my mind off stuff for the moment.

'Oh, darling, I completely forgot to tell you the reason why I wanted to speak to you earlier. Lynne and John next door have just become grandparents for the first time. Isn't that wonderful? Curtis and Holly had a little girl yesterday morning. Isn't that lovely? Lynne popped round to tell me last night. They are all obviously over the moon and the whole reason for me calling you in the first place was to see if you could think of something that I could buy them? A little keepsake of some kind.'

This news stung a little, I must admit, but I tried not to show it.

'Oh, that's nice news, I'll have a think.'

Mum was so excited for them and it made me feel even sadder and even more of a failure for not being able to give her the same joy in her life.

Raindrops appeared on the window, and Mum said she

needed to get the washing off the line and I watched her through the French doors. They were her pride and joy; she'd saved up for years for them and they'd changed the lounge dramatically. This home was so cosy and welcoming. I looked around the room and inhaled the familiarity. I couldn't remember the last time I'd done this. In fact, I couldn't remember the last time I had come home, properly home, without just popping by. Working all hours meant that I'd prioritised work and not my family, which I regretted somewhat now that they had got rid of me. I should have made more time for Mum. I really should. Why didn't I see it then? Too busy thinking of myself, I guessed, and putting work first. Always rushing, always having to get back to do something for work. And look how that had turned out.

'Stay here for the rest of the day, darling, and let me look after you. I know you probably won't want to but you could stay the night, you know. Your room hasn't changed a bit. All your things are still here. There's even some of your teenage pyjamas. I'm sure they'll still fit you.'

'You don't have to look after me, Mum. I'm a grown woman.'

She grinned wearily. 'Oh, I know I don't have to, darling, but you will always be my little girl no matter what your age. And anyway, I *want* to look after you. I'm your mum. It's my job. You could even go and see Beth tomorrow. I bet you haven't seen her for ages.'

This time last week, this scenario would have been my worst nightmare, but right now it was the best feeling in the world. I should have done this before. Why did I have to wait for a crisis to happen in my life for me to appreciate my mum?

We watched mindless TV for the rest of the evening and at around 9 p.m., I went up to my room and wrapped myself up in the duvet. Mum came up with me and waited as I used the bathroom, then she tucked me in just like old times and kissed the top of my head.

'Goodnight, my darling, and try not to worry. We can get through anything, you and I.'

'Night, Mum.'

As I looked around my childhood bedroom, which Mum had never redecorated because she said she loved the memories it gave her, my last thoughts were about how excited I had been travelling into work this morning, yet what an unexpected turn of events had changed my life.

Right now I felt like a complete and utter failure. For the first time in years, I had no idea what tomorrow would bring and that was a hugely scary prospect.

4

When I woke the following morning, I was a bit disorientated. Looking around the room, I saw pictures of Take That Blu-Tacked to the wall, and I realised exactly where I was, and why. I looked at the bedside clock and saw it was 7 a.m. I'd been asleep for nearly ten hours. I really couldn't remember the last time I'd slept for that long.

I smiled as I looked at the boys back in the day, dressed in leather and covered in jelly and ice cream, and remembered how devastated I'd been when Robbie left the group and when they split up. I was so distressed at the time, and I smiled now remembering that Beth had sent me a 'with sympathy' card, which she'd found hilarious. I thought about how they must have felt, and how hard it must have been for them at that point in their lives. After years of being together, they had to get used to a life of not being in a band and had to start all over again, a situation I felt I could completely relate to. Although I was sure they had a little more cash in the bank than I did.

But then look at what they'd achieved since then. The fab five were now the awesome three, and extremely successful in a different way. So, it just went to show that you could make a comeback and be a huge success again. If they could do it, perhaps anyone could. Did I have the strength though? I guessed I'd have to discover that.

I picked up my phone from the bedside table, the first thing I did every day – a habit I really needed to break – and noticed a text message from Beth sent the evening before when I was well and truly in the land of nod.

> Hey stranger! Spoke to your mum and she told me that you were having a tough time right now. If you fancy a coffee tomorrow with an old friend, pop on over. I'd love to see you xx

It was so lovely to hear from her. I took a deep breath. Right now I had two choices. I could wallow in bed all day and feel sorry for myself, or I could get my arse out of bed, dust myself down, get dressed and go and see Beth. It had been a while since I'd seen her last. She was a lovely girl, and we'd been such good friends over the years, even though I'd neglected her over the last few, so I knew which option I needed to take to move forward.

* * *

Bethany Jane Millington and I met three hours after I was born when Mum and I were taken back to the sunny maternity ward of Stafford Hospital where two roomies bonded over their beautiful newborns, sharing some of the most cherished and precious moments of their lives. Her parents were farmers, a lovely couple who somehow managed to be wonderful parents as well as run Giddywell Grange, a small but busy farm just on the outskirts of the village. Beth was their second child and their son Alex was two years older. They were so kind to Mum, who was parenting all on her own, after my dad, apparently, buggered off the minute she told him she was pregnant.

Our families did everything together, from those early days when our mums used to get together for coffee mornings and just stare at us babies, through to reception class where allegedly I used to cry until my bestie arrived, when I'd run in excitedly holding hands with her, looking forward to the day, through our early years at primary school and then on to high school.

As I pulled up into the courtyard in front of Giddywell Grange, I got a warm fuzzy feeling deep in my tummy as I remembered how much I loved this house and what it meant to me. I hadn't been here for a couple of years and it really felt like I was coming home. It was their family farm, which had been handed down through the generations, and had always been a welcoming, warm and wonderful place to be. The big ivy-clad stone farmhouse, set in acres of land, held so many good memories for me. It was almost like the thick stone walls were ingrained with happiness, warmth and love that oozed out to those who were in it like a warm, cosy hug.

Much of my childhood was spent there, and my teenage years had been so much fun, helping to muck out the stables and grooming the horses with Beth, doing our homework at the kitchen table while Aunty Jen made us hot chocolate in the winter and doorstep sandwiches with her homemade bread, singing into our hairbrushes and pretending to be the Spice Girls in Beth's room.

Beth must have heard the car pull up as she was standing at the front door. She enveloped me in a hug.

'Oh, Maddy, my love, it's so good to see you.'

My lip quivered and tears threatened, but Beth, tactful as ever, turned round and led the way into the kitchen. 'Come on, love, I'll pop the kettle on.'

'It's really good to see you, Beth, I'm so sorry it's been such a long time since I popped by.'

While I was living the life of Riley in the corporate world, staying in swanky hotels, dining at the most salubrious restaurants and making sure I had Christian Louboutin shoes and the latest Mulberry handbag, Beth had launched and was running a very successful doggy daycare and boarding business called Growlers at the Grange, happy in wellies and wearing a backpack where she always had dog treats and poo bags at hand.

'How's business?' I asked her. I realised that I didn't actually know much about her work and I felt quite bad. It was becoming increasingly clear to me that I'd been so wrapped up in myself for the past few years that I had distanced myself from everyone who was once close to me.

'It's going really well actually. We're dead busy. We've expanded Growlers so that we can have up to ten dogs in the daytime, and we do overnight boarding now too, so it really keeps us on our toes. Dad and I do most of the work between us – obviously Dad has the farm to run too, but he's really cut back on the actual farming now. We have way fewer animals than we've ever had before and the ones we do have we can just about cope with. He's renting out a couple of the large fields to neighbouring farmers who are keeping their own cattle on our land, and he's renting out allotments to local people. Oh, and we also have a side business where we have a totally secure field that we rent out to people who want to bring their dogs along, those who don't normally let their dogs off the lead. That's a money-maker, I have to say. Oh, and we've got the barn that we do a long-term let on too. It certainly keeps us busy. And gives us various income streams coming in.'

I hadn't realised that Beth had such a good business head on her shoulders. Perhaps she wasn't living the dull and boring life, stuck in the village, that I'd thought.

'Crikey, that sounds like a lot to do.'

'It is, and it certainly takes some juggling and keeping on top of, but we both love it. We have a young lad called Russell working some hours for us too. Really nice lad and he loves dogs, which helps.'

'That sounds amazing, Beth. You really seem to be happy and living the dream.'

'Well, I'm sure you've always thought that my life is dreary and unexciting after the work that you do and all those swanky hotels you stay in and fancy restaurants.'

I gulped. It was as if she could see right through me.

'I love it and it's just my way of life. And I've also become involved in a couple of local community projects too through the library to give me some variety away from here and because I wanted to do something to help others.' Beth had always been so very kind and it was in her blood to help others before helping herself. Just like her mum. She really was one of the nicest people I knew, and perhaps I hadn't been the best friend to her that I could have been. Like with Mum, I'd neglected our friendship, another thing I'd prioritised my job over... and for what? For them to get rid of me. I hoped I could make it up to her.

'And how about your health, hun? Are things better on that front?'

'Not really, they have decided that the best thing for my dodgy knee is to operate. The torn cartilage needs sorting out and they're going to shave some of the bone away, quite disgusting really and probably better that I'm out under general anaesthetic for it. They offered key-hole surgery but you know how squeamish I am. I'm just waiting for a date for the op to come through. That's going to be quite a challenge. And I don't think I'll get much notice either.

To be honest, it's really playing on my mind at the moment, but I'm sure we'll work something out. Dad will have to work extra hard and Russell will up his hours, but obviously the cost is going to hit the business hard. Luckily Alex is going to come over to help out for as long as his work will allow him to, but he can't stay forever; he has his own job, and Sophie, to get back to over in the States.'

Alex was Beth's older, cooler brother, who was always out with his super cool mates when we were teenagers hanging around the farm, but then he went away to uni. I don't think anyone ever realised that I'd always had the *hugest* crush on him.

'Anyway, it stresses me out to think about that so let's get back to chatting about you. What are your plans going forward? Do you have any? Or are you just going to give yourself some time to look around?'

Another great quality of Beth's was that she was very direct; there was no pussyfooting around with her. She just came straight out and asked what she wanted to know.

'Well, I suppose I'll just look around for a similar role; it's all I know really. I might see if there's something in the interim. There must be jobs out there that I can do. My redundancy money won't last me forever. One of the first things I need to do is to buy myself a computer. I desperately need to get myself set up so that I can use the internet properly instead of just on my phone, and start looking around, I suppose. I need to buy a car too; my company car will go back at the end of this month.'

'You can always use the office computer here, you know. It would be great to spend some time with you, and there's always one desk free. Would that help at all? You could even come and help with the dogs, too. An extra pair of hands around the place would never be refused if you are looking to fill your time.' She laughed and went on to say, 'I could just see you getting stuck in with the poo pick-ups. Only joking! I know you'd never get your hands dirty in that way.' Clearly she knew me well. Way better than the people who I'd worked with day in and day out and who I'd thought were my friends, but who were strangely silent right now. If they'd known me as well as Beth did, they'd have realised that one of the kindest things they could have done for me would have been to say something, even if they weren't sure what to say; sometimes a friendly word is all you need to hear.

'Not sure about picking up poo, but being able to use the internet would be amazing, Beth, thank you.' I stood to hug her.

Warmth, generosity and kindness oozed from every one of her pores. 'You're welcome here anytime, Mads, I hope you know that.'

I looked at my oldest friend properly for the first time in what seemed like ages. Beth and I had been through so much together over the years. She was always the centre of attention, the belle of the ball, the one who, when we were out clubbing and dancing to 'Relight My Fire', yelled over the music, 'I'm gonna be Lulu!' and took to the centre of the dance floor. Every single time!

And now, she was still beautiful and kind and she seemed so happy and comfortable in her own skin, and I was so blessed that she was my friend. I vowed at this point to be a much better friend to her than I'd ever been before. It had never really occurred to me before, but if we were all a bit more Beth, and spent our time helping others and making them happy, the world would be a much better place. Sometimes it's easy to lose sight of what is important.

'Well, there's no time like the present. I need to go over to Growlers and do some jobs now. Why don't you come over and I can show you how everything works and give you passwords, and then you can help yourself whenever you like. Unless you have other plans, that is.'

'I don't! I don't have any plans for the foreseeable future, to be honest. You really are kind, you know, Beth. I do appreciate it. I know I've not been around much in recent years but now I am; I'm really looking forward to spending time with you.'

She brushed my comment aside with a flimsy wave. 'Maddy, I know that you've had a tough time over the last few years with Jamie' – she paused – 'and everything.' She smiled a sad smile at me. 'I know you. And I know that you had to get through that on your own. But you have always known that I'm here for you any time of the day or night. And besides, that's what friends are for.'

* * *

We headed over to the kennels where a huge metal sign reading 'Growlers at the Grange' with paw prints either side hung outside a set of iron gates. The name always made me smirk, since Paul Stubbs at school had got told off for asking the girls to pull down their pants and show him their 'growlers'. But here it obviously wasn't a euphemism for one's lady-garden. Beth and I had laughed so much when I reminded her of this after she'd told me what she was calling the business on one of our phone calls, which had been very few and far between around that time.

'Well, hello, my darling. Come here!' Uncle Tom opened his arms to me and I walked into them. He wrapped me in a huge bear hug, which he hadn't done for years. I was trying to remember how long it had been since I'd seen him and the fact that I couldn't recall when it was told me that it had been way too long.

'Maddy, darling. So good to see you. I was hoping you'd pop over while you were here.' A hug from him felt so good, and at six feet five, he was such a giant that you couldn't help but feel safe and secure when you were cocooned in his arms. My mind wandered for a second and I imagined, like I always used to when Uncle Tom hugged me, what it would have felt like to get a hug from my own father. My own flesh and blood. I'd never know though, so I pushed that thought aside like I always did. It was something I couldn't think about because it would drive me insane again.

I was one of those people who was very good at pushing things away when they became hard to deal with. I'd done it all my life when I thought about my father and I did the same when my world crashed around me when I found out about Jamie and everything that happened at that time. I supposed it was just my way of not having to deal with stuff and once I'd got my head around it all, enough to get back to work, throwing myself into it whole-heartedly and working all the time meant that I didn't have to think about anything. Work was a huge distraction to me. But it was silly because all that stuff was still there, deep inside my mind, just with a lid on it. I knew there was a possibility that one day it could all come spilling out, but I had no intention of letting that lid come off for a good while yet.

'Come on, sweetie, let me show you around.' Beth tucked her arm into mine and we strolled into the first barn at the back of the offices.

Uncle Tom and Beth had spent a great deal of time and money making Growlers at the Grange the most wonderful five-star doggy daycare and kennels that you could ever wish to leave your dog at. Everything was behind locked doors and gates so there was no danger of escapees, and it was immaculately clean. Each pen was once a stable and therefore a good size, with an outside and an inside section, separated by a large dog flap so that the dogs could choose which bit they wanted to be in. There was a raised dog bed in the corner of each pen with a fluffy blanket on it, and a big squashy armchair in another corner, covered with a throw for those dogs that preferred to be on furniture. There was even a TV in each of the rooms. 'We find that they don't react to everything if there's a bit of background noise. And the sofas are for those more pampered pooches who are used to being on the furniture at home,' Beth explained. 'It helps those dogs that are a little more anxious.' I could have lived there myself, to be honest.

'We'll go through to the paddock areas now. It's all totally secure and off lead from here, which the dogs love.' The huge paddock had six-foot-high metal fencing all the way around and an assault course with tunnels and jumps and even hay bales, which Beth explained that the dogs loved because they hid treats in them for the dogs to forage and find, keeping them mentally stimulated as well as physically. If I had a dog I'd be so happy to leave them here.

A young man was playing with several dogs in the paddock. 'And that's Russell. He's such a lovely lad. He spends lots of time here, even when he's not working. He just loves dogs and playing and spending time with them. He's going off to university soon though. Wants to train to be a vet so is trying his hardest to build up a pot of cash. We'll be so sad to see him go and I really don't know how we'll replace him. He's such a help. His mum is Rebecca, who works at the library. I help her out on the community projects that she organises. You'd like her, Mads. I'll have to introduce you – although she'll probably try and rope you in to helping. Lovely family.' Beth smiled at me and tucked her arm back in mine as we walked back to the office. 'I'm so happy to see you, matey. I really am.'

Beth was such a good egg. I definitely needed to be more like her.

* * *

Once I'd worked out how to use a PC again – which was very different to a Mac – I found a couple of jobs that I thought I'd apply for, if only to keep things ticking over in the interim period before I got my foot back in the door of PR. I wasn't sure whether I wanted to go through a recruitment agency just yet and thought I'd see what I could find on my own. To be honest, at the moment, I couldn't face bumping into people from the industry that I'd come from and admitting what had happened. It was still something I found highly embarrassing, so I thought a change of environment might do me good while I could get my head around things.

The first was as a sales rep for a hairdressing product company. Surely I could do that with my hands tied behind my back. I had learned so many different skills over the years that I knew I could turn my hand to anything. The other job I quite fancied having a go at was a membership co-ordinator role at a gym. Now, gyms I knew well. I'd pounded the treadmill many times to get rid of unwanted thoughts during the last few years and enjoyed people-watching, so I knew the different types of gym member. Surely it couldn't be hard to recruit new people.

I spent the next couple of hours putting together a CV and got Beth to proofread it for me.

'Well, on the strength of that CV, I can't see you having any problems whatsoever getting either of those two jobs. They'd be bloody lucky to have you.' My confidence had taken a bit of a battering of late, so I crossed my fingers and fired off my CV to both companies, hoping she was right.

* * *

The hair product company was the first to come back the following day and they invited me to call them and arrange an interview. They asked if I could go in at short notice, so I agreed and planned to go along that afternoon. For the first time in a couple of days, I felt a frisson of excitement as I showered and put a conditioning treatment on my hair. I'd always used the best of hair products so it looked sleek and shiny, so hopefully they'd notice that too and it would go in my favour.

Deciding to go for a natural make-up look, I put on my favourite pinstriped trouser suit with a pretty blouse and spritzed myself with Daisy by Marc Jacobs before sliding my feet into a pair of high heels. I absolutely looked the part and envisaged myself walking through salon doors with a product brochure and wooing the managers into buying lots of gorgeous products.

I arrived fifteen minutes early and was asked to wait in reception until they were ready. Forty-five minutes later, I still hadn't gone in and I was getting more wound up with the waiting.

Eventually, my name was called and I was taken through to a conference room where a panel of three sat behind a table, with a vacant chair opposite them in which I was invited to take a seat. They introduced themselves as the MD, the sales director and the operations manager. They all seemed perfectly nice and fired questions at me left, right and centre. I answered everything pretty darn well, I thought, and felt confident that I could do the job, even though what I'd been doing for the last twelve years wasn't directly linked. I knew that the skills and experience I'd picked up over time meant that I could do most jobs standing on my head.

'Thank you so much for your time, Miss Young, and for coming in so quickly. You've certainly got lots of experience on the sales, PR and marketing side of things which is exactly what we're looking for. We'll be going to second interviews as the next stage, so you'll be hearing from us very soon.'

I shook hands with all three of the panel members and left feeling pretty damn confident. I walked out with my head held high. Maybe things were starting to look up after all and I wasn't as bloody crap as I'd thought I was after Ronington's decided to part company with me. Within days, I'd very probably got myself a new job. I'd show them that I wasn't useless after all.

* * *

That particular feeling didn't last long though as within a couple of hours of being back home, my phone pinged to say that an email had arrived. My heart sank as I read that while they felt that my skills and experience were excellent, I wasn't quite right for this particular job. There was lots of good luck for the future blah, blah, blah, but I was back to square one. No job, no future to look forward to and I felt lower than low.

I fired off a quick text to Mum and Beth, telling them both that I'd been turned down, and Mum sent back:

> Plenty more jobs out there for my beautiful girl. Onwards and upwards. Love you x

And Beth came back with:

> Well, it's obviously not the right job for you, my love, and not meant to be. Don't lose heart. The right thing will come along at the right time. And remember, there'll always be a poo bag here with your name on it!

That night, I sat in a pair of old pyjamas and stuffed my face with chocolate, feeling really sorry for myself. I drank the best part of a bottle of Pinot Grigio and took myself off to bed around 10 p.m. feeling sick from being a total glutton. I wished I'd stopped at Mum's again. I felt really lonely.

* * *

A ping from my phone woke me around 8 a.m. I'd slept in, which was very unlike me and possibly down to the wine. It was the noise that signified I'd got an email, and when I checked, there was one from Gym Fit, asking me to call them to arrange an interview. Crikey, this job-hunting lark was a proper rollercoaster on your emotions. I waited till 9 a.m. on the dot and arranged an interview for the following morning.

What the hell did I do with myself today though? I literally had nothing to do. I could have checked job sites, but doing it on my phone wasn't the best way to do it as the writing was all so blinking small.

The post arrived and in it was a letter as Celine had promised from the HR department with my redundancy settlement. One week's pay for every year that I'd been there, my holiday pay for the holiday that I hadn't yet taken that year and an extra thousand pounds on top. Sounded like quite a bit, but once I started to get the things I needed from the list I'd made, I couldn't see it lasting that long, especially when I had to buy a car.

Window shopping. That was the answer. I'd go and check out laptops and iPads. I know Beth had said that I could use hers, which was so kind of her, but I needed something to do while I was at home too. The other thing I could do was to go to the gym, but I was scared to death to bump into someone I knew who would want to know why I was there in the daytime, and I'd have to tell them my whole sorry story. I wasn't ready to share that just yet.

I drove to the local retail park and went into two different electronics shops. Not having a clue as to what the hell I was actually buying, I even surprised myself when I came out of the second one with a new Mac and an iPad. At this rate, my redundancy money wouldn't last long at all.

I spent the rest of the day setting everything up and googling

PR jobs, but also looking at blog posts about what to do when you want to change your career. I really didn't know what I wanted to do. I also checked out some other local gyms so that I could be fully prepped for tomorrow's interview.

* * *

Once more, I turned up looking the part in a smart trouser suit. I was the smartest one there and was introduced to the regional manager and the gym manager. A quick tour round the gym piqued my interest and it was explained to me that the main part of the job was to contact local companies and offer their staff corporate membership. How hard could that be? They seemed to be a really young, dynamic team and the company was really forward-thinking. Part of the role would be to manage the membership team of three people and ultimately increase their membership numbers. I felt that I'd be well suited to the job and it appeared that they did too because after being at home for two hours, a job offer landed in my inbox.

I punched the air. I could do it. People did want me to work for them. I was good enough! Thank goodness for that. I gave the regional manager a call and after a little negotiating – I asked for more money and they said no – we agreed on the offer. It was nearly half the salary I was used to getting, but a job was a job and I couldn't afford to be particularly choosy right now, so I accepted and said that I was looking forward to starting next Monday.

* * *

The days until I started my new job dragged a bit. I milled around, not really doing much, just sleeping lots and drinking buckets of tea and nursing my wounds. I still felt totally devastated that I'd been made redundant and it really hurt when I felt that I'd given so much to the company, although I was grateful that I'd found something pretty quickly. Not everyone was that lucky.

My emotions were all over the place. I spent time over at the farm when Beth was free, although she was so busy alternating between Growlers and helping in the community, those times were few and far between.

Monday came around. Wanting to make a fab impression, I had dressed in a designer suit and high heels. The club manager took one look at me, grinned and passed me a pair of shiny branded tracksuit bottoms and a manly polo shirt with the name of the gym printed bang in the middle of my right boob. Perfect placement by the marketing department. I was leant a pair of really manky old trainers from lost property and told to bring my own in tomorrow. They'd forgotten to give me that little bit of useful information. The thought of putting my feet into this disgusting footwear made me cringe as I thought of my beautiful shoes and the designer pumps I normally wore if I had to resort to flatties.

I sat at my desk and was told that at 10 a.m. there was a conference call when all the membership managers from the Midland sites dialled in and talked about what they would do for the day ahead. A further call would take place at 5 p.m. to talk about their successes. That seemed a little excessive to me, and very controlling, but so be it. I was the new girl so I'd go with the flow.

After spending most of the day being introduced to the fitness team, and the three members of staff who would be working under me, in the time we had left, I was given instructions from the gym manager to do roleplay with my team and go through some scripted questions and answers which were in the handbook. It all felt a bit daft to be honest, something that grown adults shouldn't really have to do.

There wasn't much I could contribute to the early evening call that day, and I went home wondering what the next day would entail. I soon found out, when on the morning call the next day, my instructions were to continue with the roleplay with my team until we knew it off by heart. I'd never been one for roleplay to be honest; at the PR company we just got on with stuff, but then I'd never worked at a gym before, so I ran with it. Just before lunch, the club manager suggested that we went out into Stafford town centre to give out some free day passes to the gym to break things up a bit. I was taken aback at the thought of standing around in the street – having thought that my role was to focus on corporate membership – but my team looked to me for guidance, so we piled into my car and headed for the town centre.

We chatted in the car and I got to know the guys a little better. Dave was just nineteen and a fitness fanatic and it was his first job after leaving sixth form. Ali had been working there for two years and said that she'd seen membership managers and staff come and go quickly. When I asked her whether she'd considered applying for the position, she laughed and said that the turnover of staff in the department was so incredibly high that she'd rather keep her job. She was quite happy because she got membership for free and she was a proper gym bunny. Marie was the member of staff we'd left behind in case there were any walk-in visits. Ali told me that she was twenty-three and had taken a change of direction from her beauty career as she couldn't cope with standing on her feet all day. She'd been there for one month and was still learning the ropes herself.

As we approached the town centre, the weather was looking pretty grim, with grey cloudy skies ahead, and after I parked up, we spread ourselves out along the high street. In our bright green gym polo shirts, we were quite a show. As it started to drizzle, and my carefully curled hair hung limply around my shoulders, I handed out leaflets, smiling at the passers-by and using my most enthusiastic voice.

'Hi there, can I offer you a free day pass to Gym Fit in Stafford?'

Now, I know us British people are a suspicious lot when someone is trying to stop them in the street, but I found myself wondering why people couldn't actually be nice to those just trying to do their jobs, instead of completely ignoring them, deliberately walking in a different direction or avoiding eye contact. You would have thought we were passing on a deadly virus, the way people treated us.

A group of lads in their late teens walked towards me. *These will definitely go for it*, I thought. I smiled sweetly. One of them deliberately nudged into me, knocking all the fliers out of my hand. They found it highly amusing as I picked up the scattered leaflets that were all getting wet.

'Sorry love, didn't see you there doing your Kermit the Frog impression!' More laughter drifted my way, but I held my head up and continued to smile sweetly through gritted teeth.

'We're giving away free passes today to Gym Fit. Would you be interested at all?' They fell about laughing and one shouted, 'You're not a very good advert for a gym with an arse the size of yours, love.'

I was seriously insulted – I knew the tracksuit bottoms weren't the most flattering, but I couldn't believe their rudeness.

I huffed Miss Piggy style and turned in the opposite direction. A pretty young lady walked towards me with a pushchair.

'Hi there, can I offer you a free pass to Gym Fit?'

She turned on me. 'You calling me fat, you cheeky cow?'

'God no, not at all. I just thought you might like to come and try us out. Maybe grab the chance to have a bit of "me" time.'

'No! Fuck off!'

Charming! I looked over at my team who were getting similar

abuse from passers-by. I couldn't believe the reaction we were getting. Why couldn't people just be nice?

I rounded my team up and decided that we'd go to the nearest coffee shop to warm up and get out of the rain. They told me that this was quite usual behaviour from the general public and that they rarely got people to even take a flyer, let alone come for a free trial.

Downhearted, we headed back to the gym and the manager asked how we'd got on.

'Completely bloody awful, to be honest,' I replied.

'Oh well, tomorrow is another day. Perhaps you could try a different town centre or a different approach. The one you are using is clearly not working.'

Slightly disappointed by the lack of encouragement and empathy, I found the sales call that took place at 5 p.m. wasn't the most positive, either. The area manager ended by saying that there would be consequences for the teams that had the fewest sales at the end of the week and that our priority was roleplay again the following day as we were obviously not getting our sales patter right. Great. Now I had that to look forward to.

I realised that at Ronington's, I was pretty much left to my own devices. I worked out my own plan and just got on with it, without any supervision and certainly no need to do roleplay. I was thirty-seven, for goodness' sake. Did I really have to sit and do roleplay with a team to work out how to get new customers? There were so many other ideas I had that I knew would work.

That evening, I got my notepad and pen and sat for an hour and a half jotting down a ton of ideas, planning to bring them up during the conference call the next day. That lifted my spirits a little. After all, PR and marketing was what I did, and I knew that I knew my stuff. I went to bed that night feeling a little more positive than I had earlier that day.

On the conference call the following morning, I suggested that we could contact some of the larger companies in the vicinity of the gym and ask whether they had an open day, or a staff health day, or whether we could introduce one. Maybe a health check or even just give out our free day passes and ask people to come along and see what facilities were on offer. I was met with deathly silence.

'Thank you for your input, Madison, but I'd rather you just got on with what I've asked you to do rather than waste time coming up with random ideas. You are paid to do as you are told. Please do it.'

Slightly disillusioned that I wasn't using my skills to the full, which I understood were the reason that they'd taken me on, when I went back to the sales office, I made an executive decision and decided to sit down with my team and chat the ideas through with them. They loved my ideas. We were all fired up and cracked on with making calls to local businesses, setting ourselves little targets along the way, and it was fun. I thought that everyone loved a bit of initiative, and when I could show her our results, the area manager would be really impressed.

On the 5 p.m. call, when she asked about our success for the day, I told her we'd made several appointments for people to visit the following day because of the activity we'd done. There was deathly silence for about thirty seconds.

'I told you what to do today! Did you not listen? What on earth did you think you were doing?' she bellowed down the phone line. I was mortified, knowing that ten other membership managers were on the call.

'I used my initiative and we got results,' I stuttered out.

'I have never known anyone as insubordinate. I'll be coming to your gym tomorrow and I'd like to see you privately.'

Well, I'd obviously made a cracking impression on her. Why

hadn't I just done what she'd told me? Why had I thought that my ideas were better than hers? I could have kicked myself. I just wanted to do a good job, and that was what I explained to her when she came to the office on Thursday afternoon.

'I've decided that you and your membership team will report to Dudley Gym Fit tomorrow morning at six a.m. and you will do an hour's boxercise class.'

I giggled but when she glared right back at me I realised it was no joke. Dudley gym was about forty-five minutes' travelling time from my house at that time in the morning, which would mean leaving home at 5.15 a.m. at the latest. Surely she wasn't serious.

'Perhaps after that, the next time you're thinking of using your initiative you might think again and do as you were told in the first place. We don't pay you to think.'

She was only about twenty-eight, clearly one of those who was keen to get on and push her way through the ranks, not caring who she left behind in her wake. I'd seen that type before and suddenly from nowhere, I found my voice. She might be my boss, but that didn't mean she had the right to speak to me this way. I decided I'd try to explain once more.

'I was using my initiative, that's all. I have a PR and marketing background and know that these things work. In fact, we have made ten appointments this morning alone with local businesses who are really interested in us working with their staff. If we can help them to have healthy staff, it's great for their absence figures, and if they get benefits from being a member of the gym as part of their wages, people are going to want to work there. That's had more effect than standing in the street handing out leaflets. I'm sorry, but I think that to be punished in this way is a little unfair.' *Bloody massively unfair* is what I wanted to say, but thought I'd better tone it down a bit.

'Well, your team will have you to thank for getting up early and training, won't they?' She was venomous. How did someone like her get a job like that? My blood was beginning to boil. I made a split-second decision which I knew I might come to regret, but right then I didn't care.

'I'm sorry, but I won't be going.'

'You *will* go!' she yelled at me.

'I'm sorry but to be totally honest, this is probably the crappiest job I've ever had in my life. I've had to dress up like Shrek, stand in the pouring rain, been told to fuck off, been told I have a fat arse, and all that when the pay is rubbish. I've tried to get new members into the gym but we can't make people come doing it your way and then, when we find a way that does work, you think it's OK to punish us for that. No one deserves that.' I was on a roll now and the words wouldn't stop pouring from my mouth.

'The people that you have working in the team here are bloody good people and this is how you treat them? They don't deserve it. I don't want to work for a company like this and certainly not for a person like you.'

She was bright red in the face, furious with me. I didn't think anyone could ever have spoken to her like that in her life.

She went to speak but I held my hand up, palm towards her, to silence her. 'Let me stop you there!'

And I picked up my handbag from the side of my desk, grabbed my jacket from the back of my chair and walked out of the double entrance doors to Gym Fit for the last time.

* * *

I couldn't face going back to the apartment, so I dropped the car off into my parking space and decided to go for a walk to cheer myself up. I couldn't believe that in less than a week, I was out of work again. There was a children's park just down the road from the development and I found myself heading there as I did so often when I needed to clear my head. Sitting on an empty bench overlooking the play area probably wasn't one of my brightest ideas. A pretty little girl in denim shorts and a flowery long-sleeved t-shirt played in the sandpit while her mum took her phone out and snapped lots of pictures. The daughter ran up to her mum and, chuckling, flung her arms around her neck and threw her body weight at her. Her mum laughed as she fell backwards and they hugged tightly and she showered her mum with kisses.

It felt like a stab to the heart, and a lone tear rolled down my cheek as I thought about what might have been if my life had turned out differently. Whether I'd have made a good mum. It was a question I'd asked myself many times.

That first tear must have broken the seal, and more streamed uncontrollably as reality started to sink in. I had no job. I had no children. Nothing to get up for. No purpose in life. That panicked feeling came crashing over me again and I grabbed onto the bench for support.

A cold, wet nose nudged my hand and I looked down to see a beautiful furry face staring at me.

'Excuse me for poking my nose in, but are you OK, my lovely?'

I turned my head towards the sound of a woman's voice, and had been so deep in my misery that I hadn't even noticed that someone had joined me on the bench. I soon realised that it was the dog-walking lady that I saw sometimes from my window. She was older close-up than I'd originally thought, but even prettier than she looked from a distance. Her blonde hair was swept back Grace Kelly style in a sleek clip, revealing naturally high cheekbones and perfect rosebud lips.

I tried to speak, but nothing came out and my breath just wouldn't come.

'Just breathe, my dear. Deep breaths; look at me and do it with me. In, two, three. And out, two, three. And again. In, two, three. And out, two, three.'

She took my hand and smiled at me as I looked at her intently, and after a few seconds of repeating what she told me to do, my breathing steadied and finally I felt able to speak.

'Thank you. So kind of you. I'm not sure what came over me.'

'Well, something has certainly upset you. I live just round the corner. Why don't you come and sit in my garden and I'll make you a nice hot sweet cup of tea? It looks like you need one. Perhaps you might want to talk about what's upset you. A problem shared is a problem halved and all that. But if you don't want to share, you can just sit and gather yourself together.'

'Thank you so much, but please don't let me interrupt the rest of your afternoon. I'll be fine, honestly.'

She picked up my jacket and my handbag from the bench and handed them to me.

'You are far from fine, young lady. You're shaking like a leaf and you're not interrupting anything at all. I was only popping to the shop anyway for something to do to fill my time. Sometimes in life, we need a little helping hand, and this afternoon I'd like to be yours. I'm Alice, by the way.' She tucked her arm into mine and led the way steadily. I was glad of her support as I was still feeling a little wobbly, and I introduced myself.

Just around the corner, tucked away, was the prettiest little picture postcard cottage I had ever seen. We walked through a low gate and along a winding path weaving through a small but perfectly formed front garden full of glorious flowers in bloom to a vintage green front door. Just being in that garden was making me feel a whole lot calmer.

'If you want to take yourself through to the back garden, go through that side gate. I'll be round in a minute or two.'

I walked through the big gate, which looked like it led to a secret garden. Taking a seat, I looked around me and noticed that it flowed effortlessly into another beautiful garden space, with a vegetable patch at the bottom, a small pond and a decking area with outside seating. I listened to the wooden wind chimes tinkling away as I turned my head towards the warm early spring sun. My breath slowed down to somewhere near normal and I felt much steadier.

'Here you go, tea and biccies. My grandmother used to swear that it solved everything.' She placed a tray with two pretty Emma Bridgewater mugs and a plate with a selection of biscuits on the table, and my tummy rumbled as I realised I had never got around to eating lunch today. The golden Cockerpoo I was so used to seeing her walking was now scampering around her legs.

'You really are very kind, Alice. Thank you.' I put my hand down and ruffled the fur on the dog's head.

'Ah, it's a pleasure to help. I lost my husband suddenly earlier this year and I've had times when I've been out and had a little panic attack and not known what to do with myself. I wish that someone had helped me, so I wanted to stop and help you. You looked like you were having a bad day!' She passed me the plate and told me to help myself. I was actually quite starving. Sadly, I was not one of those people who went off their food when a trauma occurred. There wasn't much that would put me off eating, which was probably why I was an ample size fourteen. Something else that Jamie had always wanted to change, encouraging me to go to the gym all the time.

'I'm so sorry to hear that. It must be hard to adapt.' I picked up my tea and took a sip. Hot and sweet, just how I liked it.

'It is. We'd just celebrated our ruby wedding anniversary when I lost him. I wake up sometimes and forget he's gone. When I reach over to touch him, it hits me all over again. Good job I've got this little monster here to make me get up in the morning or some days I'm not sure I'd actually leave my bed.' She stroked the Cockerpoo tenderly on the head and passed him a treat, which she had also brought out on the tray. 'Baxter here keeps me sane, don't you, my darling? So do you want to talk about what's upset you, or would you rather not? Sometimes it helps to talk things through though.' Baxter surprised me by jumping up onto my lap and snuggling down for a cuddle. He really was a cutie.

Alice smiled. 'Dogs always seem to sense when someone is upset.'

I tickled him gently behind his ears as he nuzzled his head further into my hand, and as I smiled at him, he looked up and I'm sure he winked at me. 'Well, I don't really know where to start, to be honest. I've recently been made redundant, applied for two jobs, got turned down for one and taken on at another, which was the worst job I've ever had, and about an hour ago I walked out on that. I've given my life to my last company for twelve years and I've never walked out of a job. And to be honest, I really don't know what I'm going to do.'

I could feel myself welling up again. Hearing it all out in the open made me realise how crappy my life was.

Since being made redundant, I had been struggling with the feeling that I just wasn't needed anywhere, and I had come to realise that this was something that was really important to me in life. Without it, I felt bereft. When I was at work, someone always needed me. If it wasn't the sales department asking about sales figures or budgets, it was the creative department, needing to know what artwork and text should look like. And Celine needed me. She had no idea who our best clients were, or who was lined up for future projects, and sometimes she just needed me to boost her ego and make her feel better, but since the day I walked out the door, no one had needed me.

Redundant. The word was so harsh, so final. I looked it up in the dictionary and it said that the definition was: *Not or no longer needed. Superfluous to requirements. Unwanted.*

I couldn't imagine crueller words. No wonder my self-esteem had taken a bit of a dent.

I'd found the transition between working all the time and then not having a permanent job really hard. My phone never rang. My emails never pinged. God, it was so quiet and I wasn't used to it at all.

Right now, I felt as if I was worth absolutely nothing. And I kept coming back to the question of why Ronington's hadn't fought harder for me to stay. How could you give your all to a company only for them to just get rid of you at the drop of a hat? I was devastated that I'd been treated this way after everything I'd put into the business. Didn't all those hours and all that dedication count for anything? I clearly couldn't have been the person I'd thought I was. Perhaps I was just deluded. I obviously wasn't capable enough for them to want or need me. I must have been totally useless for them to let me go completely. I must be, or surely the hair company would have taken me on and the gym job would have worked out. I'd never felt more confused or let down, and I didn't know if it was me or them.

And then there was the guilt I felt. Could I have done more to help our jobs survive? Had I let people down by not doing enough to keep things together? Was it all my fault? Poor Alice; I'm glad I didn't blurt all of that out. I didn't want to burden her too much, so I was glad those thoughts were all in my head.

'Do you know, Madison, I've learned that there are two ways to look at everything since I lost my Des. You can sit and wallow, or you can see everything as a chance that's been given to you, that some people never get... and that's what I've chosen to do. While we think we are having a bad time, there are others in the world who are taking their last breath, and I try to remember that and be grateful that I'm still here with a life to live. I firmly believe that we owe it to those not as lucky as we are to live it to the full. And for you, my dear, yes, this must have come as a terrible shock, but maybe when that wears off, you'll see it as an opportunity to do something different with your future.

'I'm going to visit my sister Emily in a week's time in Australia. She's been there for years and has sent a ticket for me to go over. I've never been before and I am so looking forward to seeing her. Although my blooming dog-sitter has just cancelled on me, but sorting that out is my job for today and once I've done that, then I'll be packing and off! Des wouldn't want me to sit here and dwell on it. He'd say, "Alice, you can have a pity-party, but get it over and done with quickly, and until we meet again, go and enjoy your life. Don't be sad at what we had; smile and think about all those wonderful memories that we made." I can just hear him saying it now.' She smiled. 'Life has a funny way of showing you that it's for making memories, and perhaps now is your time to make some new ones.'

I thought hard about the last time I'd made a memory that wasn't work related, and couldn't for the life of me think of anything.

We finished our tea and I said that I must get home, not that I had anything to go home to or for, but I felt like I'd already taken more of this wonderful lady's time than I should. I bent to stroke Baxter and he licked my hand. He really was a sweetheart. I told Alice that my best friend Beth ran a doggy daycare business and might be able to look after Baxter while she was away.

We exchanged phone numbers and I told Alice that I'd speak to Beth and be in touch. She gave me a gentle hug as we said good-bye. For the second time recently, I was reminded of the fact that people didn't touch me very often. I lived alone and didn't really see many people, and a hug was a rarity. It was actually really rather nice.

'Be kind to yourself, Madison. You've had a massive shock and some major things going on in your life. Be easy on yourself.'

As I walked home I wondered if the universe was way cleverer than we gave it credit for. Whether people came into your life at a time when they were meant to for a particular reason. Alice had made me feel that perhaps being made redundant wasn't the worst thing in the world, but maybe it was just a chance for me to have a bit of a shake-up of my life and make new memories of my own. And that thought actually didn't seem quite as bad as it had an hour ago.

I went home and threw a ready meal into the microwave. I knew that now I had more time on my hands, I should be eating more healthily, but right now I didn't have the energy to cook. And I was pretty rubbish at it anyway. Flicking through the TV channels made me realise how I didn't really follow anything on TV, so I opted for the first Bridget Jones film; I'm not sure whether it made me feel better or worse, but it did make me realise that crap happened to Bridget too.

5

When I woke the next day, reality hit me again. I had no job, no income, no purpose; I felt like I had no identity. I needed to do something about it.

The one thing I did have right now was time. For the first time in what felt like ages, I put on my dressing gown and slippers, plonked myself on the sofa with a bowl of cereal, grabbed the remote control from the coffee table in front of me and put on morning television. I didn't normally sit down and eat breakfast, maybe grabbing a protein bar, sandwich or a low-fat flapjack along with a skinny latte from the local drive-through Costa or garage on the way to work. There was a feature on the show about a woman who had been the victim of domestic violence for years before one day murdering her abusive husband. I wondered what on earth the catalyst had been that had tipped her over the edge. Her friends came on the show, talking about how they'd known that something was going on but that she wouldn't admit it, which got me thinking about how long she'd put up with his behaviour and their backstory. It made me realise that I was always quite quick to judge people in situations such as this and I couldn't believe that they'd let a situation go on for so long, but perhaps you just really never knew what went on in people's lives and shouldn't make judgements.

* * *

I decided that later I would pop over to Growlers and check out some more job sites on the internet. Perhaps I just needed to get straight back into the PR scene. That was what I would look at today, rather than trying something random and new. It would be nice to have some company, and I also wanted to see whether there was any chance of getting Baxter a place. I felt I should repay Alice's kindness and wise words with the same. I was feeling so sorry for myself, I completely forgot yesterday.

I texted Beth and asked if it would be OK to use the office, and she texted back.

Don't be long. Kettle's on!

When I arrived, Uncle Tom and Beth were looking very serious and I wondered what I was walking into. I soon discovered that Beth's hospital appointment had come through and they needed her to go in a week on Monday for her operation. She was stressing about how they'd cope at the farm and kennels. The doctor had said that she'd be on crutches for at least four weeks, certainly not able to drive for a good while after that, and would be needing physio for three months before she was back to work as she had a physical job. She'd be able to manage the office-based duties when she was feeling up to it, but she was really worried about how they'd manage the manual work. Russell would do extra hours, and at some point Alex would come over from America, but it was quite short notice and he might not be able to come straight away.

Beth put her head in her hands. 'What are we going to do, Dad? God, I wish Mum were here right now.'

Heartbreak and devastation had hit their family a week before Beth's sixteenth birthday when Aunty Jen was tragically killed in a horse-riding accident. I knew how much Beth missed her mum, particularly when she needed to make a big decision in her life.

He rubbed her shoulder and rested his chin on the top of her head. 'I know, darling. I do too. But we'll sort it out somehow, don't worry. You have to have that op and we'll just have to manage. Let's wait until Alex is up. He's five hours behind, so we'll call him after lunch and see when he can get here. We can't really do anything until then. Then we'll make a plan.'

She smiled back at him but it didn't reach her eyes.

I made a split-second decision. 'I'll do it!'

They both turned to look at me and gave a double-take.

'I'll help!'

'You? Really?' Uncle Tom started to titter. 'You do know this is a farm, don't you?'

'OK, very funny. But yes, me. Why not?'

'Darling, you know we love you, but it's not really your thing, is it? Apart from mucking out the horses when you were a teenager, you haven't been near a farm for years. Walking around in jeans and wellies all day cleaning up dog muck and cleaning out the chicken shed? That's not really your style, is it? And I didn't think you even liked dogs that much.'

Beth looked thoughtful. 'Wait, Dad. Let her speak.'

'Look, you need help. I have time on my hands. I have my redundancy money so don't need paying. And honestly, just how hard can it be?'

Uncle Tom stood and hugged me. 'Madison, my darling, if you

are really one hundred per cent sure, I think you could just be the answer to all our prayers. However, I do insist on giving you a wage for working here. We'll sort something out that we're all happy with.' For the first time in a couple of weeks, I actually felt useful and knew that I would be able to help them. And that felt good.

'Well, there you go then. All sorted. Now, where's that cuppa you promised me?' Beth grinned and headed for the kitchen.

'Thank you, darling. This means the world to us. It really does.'

'I won't let you down, Uncle Tom. You both mean so much to me and it's the perfect solution for all of us.'

'To Growlers, Giddywell Grange and us!' We toasted the arrangement with three mugs of tea.

Suddenly realising that I'd forgotten something important, I asked them whether they had space for another dog for next week and after I told him the story about Alice and Baxter, Uncle Tom said he'd be delighted to take Baxter for as long as she needed. We sorted out a plan for Alice to come along to have a look later that day, and then I would stay afterwards and have a chat about what else I needed to do to help.

I couldn't wait to ring Alice and tell her that everything was sorted, and I knew that I'd be able to keep an eye on Baxter for her too if I was helping out a bit. He really was an absolute darling. I sent her a quick text asking if I could pop round after lunch as I had some great news to tell her, and she quickly replied and said that around 2 p.m. would be perfect and she'd make sure the kettle was on. I didn't think I'd ever drunk as much tea in my life since I'd been made redundant.

* * *

When I arrived at Alice's house, Baxter ran in circles around my ankles and kept brushing himself against my legs, and I was flattered when Alice said that he only did that with people he really liked. I stood leaning against one of the kitchen cupboards while she laid the tea tray, and I told her that I'd managed to bag Baxter a spot at Growlers if she wanted it. As Uncle Tom suggested, I asked if she'd like to come and have a look round this afternoon and make sure she was happy with it before she made her mind up.

Her face lit up and she stepped towards me and threw her arms around me. 'I knew you were lucky when I met you. I had a feeling.' She grinned. 'I trust you already, so if you say it's OK, then I'm happy for Baxter to go there, but yes, it would be lovely to see where he'll be staying. I do worry about him being away from me.' She reached down and gave him a treat from her pocket. He scampered off to his bed by the back door and munched away.

'Well, I'll be able to visit him and I'll be working there quite a lot over the next few weeks, so I can even text you pictures of him to reassure you.'

'Oh Madison, I'm so happy. I was really worried that I might not be able to go. It's a huge thing for me to leave him behind while I visit my sister, but knowing that you'll be on hand makes me feel so much better. Let's have a quick cuppa, then can we go and have a look? Do you think it would be OK if I bring him along?'

'Of course, Uncle Tom said that dogs settle in better when they've already visited and know the place, and he's going to be there to show us around. He's looking forward to meeting you both. I'm going to be stopping there for an hour or two afterwards, so is it OK if you follow me in your car?'

'Of course, and honestly, Madison, you've really taken a weight off my shoulders today. I hope you realise what a difference you've made to us.'

My heart lifted and for the first time in a long time, I realised that helping others was a good thing to do.

Perhaps I wasn't a nobody after all. If Alice thought I had made a difference to her, then perhaps I could make a difference to others too.

I vowed that from here on, I was going to do at least one thing every day for someone else. I was going to do something that would make a difference to someone and brighten their day. It could be someone I knew, or it could be a random stranger. And it would give me something to focus on for the future. I felt like I'd spent so much time looking out for Ronington's and my position there that I had forgotten about the important things in life.

6

When we arrived back at the farm, it was as if I was seeing it through a new set of eyes as we drove into the courtyard and arrived at a set of six-foot gates. We both parked up and negotiated our way around some clucking chickens and a very noisy but friendly cockerel who didn't seem to realise that he was only supposed to cock-a-doodle-doo in the morning, as he seemed to cock-a-doodle-doo all day long. Uncle Tom always said he was just protecting his ladies like a true gentleman should.

A huge brass bell hung on the wall of the barn to the right of the gates. I gave it a tug and it rang and echoed around the courtyard for what seemed like ages. Alice and I laughed at how loud it was and how it seemed to set off the dogs barking in a chain. I heard the noise of a bolt sliding across and another gate shutting, before Uncle Tom appeared and invited us through to reception.

He bent down and tickled Baxter behind the ears, and Baxter licked his face. Uncle Tom never batted an eyelid. He was used to all sorts of dogs and loved them more than humans, I always felt. There were always dogs running around on the farm in the summer when we were kids, and curled up on their beds beside the fireplace in the winter.

'And you' – he stood and turned – 'must be Alice. Good afternoon and welcome to Growlers at the Grange. Come through, come through.' He led us through the back of reception out to the stable block, with Baxter trotting happily alongside us.

Alice nodded and smiled at me, and I could see that she was really happy with what she was seeing.

'The dogs are all off lead from here, and it's totally secure, and they can run around to their hearts' content.' He guided Alice through to the fenced paddock and explained about the activity centre that was set up.

'We spend lots of time in here and the dogs love it, and it helps to tire them out both mentally and physically. My daughter Beth, who the business belongs to really, would rather spend her time out here playing with the dogs than doing the paperwork side, so that's my domain really. And Maddy here is going to be helping out, as much as we can persuade her to, while Beth is recovering from an operation. So what do you think, Alice? Do you think Baxter will be OK with us?'

'Oh, Tom,' she said with tears in her eyes. 'It breaks my heart to leave him behind, but my sister has been in Australia for over twenty years and I've not seen her in person for all that time, and she's paid for me to go over to see her. I thought I was going to have to cancel, but luckily for me, I met this young lady.' She smiled and touched my arm tenderly. 'I really do think some things are meant to be. If I hadn't met Madison and had that conversation with her, I might have cancelled my trip. I feel a million times better knowing that he'll be coming to such a wonderful place, with such lovely, caring people.'

'Well, we're so pleased to be able to help. And I promise you that we'll look after him. He looks like he's taken a shine to Maddy already! Look at him, he won't leave her side. I think she's becoming quite fond of him too.'

Alice smiled at me as I was kneeling down rubbing his ears and he was leaning into me.

'I don't think he'll have any problems here, Alice. Let's go and sort all the paperwork side out and we might even be able to persuade Maddy to make us a cuppa.' He winked at her and they all turned round as Baxter started to bark, circled round three times, squatted and did a huge poo. Uncle Tom laughed as he pulled a poo bag from out of his coat pocket and picked it up, while I turned up my nose and asked myself again why I'd decided to help out at a doggy daycare and wondered how much of my day would consist of picking up crap. Although, I pondered, maybe that was not so different to my old job – just a different type of crap.

But then Baxter made me giggle when he came and stuck his nose right in my face. Alice apologised and said he had no concept of personal space and was just an 'in your face' type of dog. I ruffled the fur on his head and when I looked at Alice, who was watching how I reacted to her furry friend, she smiled at me. I knew we were able to help her at what was, to her, a really hard time, and I thought that there were definitely worse jobs in the world. Time to put the kettle on. Again.

7

The next week flew by as we all started getting into a routine at Growlers. While Beth was still around, she taught me all she could regarding the office work, so I could get to know every aspect of what she did from the business side of things. Then she could help Uncle Tom and Russell to carry out all the physical duties, while I kept the office side going, and they'd show me those ropes next week. They'd spoken to Alex and he was going to be able to get over a couple of days after she'd had her operation, so we worked out a rota to cover the first couple of weeks of her being away from work.

The day of the operation soon came round and it was really emotional to say goodbye to her as Uncle Tom bundled her up in his tatty old Land Rover and took her off to the hospital. He was beyond worried until he got a call to say that everything had gone as well as could be expected and that Beth was sleeping and very groggy and that it would be better if he visited the following day. She still wasn't with it the following day so his visit was short and sweet, but he was definitely feeling better now that he'd seen her.

Mum popped over early evening with her slow cooker full of

the most divine-smelling chicken casserole, and we didn't realise how hungry we all were until we sat around the farmhouse kitchen and tucked in. We arranged a visiting rota for the hospital so we weren't all there at the same time and so that Beth wasn't alone for too long. Fingers crossed, she'd be allowed home within a few days to start her recovery.

The next afternoon on my visiting shift, Beth seemed much perkier than I'd thought she'd be.

'Well, I'm glad you've lost your job!'

'*Beth!* You can't say that.'

'Well, I am. And because I'm ill I can say what I want! It's like being an old person who doesn't give a shit who they upset with what they say. I love it!' She grinned. 'Perhaps now you'll spend time doing other things than work, Maddy. And just think – you can spend more time with me right now. You would never have done that if you were still working. Sometimes things happen for a reason, but we don't know why.'

'I don't know how to do anything apart from work.' I laughed.

'I know you've always thought my life was really boring compared to yours, Mads.'

'I never said that.'

'You didn't have to say it. You always looked down your nose at me when I told you what I was doing. I could never compete with your world of glamour and money. All you've ever done for the last few years is work your backside off to make someone else's dreams come true and to make their business a success. What do you do for you, Mads?'

'But I've had to do this; it's important to me to be a success. It's all that matters to me.'

'But why, Maddy? What can be more important than having a great life and doing something you love? I've never really understood why you pushed yourself so hard.'

'Because,' I answered, almost whispering the words. 'Just because.'

'Who do you feel the need to prove yourself to?'

'Please Beth, just drop it. It's not important.'

'OK, I'll drop it for now, but don't think I won't come back to this when I have more energy. You've been so busy making a living that you've forgotten to make a life for yourself.'

Beth's words cut me to the core as the realisation dawned on me that she was absolutely right. As soon as someone asked me to do something, I'd say, 'I'm sorry, I'm working,' or mostly, 'I don't have time.'

'We all have twenty-four hours in a day, Mads, even Richard Branson and Beyoncé. It's what we choose to do with it that makes all the difference.'

I looked at my friend. Beth had been with me all my life, even though over the last few years I'd not really been the best friend to her. I realised that for a long time, our friendship had been very one-sided. If Beth had organised something then I'd go along, but I was always way too busy to actually arrange something myself. I asked myself exactly what I had brought to our friendship and for the last few years, the answer was actually not a lot. But when I asked what Beth had brought to our friendship, the answer was... everything.

'What are your dreams and desires, Mads? What do you want out of life?'

'I really don't know any more. I thought I did. I thought that working at Ronington's and throwing everything I had into their business was what I wanted, and I *do* think I've lost my hopes and dreams somewhere along the way. I suppose I've been busy helping someone else to build their dreams instead of thinking about my own. And to be honest, since they let me go, until I started working at the farm, I was feeling pretty bloody useless.'

Being made redundant was one of the worst points of my life. I didn't think I'd ever felt so low, not even after what had happened with Jamie. I never saw it coming that morning; never suspected the rollercoaster of emotions that awaited me. One minute I was elated at the prospect of being promoted, then plunged into shock at being told that I wasn't good enough to keep my job and that I was being let go.

Talk about a kick in the teeth.

Seeing that her words had had an impact on me, Beth decided to relent a little and get back to business.

'Over there on the bedside table is a list of things that I need you to do to cover for me while I'm out of action. I don't want you to look at them yet, but I do want you to take the notebook home with you. Basically, I need you to do these things. Non-negotiable. If you don't do them, then lots of people will be let down. Good people who need help right now. And I think it'll do you good. You've been walking round with blinkers on and I really want you to throw yourself into the stuff I've written down. It's nothing major, just stuff that I do every week to help out in the community. But if I don't help them, then no one will, so it's all down to you. It'll be good for you too!

'You might find these tasks dull and boring, but these people need someone to help them. They depend on me. And maybe somewhere along the way, they might just trigger off some ideas that will fire you up and inspire you. You've lost that passion and spark that you had all those years ago, Mads, and I want to help you get them back. And let's face it, there's bugger all else I'm going to be doing for the next few months, is there?' She waved her hand up and down her body and sighed loudly.

That feeling of panic and nausea was coming back. My heartbeat started to quicken. Apart from working at Growlers, I had nothing else planned for the immediate future and it was pretty darn scary. What Beth had said to me, about losing my spark, hit home too. And if I was really honest with myself, maybe I'd lost my identity before I'd been made redundant. Even though I gave the impression that I was living my best life, was I really? Work was my everything and there was nothing outside of it. Beth was being quite brutal with her words, and it hurt, but she was actually right. This was all totally outside of my comfort zone, but perhaps it *was* time that I explored more options.

I scraped a hand through my hair and had a fluttery feeling in my tummy. I took a deep breath.

'OK, let's do this!'

8

Waking up to a manically enthusiastic message from Alice telling me what a whale of a time she was having in Australia already was such a lovely way to start the day. On her first day there, she'd apparently already been cuddling koalas in a zoo in Brisbane, and her list of things to do while she was there included snorkelling at the Great Barrier Reef and visiting Byron Bay. Then they were going to spend a few days in Sydney visiting friends, attend a concert at the Sydney Opera House and walk the Harbour Bridge. She was even going to visit the set of *Neighbours*. It sounded like an exhausting holiday to me with tons of travelling, but I had to admire her lust for life; it filled my heart with joy. She was doing way more on her visit to Australia than I'd ever done on any of my holidays, where I normally spent my relaxing time on the beach reading a business or personal development book or listening to one on audio. I quite liked an audio book, especially when I was in the car. I never wanted to waste time listening to the radio and those crappy chart songs.

I hadn't even had a holiday for the last couple of years and I was quite envious of Alice. We arranged a Skype call for when I was at work so she could see her beloved furry friend.

Great news awaited us when I contacted Uncle Tom after breakfast to see how Beth was. He'd rung the hospital and was told that she was recovering well and would be able to come home the next day as long as she followed the specific rules and regulations. There was no reason why she couldn't remain happy and healthy in her own environment until we reached the next stage of her journey where her physiotherapy started and her recovery could continue.

Delighted with this news, I promised to pop in later and see her, but I had to cover one of Beth's community projects first. I had to report to Stafford Library at 10 a.m. and was told that all would be revealed when I got there.

It was years since I'd been inside a library and I hadn't read a novel for a long time.

Being the dutiful friend that I was, and ready to fill Beth's shoes temporarily, I turned up at the library just before ten and reported to the information desk. 'Hi there, I'm Madison Young. Beth Millington sent me.'

'Ah, Miss Young, we've been expecting you. I'm Rebecca. Thank you so much for helping us out with our community reach programme. It means so much to get people like you to help us.'

Community reach... what the hell was that when it was at home? 'Do you mind if I pop to the ladies'?' I asked the dark-haired pretty librarian. Being a librarian must be the most boring job in the world, I thought. I excused myself and went off to find the ladies'. While I was washing my hands, a poster on the wall caught my eye.

Community Reach

Do you have a few hours each week to help people who can't get to a library?

There are a number of people who are physically unable to come along to get books from us, but who love to read.

We want to make a difference in their lives. Can you help?

If so, we'd love to hear from you so that we can make someone's day.

Now I knew a little more about it, it still seemed like something really dull. But in fairness, I had all the time in the world, and I had promised Beth that I would trust her and go through with anything I was asked to.

Begrudgingly, I went over to Rebecca and asked her what I needed to do next. She gave me an empty cardboard box and a list of titles and instructed me to find the books on the list and put them in the box, then bring them back to be checked out.

As I searched the shelves, I read the descriptions on the back covers and some of them actually piqued my interest, which surprised me. There was a real mix of genres, from a psychological thriller about a girl who woke up to find her son missing, a romcom about a girl who fell in love with her arch enemy and another a fantasy romance where the hero alternated between being a faerie king and a normal person. Perhaps I should give reading a go. I used to love it as a child. I still didn't really know why I was putting these books in the box, but as Rebecca date stamped them at the desk, she gave me an address.

'So, you are going to Mr and Mrs Darby. Their address is 136 Glasscroft Close. Here's the postcode too. All you have to do is take this box of books and pick up the ones they're returning and bring those back. That OK?'

Simple then, nothing difficult in that. I'd be in and out within a minute or two, I guessed. Best go and get on with it.

I loaded the books onto the back seat of my car and set the satnav for the postcode I'd been given. As I parked outside 136 Glasscroft Close, I looked up at the house. It was a beautiful Georgian building, but looked very tired. Grabbing the box of books from the car, I noticed that the garden was overgrown and the front door looked like it needed a lick of paint.

I knocked on the door and waited. And waited. After what seemed like five minutes but was probably not anywhere near that long, I went to turn to walk back to the car. If they couldn't be bothered to answer the door, then I didn't have time to hang around waiting for them. Although, I did really, didn't I?

'I'm coming.' I heard a muffled sound from behind the door and it eventually opened as far as the chain would allow it. 'Hello?' The wrinkled but clearly once beautiful face of a little old lady peered at me from behind the door. 'Can I help?'

'Hello, Mrs Darby. My name is Maddy and I'm here from the library community reach programme. I've brought you some books.' The penny was finally starting to drop with me.

'Ooh goodness me, how wonderful,' she exclaimed. She shut the door and I could hear her taking the chain off. I balanced the box of books on one arm and showed her an ID badge I had on a lanyard with my free hand.

'I don't care who you are as long as you can cheer up my Ron.' She smiled at me and then shuffled along behind her walking frame down the hallway into a kitchen.

'Would you like a cup of tea, dear?'

I was about to say I didn't have time. It was more of a habit than anything else, and I realised that I did have time. All the time in the world. I had no other plans today and, just maybe, having a chat and a cuppa with this lady might brighten her day. And it felt good to be doing something for someone else for a change.

'Yes please, that would be nice,' I replied, but as she was clearly struggling to lift the kettle and manoeuvre around her walking frame, I took it from her.

'Let me. Why don't you sit down and let me make you one, Mrs Darby.'

'Ooh my dear, how lovely. I can't remember the last time someone made me a cup of tea. Thank you. And please, call me Leila.' She plonked herself down onto one of the kitchen chairs and directed me to the cups, spoons and teabags. 'We'll take one up to Ron if that's OK. It's been a while since his last one. Can't let him have too much to drink, it's so much trouble to get him out of bed and into the bathroom.' She laughed. 'It wears us both out.'

We chatted easily as the kettle boiled. Leila told me that she and Ron were childhood sweethearts and had been married for seventy-five years. They were both ninety-six. They had two children with families of their own, giving them five grandchildren, but they all had busy lives and they didn't live in the local area so weren't able to help out much.

My heartstrings twanged when I thought about how little I knew about my own grandparents. Mum had told me that they'd had a falling out years ago and she flatly refused to talk about it, so over the years I just stopped asking. While I respected her decision, it was my life that was affected too and I wondered again whether there were still people out there related to me, struggling along in their lives. Or had they left this world already? Would I ever know? Did I have a whole family still to be discovered? And would I ever discover them, or would my questions go unasked and unanswered for the rest of my life? Mum and I were a family, and a great one, but I always wondered about the people that I'd never met.

I made tea for three and carried the tea tray to the foot of the stairs where a stair lift took over the bottom of the hallway. Leila shuffled down the hallway and suggested that she made the journey first, then send the chair back down, and I would rest the tray on the top of the box of books and send it up again. Leila laughed as she alighted the stair lift at the top of the stairs. 'Bloody slow but it does the trick. And as Ron used to fart with every footstep on the way up, it's way more pleasant than following him up. Don't get old dear, it makes you very windy!' She winked at me.

'Nearly there, Ron my love. Make sure you're decent. I have a young lady with me who doesn't want to see your wrinkly old soldier hanging out of your pyjama bottoms, thank you very much.' She grabbed another walking frame on the landing, and I squeezed past the stair lift as it made the trip with the books and tea.

Leaving the box of books for a moment, I carried the tea tray into the room that Leila had disappeared into, where she told me to put it down on an old oak dressing table.

'Just the job,' came a man's deep voice from behind the door.

'And you must be Mr Darby. Good morning. I'm Maddy.'

'Call me Ron, my dear. Mr Darby makes me feel old!' He winked. 'Hello, Maddy, what brings you to Glasscroft Close this morning? Not that I'm complaining about getting visitors. We don't get many these days, do we, Leil?'

Leila plonked herself on the bed next to her husband and took his hand in hers and patted it, her eyes full of love as she shook her head gently. A lump formed in my throat. When I was younger, my dream was to grow old with Alex, and then when I met Jamie, I thought it would be us. But now, it's just me. All alone.

Remembering the books, I scooted back to the landing and returned with the box and put it on the edge of the bed.

Ron's eyes lit up like the Blackpool illuminations and a grin spread literally from ear to ear. 'Ooh, you've brought books. Do I get to choose one?'

'Not one, they're all for you if you want them. There's a selection of the genres that the library ladies know you read.'

'Goodness me! *All* of them?' Ron looked like a child in a sweet shop. 'Are you sure? All of them. There must be twenty books in that box. Really?'

My heart warmed to the happiness that was etched on his face as he started to search through the box and there were oohs and aahs coming from him as he took them out and read the blurb on the backs, with his glasses perched on the end of his nose.

'As you can see, Ron is mainly bedridden and we can't get to the library these days, so someone suggested that the library could come to us. We normally have a lovely young lady called Beth deliver our books.'

'Ah, Beth is my best friend, but she's not able to get around much at the moment as she's had an operation. I've known Beth all my life.'

'Such a lovely girl. What she has done for us has given us both a new lease of life. We're both avid readers and because we don't have a fat lot else to do in the day, we devour books. We're both very lucky to be blessed with good eyesight, which is unusual at our age and which we are so grateful for, as reading is our escapism. I don't think people realise how important this community service from our library is to people like us. You've made us so happy, Maddy. If you hadn't have come, we might not have been able to get any more books till Beth was better, and I'm not sure how long that might be. Please do give her our love, won't you. And Maddy, we honestly can't thank you enough. We can't get out much into the world any more, but books bring the world in here to us.'

What a lovely way to look at reading, I thought.

'Is there anything else I can do for you while I'm here?' I asked.

Ron looked at Leila and raised his eyebrows, but she shook her head.

'No, it's fine, thank you, you've done more than enough already,' Leila replied.

'It's no problem, honestly. I have a day of no plans, so make the most of me while I'm here.'

'Well, there is something, dear, if you really wouldn't mind. On top of that wardrobe is a small suitcase which I'd love you to get down if you can reach it. I keep meaning to climb up on that bedroom stool, but Ron keeps telling me I'm not to.'

Being tall was something that used to drive me mad when I was at school. I used to get picked on and called 'lanky legs' and I hated it. But right now, it was very useful as I reached up above the wardrobe and pulled the suitcase down, along with a cloud of dust. Ron started to cough, and Leila asked me to open the window a tad. 'Come on, Ron, steady on. You know when you cough like that you have to concentrate and control your bodily functions.'

Leila turned to me and giggled. 'Honestly, my dear, at our age, anything can happen.'

He took in some fresh air and got his breath back as she gently patted his back. He took a sip of his tea and I pulled the window to again, so that he didn't catch the draught.

We chatted easily while we drank the tea. I thought they were a lovely couple. Looking at my watch, I noticed that an hour had passed since I'd arrived, so I collected the cups, took them downstairs and swilled them in the old Belfast sink, leaving them on the side to drain. I gave the sides a wipe down with the dish cloth. Leila might think their eyesight was good but an extra wipe would get rid of some of those crumbs that had been left behind.

When I popped back upstairs to say goodbye, Leila had climbed back onto the bed and was lying next to her husband, snuggled into his shoulder. Ron took my hand in his. 'Thank you, Maddy, you really have made my day. I'm so looking forward to reading these books. I love a good murder, the more gruesome the better. And Lei loves all these bloody daft romances that you've brought her too. Hope there's no saucy books in there. I don't want her getting ideas and ravishing me. I don't think my heart is up to it these days.' He winked at me and Leila just laughed at him.

'I cannot thank you enough. This suitcase is full of photographs and we're going to spend the day looking through them. What a delight.'

'Is there anything else I can get you?' I asked.

'No thank you, dear,' smiled Leila as she patted her husband's hand. 'I have everything I will ever need right here in this room.'

I swallowed down another lump in my throat and thanked them for their time. They thought I'd done them a huge favour, when in fact, it was totally the other way round. Letting me into their lives was a true reminder that what to some was just a small task in a day could be the most important thing in someone else's world. If only more people knew about this service. There must have been lots of people like the Darbys who needed company and would have liked someone to pop some books into them. I could really appreciate the value of the community outreach programme now I had seen the joy it could bring for myself.

Today, in just a short time, I felt like I had done something worthwhile. I hadn't felt that sense of satisfaction since being made redundant.

I offered to let myself out so that they didn't have to move, and as I picked up the box of books to be returned and closed the front door gently behind me, I heard Leila and Ron reminiscing over treasured memories and years gone by.

* * *

As I closed the gate, I looked again at the overgrown garden and mused about what a beautiful house and garden this must have once been, when a thought popped into my mind. Young Russell from the kennels was always saying that he wanted to earn some extra cash; he was hardworking and keen. I wondered whether he might like to come and mow the lawn and give the garden a tidy-up. I was sure they'd appreciate it. I'd be happy to pay him to do it; it would be my treat to the Darbys for brightening up my day and showing me what love could be.

My mind was working overtime as I drove back to the library, although I was returning with a lighter heart than when I'd left first thing this morning. My father had suddenly popped into my mind.

Father. It was a strange word to me. My biological father had never been a real father to me. He'd certainly never been a dad. I wondered whether the word 'father' really applied to him at all.

Even though Mum and I hadn't talked about him for years, it didn't stop me wondering about him and imagining what it would be like if I ever met him. I didn't even know if I'd ever want to. He came to me in dreams quite often, although I could never see his face. I walked past people in the street and wondered if he looked like them. Perhaps *I* looked like *him*. Did I resemble my half siblings – if I had any? Was there a whole new family out there I knew nothing about?

And then there was Mum to consider. How would she feel if I ever did want to contact him? Did she ever wish that I hadn't come along and spoilt everything for them? Would they have stayed together? I wondered if she regretted having me. Would they eventually have had a different family? Would they be like the adorable Darbys that I'd just left? It was all totally mind-blowing when I opened myself up to the questions.

Perhaps I needed to open a new notebook and start a list with all my questions in it. It might be cathartic to get them all out of my head. It was giving me a headache and also sleepless nights.

But did I really want to know the answers to my questions? While it was still all unanswered, I didn't have to deal with it. And let's face it, I'd managed for this long perfectly well without a dad, so I didn't really need one. I had Mum, after all, and she'd been everything to me all my life even though I'd neglected her in the latter years. I suppose there was a part of me that made me totally self-sufficient, the same way that Mum did, as that seemed to be the only way that you wouldn't get hurt. I knew though in my heart that at some point we'd need to talk more about it. It was just about finding the right time.

If only I had a name, I could have done some digging around on Facebook. But then again, if I found someone, it would open up a whole new can of worms. And was it really what I wanted? I could never undo it once I'd started, which was why I'd never gone further in the past. Maybe it was better just left buried.

Oh God! I just didn't know. It was way too confusing for this mind to take right now. Good job really that I didn't have to think about high-powered executive work at the moment too as I'd never be able to concentrate.

Rebecca saw me struggling to balance the box of books. She came and held the door open for me, bringing me back to the present.

'How did it go?' she asked.

I couldn't stop myself as I burst into tears. I seemed to be so tearful lately.

'Emotional, isn't it?' She put her hand on my arm and guided me over to the office area behind the counter and made me a cup of tea.

'They are such a lovely couple, and in their old age they have everything they could ever want.' I couldn't find the words to explain how much the Darbys had melted my heart and made me feel really melancholy.

'Thank you for your help today, Maddy. I did wonder whether we'd still be able to offer this service with Beth being off. I'm so grateful to you for stepping in.'

'Is that it? Can I help some more? Can I do it again?'

Rebecca laughed. 'Of course you can, Maddy. Let's go and check the rota and see if there are any other visits this week that need covering. We truly are grateful for your help. We've just lost a support worker who has got a fulltime job, as well as Beth's operation affecting us, so you coming along is perfect timing.'

'It's me who should be thanking you, Rebecca. Today has really helped me to feel valuable again. Since I was made redundant, I've struggled to find my place in the world. I only knew work. I was a proper workaholic, too. Would you mind if I took a look around the library while I'm here?'

'Of course not. Help yourself. Are you a reader, Madison?'

'I haven't been for a long time. I used to read lots when I was younger. Always used to lose myself in a book. Perhaps I need to start reading again for pleasure. My mum is such an avid reader. I sometimes wonder how she ever gets anything done around the house when she's always got her nose in a book.'

'Ah well, there's nothing better than a good book to take you away from everything. You should try it. You'll see.'

I meandered around the library and chose three fiction novels to take home in different genres just in case I didn't get on with them. One was a fluffy romcom, another was described as heartbreaking women's fiction and the other was a psychological thriller. I wasn't promising to read them all, but I'd give it a go.

When I arrived home that lunchtime, I made myself a cup of tea, sank into the sofa and tucked my feet up. I covered myself with the mohair throw which was always on the back of the sofa – for decorative rather than practical purposes until now – and spread the books out on my lap, deciding which one to read first.

I promised myself just a few chapters as I knew I had things to do, but before I knew it, it was early afternoon and I needed to get a wriggle on as I was due over at Growlers at 3 p.m. for a few hours. For the first time in a very long while, sitting and losing myself in a book had felt relaxing yet at the same time exhilarating. I hadn't thought of anything else for the last few hours, totally immersing myself in the story. Perhaps there was something to this reading lark after all.

* * *

As I had been doing for the last few days, I made sure that Baxter was my first port of call when I arrived at Growlers. He was so happy to see me, jumping up at the kennel door. I let myself in and sat with him for about fifteen minutes before letting the dogs in the field for their afternoon exercise session. Some had to be walked separately, as they didn't mix well, but those that did all went together and played boisterously with each other. I threw a tennis ball and yelled 'Ozzy, come' to a large Rottweiler, just like Uncle Tom had taught me, and laughed as he thundered towards me. I stood my ground, knowing that there was no way he would run straight at me. How wrong I was. I was completely winded as he knocked me flying and I fell backwards, bum first, into a paddling pool full of cold water. I heard chortling from reception and Uncle Tom was holding his side and laughing so hard. After my dignity was restored, I returned to the office where he gave me a big hug and made me feel so much better, if a little stupid.

'Maybe next time, move out of the way, just in case, Madison.' He laughed.

* * *

That evening, after I'd filled more poo bags than I ever thought possible and thrown more tennis balls than I thought existed in the world, I popped into the hospital to see Beth, but when I arrived she was asleep. Glad that I'd brought my book along with me, I settled in to read but after just one page it was almost as if she sensed that I was there. She turned her head. 'Hey, thanks for coming.' She was still really groggy.

'Hey, gorgeous, sorry I woke you.' I tried to think of something to say that wasn't 'how are you?' – a rather ridiculous question right now but one that most of the time you couldn't help but ask.

'I'm sorry if I look like shit.' She tried to move around to make herself more comfortable and even that exertion looked like it exhausted her. I jumped up to hold her forward while I adjusted the pillows and propped her up.

'You could never look like shit, Beth. You even look fabulous in a hospital gown with your arse hanging out the back. Are you in pain?'

She giggled but I could see how much it hurt her. 'Thank you for saying that but I know I don't. Luckily I'm off my tits on morphine so I can't feel a thing right now.'

I smiled. It was great to see that she hadn't lost her sense of humour despite what she'd gone through.

'Don't take the piss! Actually, someone could come and take the piss, because I've got a catheter in and I'm sure I probably stink of wee! I think they need to empty it!'

'Don't worry about that, I love you even if you do stink of wee.'

She enjoyed hearing all about my morning with the Darbys and I told her they'd sent their love and how much their visit to them had warmed my heart.

'You can't beat the feeling of knowing that you are helping someone,' she said.

'You're right, you know. I know I've helped people in a work capacity but this is kind of helping someone to live, and today just filled my heart with joy.'

'I knew it would. I just knew it. So what are your plans for tomorrow?' she asked.

'I'm doing a full day at doggy daycare tomorrow. So that'll be a test for me,' I laughed. I'd agreed with Rebecca to go back to the library the day after tomorrow for my next project and told Beth that all I knew was that I was going to see a Mr Parkes. Beth smiled. 'Ah! Mr Parkes. Can't wait to hear all about it.'

When Alex and Uncle Tom walked through the door, we were laughing raucously, reminiscing about our very first holiday abroad. What we thought was going to a be a little fishing village, filled with Greek character and charm, had actually turned out to be party central and filled with booze, drugs and boys. Blimey, we grew up a lot in that fortnight, seeing things that we could never unsee.

I reminded Beth of the time she squealed in horror when she got pulled up onto the stage of a nightclub by the compere and told that she'd been chosen to be a judge in a Mr Wet Y-Fronts competition and she ran off and hid in the toilet. We never left each other's side for the whole time we were there, petrified that we might be led astray. Two naive country bumpkins from a little village in the sticks of Staffordshire thrust into a world that we never imagined even existed. But oh boy, did we have a good time! We laughed about Thanassis, a full-blooded, eighteen-year-old Greek boy who followed Beth around from dusk till dawn, desperate to woo her and who kept trying to lure her up dark alleys to snog her. And then there was Aki, the drop-dead gorgeous jet ski instructor, who spent the day strutting up and down the beach in his Speedos, thinking he was God's gift to women, while all the teenage girls on the beach drooled over him. Such amazing memories of a belter of a holiday, never to be forgotten.

I glanced at Alex, who was shuffling from one foot to another in the doorway, and caught my breath. I'm sure I must have been staring. He was even more handsome than I remembered, and I felt my cheeks flush as I took in his salt and pepper hair, stubbly beard, the dark denim jeans, white open-necked shirt and his hands hidden in the pockets of a – clearly very expensive – tan leather jacket. He oozed sophistication and charm but the best part of all was that he had absolutely no idea. He smiled at me and the room lit up. He had always had the most beautiful smile I had ever seen.

We'd had a couple of 'moments' over the years and I wondered whether he remembered. The first was at my eighteenth birthday party, which was held at the farm. Mum and I were spending the night there, and all the oldies had gone to bed and there was just me, Alex and Beth left up. Alex and I plonked ourselves down on the sofa out in the conservatory while Beth was clearing up in the kitchen. Our thighs were touching and as I turned and looked up into Alex's deep blue eyes, my breath caught in my throat. He was gorgeous and I had loved him all my life. It was as if time stood still as he gently reached out to me, put his hand to my cheek, and lowered his head to mine. Our lips were mere millimetres apart. His stubble brushed against my chin and the smell of his musky aftershave made my body tingle with anticipation. All my inhibitions were flung out of the window with the three pints of cider I'd drunk and I just wanted to snog his face off.

I closed my eyes, waiting for his lips to touch mine, a dream I had waited for ever since I could remember. I thought that my body was going to spontaneously combust through anticipation.

At that exact moment, bloody Beth came flouncing into the room, totally oblivious to our situation, and flung herself across our laps, declaring my birthday party a huge success. Our 'moment' was lost but I'd never forgotten it. Alex went back to university a week later and I didn't see him for months. When he graduated, he landed a job as an architect in New York, and it was there that he met Sophie.

The last time I'd seen him was when he flew back for their grandma's funeral with her. She was absolutely stunning with her thick, shiny, long chestnut-brown hair and huge hazel eyes, which peered out from under her perfect fringe, her make-up flawless, on skin that didn't have one imperfection. A little bit of me hated her guts. Especially because at that particular time, my skin from the neck up was completely blotchy and I probably had mascara streaks from all the crying I'd been doing that morning.

As we stood at the church and said our goodbyes to a lady who had always been in my life, I looked across and saw Sophie draping her arm around her husband's shoulders and pulling him close to her, and I wished with my whole being that it was me who was comforting him, not her. But it wasn't and I vowed that I had to be nice to the woman that the man I secretly loved had chosen to be with.

We were all so distressed at the time, and when I tried to give the family some time to be together, Uncle Tom insisted that Mum and I stuck around, saying we *were* family. Mum did everything she practically could to help them, preparing food so that they didn't go hungry, even helping out at the farm where she could to make their lives as easy as possible. I now felt bad because I hadn't wanted to get my hands dirty. I was all power suits and immaculate grooming in those days, just trying to impress everyone, and looking back now, I really should have done more to help.

I do remember Alex coming out of the toilet at the farm one

day just after the funeral, as I was standing outside waiting to go in. He looked so sad, and I gave him what started as a friendly, sisterly hug, which neither of us pulled away from, and it developed into something that made my heart pound. He didn't seem to want to let me go. He held me close to his chest and sighed as he reached one hand into my hair and rested the other under my chin, tilting my face to look up at him. Once more, I got lost in those gorgeous blue eyes and time stood still for what seemed like minutes, and when he looked at my lips and moved his head just a tiny bit closer, I held my breath and closed my eyes. We pulled apart sharply when we heard a cough, and from nowhere Sophie appeared and it all got a little bit awkward. After that, I felt like he couldn't wait to get away from me. She just glared at me and walked back into the kitchen. She'd never liked me. Perhaps she could sense my crush. I had gone as red as a beetroot, so I presumed so.

I blushed again now just thinking about it, and as I looked up, his eyes met mine across the room as I was brought back to the present. He smiled at me and fireworks exploded in my tummy.

Kissing Beth on the head, and saying goodbye to everyone, I left her with her family and went home to my flat. Walking through the door, and placing my handbag on the coffee table in the lounge, I looked around and I realised again that it didn't have any warmth or depth as a home. It was very minimalistic and almost clinical. Probably because I didn't spend much time there, but staying over at Mum's, even though I'd only done so on the night I was made redundant, had made me feel a little bit differently. I loved the laughter I felt every time I walked through the front door of Giddywell Grange.

Mum's house, my childhood home and the place I would always call home, was warm and cosy, with photos everywhere celebrating the hundreds of wonderful memories that we'd made throughout the years. I suddenly realised that perhaps it was time for me to make some changes in my life after all. Perhaps the time had come for me to move out of this ultra modern apartment and move into something a little bit more homely. Perhaps I needed a new start somewhere fresh. I suppose it wouldn't hurt to see what was around. Maybe it was my time to start a new chapter.

* * *

The next day was a day mainly of office work. There were lots of bookings to organise and people to show around as it was well into the summer holiday period now and people were booking last-minute holidays then desperately trying to find places to look after their dogs. I always wondered whether you booked the holiday first then tried to sort somewhere for your dog, or sorted the dog out first and booked your holiday around them. The phone was ringing non-stop. It was clearly a thriving business and tons of people were ringing up to see whether we did grooming too. I needed to mention that to Beth when she was feeling up to it. Maybe she could get a groomer in, or Beth could even get trained up, although I doubted whether she'd have the time. Russell and Uncle Tom did most of the exercise sessions and cleaning the kennels out. I was shattered that night and soaked for ages in the bath after pouring in a hefty slug of Jo Malone English Pear and Freesia bubble bath, because I was sure I smelled of disinfectant. Then I fell into bed and was asleep within minutes.

* * *

The next morning, when I arrived at the library, I was given an address, not too far from my own actually, a ground floor apartment in a trendy block the other side of the waterside complex that I lived in, and a sealed box to take with me. I was really curious to know what was inside but Rebecca just said it was some 'stuff' to give to Mr Parkes.

Bearing in mind that the last couple I visited were both ninety-six, I was most surprised when I knocked on the door of No 7 Chase View and was greeted by a strikingly handsome man peering at me from under a mop of surfer-dude-style golden curls. Perfectly groomed stubble framed the face of an angel, with piercing green eyes. He was smartly dressed in jeans and a sage green jumper, which matched his eyes perfectly. The last thing I noticed about him was that he was in a wheelchair. 'Hi, I'm Stuart.' He held out his hand. 'You must be Maddy. Rebecca told me that you'd be popping along today.'

I smiled. 'I am indeed.' He turned and spun the chair round and wheeled down his hallway towards a modern kitchen, which had clearly been adapted for a wheelchair user. I placed the box on the kitchen table and asked if it would be OK there.

'Sure. You'll stay for a drink?' It was more of a statement than a question and I nodded, mesmerised by his handsome face. There was something that I couldn't quite put my finger on about him though. He didn't seem to look me in the eye.

'I presume that's a yes.' Stuart wheeled over towards the kettle on the side and seemed to feel his way across the work surface to the switch and felt around for the mug tree.

I realised at that point that Stuart was blind. Now it all made sense. I'd never come into contact really with anyone who was blind before. Not intentionally, but there was no one in my circle of contacts. I didn't really know how to react; should I help or would that insult him? Would he want me to help, and then what if I didn't offer? Oh crikey. How did I deal with this? Rebecca was really pushing my comfort zones today.

I decided to take the bull by the horns and offer to make the tea, and he smiled and said it would be lovely as he was forever scalding himself. He told me over a cuppa that he'd been injured in a car accident. When he woke up from a coma, he had discovered that not only was he never going to walk again, but that he had lost his sight. While his parents were normally around to help him, he had insisted that he could cope at home while they went on a week's respite. His friend, Rebecca, said that she'd arrange for home visits to keep him occupied, and he had friends popping in all through the week to make sure he was managing.

'It can get a bit boring, never getting out unless someone takes you, and it's also quite tiring so it's nice to have people popping in. Beth comes to see me a lot, she's a great friend. And I can't keep relying on my parents; they're at a time of their life when they should be out and about enjoying their retirement, not going back to the toddler years being burdened with me.'

How awful for him to feel this way. I imagined going from being independent one minute to not being able to help yourself the next. It made me realise how much we take our health for granted.

'Won't be long though until I get my guide dog. He's just going through his final training paces at the moment. I'm told it'll give me a new lease of life and I can't wait. I don't like being blind, but there's bugger all I can do about it so I have to make the most of everything, don't I? I suppose it could have been worse. I might not be here at all.'

What a way to look at life. And here was me feeling sorry for myself just because I didn't have a job any more. And even that wasn't permanent, as I was sure I would be working again before long.

'While you're here, tell me what the weather is doing today, Maddy? I like to create and imagine a picture in my head.'

An idea began to form in my mind. I had time on my hands,

and he needed someone with time. 'It's a beautiful, bright spring day, Stuart, blue sky, not a cloud in sight, the sun shining and warm enough to really feel it. I know we've only just met, but I don't suppose you fancy a walk with me, do you? I have no real plans today and it would do me good to get out in the fresh air. We could even grab a bite to eat at the café in the middle of the complex. It's coming up to lunchtime. Unless you have other plans that is, of course.'

'You sound like you know the area pretty well, Maddy. How's your wheelchair driving?'

I explained that I lived on the other side of the waterside, which only looked across the way but was a ten-minute drive. 'Not sure, but if you fancy finding out, I'm happy to give it a go,' I replied. 'But please don't be grumpy with me if you end up on the pavement!'

He laughed and I was glad he had such a great sense of humour. He wheeled into the hall to grab his jacket from the banister. 'Come on then, what are you waiting for?' He waited by the front door as I grabbed my coat from the back of one of the kitchen chairs and followed him down the hall. 'Before we go, Maddy, I need to ask you something really personal.'

Oh god! I thought to myself. *What the hell is coming next?*

'What colour is your hair?' he asked.

'Dark blonde with lighter highlights,' I replied, relieved that his question wasn't too difficult.

'Nice. I think you are probably very pretty, Maddy. At the risk of sounding like a pervert, what are you wearing? And I don't mean your under-crackers!'

I giggled. 'Blue jeans, silver trainers, and a black leather jacket over a black t-shirt.'

'OK, we can go now!' He smiled. 'I just wanted to know whether I need to be embarrassed or not to be seen out with you!'

I wish I knew what came over me when I bent close to his ear and whispered, 'Oh, and I forgot to say. I'm wearing really sexy black underwear too.'

Stuart roared with laughter. 'Oh, I like you already, girl.'

'Glad to hear it,' I replied. 'Although the honest truth is that it's a manky old greying bra and big granny knickers.'

'Watch it, lady, you'll be raising my blood pressure with that bit of information,' he replied, still tittering to himself as I rammed the wheelchair into the architrave around the front door on my way out, muttering 'whoops!'

We kept to the pavements, and luckily the complex was quite new and the walkways smooth and quite wide, so wheelchair-friendly, without too many dips up and down, although it was a shame that people weren't particularly considerate. They parked on kerbs in some places so closely that you couldn't get a wheelchair past and it really wound me up, and I huffed and puffed as I had to go down a kerb, around a car, and back up a kerb again more than once. And the dog mess! What the hell was that all about?

'Why don't people with dogs think that they have to pick up their dog mess? Dirty buggers! It's disgusting and if someone with a wheelchair drives through it, it's just going to get everywhere and could even get back into your house when you get home.'

'I used to get upset about it too, but I've now discovered that there's no good that comes from it. The only person that gets annoyed is you. Do you think that the person whose car it is cares and spends the day being wound up? Do you think the person whose dog just shat on the pavement cares about my wheelchair? We just have to realise that people are so busy wrapped up in their own lives that they don't think. It's not deliberate. So it's best to just let it go.' He was talking such sense. It was a lovely way to look at it, much better than getting all annoyed and tense about things.

'Tell me what you can see, Maddy; humour me and be my eyes.'

I pointed out every little detail of the apartment complex and noticed things that I'd never even seen myself before, from the mixture of beige-coloured and red bricks and grey slate roof tiles of the buildings we were passing with their grey aluminium window frames, to the green, short grass and the bright yellow of the wild dazzling daffodils and vibrant multi-coloured tulips, which brightened up the hedgerows. And as I described things to him, it was as if all my other senses were coming alive too.

Along the waterfront, the lake that I'd always seen as murky was actually clear in parts and there were radiant water lilies at the lake's edge, with pretty pale pink flowers – although there was also the odd carrier bag, a bicycle wheel and some other debris that I didn't bother going into detail on for fear of shocking him, and I didn't want to look too closely at it myself, to be honest.

I described the shapes that I could see in the clouds in the sky and we laughed easily as I told Stuart how my mum always used to take the mickey out of me because I used to see animals in the clouds as a child and she never could. I always said she needed to have a much better imagination. She always said that mine was way too over-active.

I smiled as I saw a mother duck with seven little babies following in her wake, describing how small and fluffy the chicks were and how they were rushing along to keep up with their mother so they didn't get lost. And how busy the mother duck seemed to be, waddling along at quite a pace, glancing back from time to time to check that they were all still there.

I'd always thought – ignorantly, I now realised – that trees were just green, but now I was looking at them in a different way, and describing them to Stuart made me realise that there were so many different shades of green, as trees and bushes that had lost their leaves over winter began to grow new leaves in various shades and buds began to open. Pretty pale pink blossom on the cherry trees painted even more colour into a landscape that had come alive for me.

Describing these tiny little things that I took for granted every single day of my life made me so very grateful that I had the gift of sight, when so many other people didn't. We really don't appreciate what we have and should show more gratitude in our lives for the things we do have, instead of thinking about the things that we don't.

We soon arrived at the little bistro café at the centre of the complex and I described the red and white canopy that covered the cast iron tables and chairs outside as I pulled the wheelchair up against a table. A pretty waitress came out to take our order and she flirted outrageously with Stuart and saw how handsome he was. She never even noticed that he couldn't see her.

I read the menu out to Stuart and we both chose a chicken panini and decided that we'd share a bowl of chips. He was so easy to chat to and we passed the time of day easily while waiting for our food.

This walk with Stuart, describing the surroundings to him, made it feel like I'd woken up and could see things that I'd never seen before, and in full technicolour too. And once more I counted my blessings.

Stuart talked about Hudson, the guide dog that he would shortly be getting. They'd been bonding over the last few months and the dog had been to stay a couple of times. Stuart was looking forward to getting some of his independence back and giving his parents a break from constantly looking after him.

He explained how most people would look at Hudson as just doing his job but Stuart saw it as opening up the world again and being able to experience things that he'd been missing out on. He was also looking forward to the emotional side of having a furry companion, that wag of a tail and lick of a hand that could brighten your day when you were feeling a bit down.

'I'd love a dog at some point, but until I lost my job recently, it's never really been the right time.'

'But maybe there'll never be a right time if you wait for it to come along. Perhaps you just have to find the right dog and fall in love with him or her and everything else will sort itself out. I've spent my life saying that I'd love to do things one day, but then I had my accident, and it made me realise that I probably will never be able to do those things now and I should have done them when I had the chance. You have to grab life with both hands, Maddy, and do the things you want to do, now. Because you don't know what tomorrow brings. I'll never forget that famous saying "Yesterday is history, tomorrow is a mystery. Today is a gift and that's why they call it the present." And it's true. Don't let anything get in your way.'

We meandered back to his apartment, once again with me wittering on about every small thing that I thought he might like to know about: the colourful wild flowers growing in the hedgerows, the bumble bees hovering and darting from one flower to the next, the greyish-brown heads, white cheeks and black bibs of the sparrows dancing around from tree to tree.

When we returned, Stuart had a huge smile on his face and some colour in his cheeks after having had a lovely morning. I knew that once again, the feeling of helping someone else was actually one of the most satisfying and heart-warming experiences that I'd ever had. I had never felt like this after a day working at the agency.

I made sure that Stuart was settled back in at home before I left. What he'd said about grabbing life was so true. Since I'd been made redundant, I'd been feeling really anxious about all sorts of things, but I couldn't let that anxiety take over like I had let it before and stop me from working out what my dreams were and setting out to grab them.

I was desperate to get home so I could ring Rebecca at the library to see if there was any way that I could be put on regular calls to both Stuart and the Darbys, who I felt had taught me more in the last two days than I had actually learned for a very long time. And I was also keen to tell Beth that she was right and that the goals I had been pursuing, thinking they were making me happy, actually hadn't made me happy for a long time, even though I thought they had.

* * *

I popped into the hospital on the way back before starting my afternoon shift at Growlers and was totally delighted to find Beth looking much brighter. She was waiting for the doctor to do his rounds and it was possible she'd be able to come home today. She was delighted to hear about how I'd got on with Stuart and was pleased that I was thinking of doing some more community projects too. Giddywell was getting under my skin and the thought of helping people really was growing on me. It helped others and made me feel happy. Win win!

* * *

Uncle Tom was waiting for me at the gate.

'Ready for Growlers then, lovely?'

'Ready as I'm going to be,' I replied with a huge grin.

'I've put these aside for you. Save your nice clothes getting too grubby. Don't want you getting a wet bum again now, do we?' he chortled, and I just grinned at him.

'Now you're going to be a fully paid up member of staff, instead of helping just in the office, I thought we'd better get you kitted out properly. I'll go and pop the kettle on and leave you to get togged up, and I'll see you out in the yard in five.' He scooted off pretty quickly, before I could see what he'd hung over the gate. I realised why when I picked up a pair of wax dungarees with the Growlers logo on the top pocket and a pair of green matching wellies. At least he'd got the right size on those, which was more than I could say for the dungarees, which would have fitted a giant. It was a good job there wasn't a mirror around; I must have looked hideous.

A loud wolf-whistle stopped me in my tracks as I turned to see, of all people, Alex. Oh, bloody great!

'Mad, you look, erm, stunning.' He flicked up his phone and took a picture before I had a chance to say a thing and grinned at me. He was gorgeous but I was going to kill him.

'I hate you, Alex Millington. Delete that picture right away!'

'Will not! I'm going to put it on Instagram right now!'

'Don't you bloody dare.' I leaned forward to grab the phone off him and he held the phone up above his head, so I had to reach even closer and up the length of his arm to grab it. As I did, he grasped my other wrist and I stumbled and fell against him. I could feel the warmth of his body, even through my gorgeous wax dungarees, and I shivered. He looked deep into my eyes and time stood still. Every nerve ending in my body tingled. We were literally millimetres away from each other. I could just reach up and kiss those lips and – oh God! – I really wanted to. As I bit my lip, his eyes lowered to my mouth and I'm really not sure if it came from him or me but I heard a groan.

'Ah, there you are. Is Alex teasing you again? He was always doing that to you when you were a teenager. Put her down, Alex. She must hate you. Here you go, Maddy, a nice cuppa for you.'

Uncle Tom passed me a thermal cup and I laughed nervously and blushed as I brushed invisible dirt from my legs with my free hand. When I snuck a glimpse of him again, he had a smirk on his face and he was still looking at me with a sparkle of mischief in his eye.

'Right, Alex and I just have to get some paperwork sorted, so I'll get that out of the way while you take your tea out to the kennel barn and you can go and let the dogs out. They're ready for their exercise session. If you want to go and take them over to the first field and then while you're out there with them, I can go in and mop the kennels out. I won't subject you to that today. They've all had their breakfast and a little snooze afterwards so they'll all be ready for a play. Russell is due in soon too and I'll send him out to help you.'

They ran around like lunatics to start with and we used a ball flinger and a flying disc to get them chasing around the field. Baxter was having such fun and I got my phone out and took a couple of snaps and texted them to Alice. I knew it would put her mind at rest. After an hour or so, the dogs were panting for a drink so we filled the troughs with fresh water and sat down on a bench in the corner of the field for a rest as they drank, chatting easily about Russell's plans for uni. Baxter came and lay down by my feet. He was a lovely little fella and I really did have a soft spot for him.

That evening, when I got back to the flat and turned on the TV because I hated silence, I wished that Baxter was snuggling up to me on my sofa. I had never felt so lonely.

9

The following morning, when I arrived at the farm, Uncle Tom raised a hand in a wave.

'Beth's in her bedroom, darling, go on up,' he yelled before heading for the doggy daycare. I was so happy when I called him last night to learn that she had been given the all clear to come home. Alex had arranged to pick her up so that she didn't have to get into Uncle Tom's smelly old Land Rover. I was glad to hear this – I was sure she could have picked up all sorts of infections from it.

Breathing in the old familiar smells as I entered the farmhouse felt like a warm blanket being wrapped around my shoulders. I headed up to Beth's room and used the hand sanitiser before knocking on the door. 'It's me, babe, are you decent?'

'As decent as I can be right now. Come on in.'

Beth was looking much better and said she felt a million times brighter being at home in her own environment.

'And look at you, Mads. You are full of enthusiasm and spark. Your cheeks are red and your eyes are sparkling. I haven't seen you like this for a very long time and it's so great to see. I'm so pleased you enjoyed my little community jobs. I love my business but it's great to get out and about and help people too. I didn't know what to expect when I started, but I immediately loved it.'

'I feel great, to be honest, Beth.' I hadn't realised that for myself until she just said it, but I did feel better than I'd felt for a long time. I felt at ease with the world, lighter than I'd felt for a while.

Beth turned the volume on the bedside radio up. 'Hallelujah' by Leonard Cohen was on and we smiled and swayed to the music as we remembered how we used to sing it at school. We sang along, remembering every word.

The school choir was always my thing. I had loved to sing from a very early age and I'd joined a choir after university but then work got in the way. I'd be in a different part of the country and unable to get to practice and I couldn't keep letting the others down, so I gave it up and hadn't sung properly in a choir for a very long time.

'You have a beautiful voice, Maddy. You always have.'

'Aw, Beth, that's so kind of you to say so. I'm a bit out of practice, to be honest.'

'Well, it's funny you should say that. I have another little job for you to do at the weekend,' she explained as she handed me a piece of paper and a CD. 'This is a backing CD and all you have to do is turn up at Meadow View Care Home at two p.m. next Saturday afternoon. The address is here. You need to phone ahead and speak to the activities co-ordinator to discuss what you are going to sing.'

'Sing! Me? In public? You are kidding, right?' My lips pressed together and I grimaced. The only singing I did these days was in the shower. My breathing was starting to speed up again and that familiar pounding of my heart seemed to be getting louder and louder in my body.

'Darling, you have the voice of an angel and you know it. I haven't heard you sing for years. They have a piano there, so you'd better brush up on your keyboard skills too.'

'But-but...'

'But nothing, Maddy. Haven't you always trusted me? Have I ever once let you down in my life?'

'Well, there was that one time you kissed Martin Bennett when you knew I fancied him.'

'Darling, we were ten and at school. And I've always told you that he kissed me, not the other way round. So I'll ask again, do you trust me?'

'Of course I do, but—'

'So please trust me again. I would never get you to do something unless I was sure you'd end up loving it. You know that.'

My breathing started to steady and I realised that what she was saying was true. Even though I hadn't always been around for her, she'd always been there for me.

'Look, Maddy, I know we haven't seen much of each other over the last few years, and I know that you found it difficult to come back to Giddywell for a while, but I hope you feel differently now.'

'Thank you, Beth, I really do appreciate that. I can't explain very well why I stayed away. I just felt like a complete failure when my relationship broke down. Giddywell was always my happy place and I didn't want to poison it with my grief.'

'Oh, darling, please don't ever feel like that. Giddywell is always a place that I hope you feel you can come back to. Anyway, I asked you before, do you trust me?'

'OK, OK.' I held my hands up in surrender. 'I trust you. But I may have to wring your neck if I make a fool of myself.'

She smiled and held my hand. 'You are silly, darling; you could never make a fool of yourself. You are too lovely. I just wish you could see what I could see. And it's not like it's a full-blown concert on a stage. It's just a few old people in a nursing home. Now if you really love me, I could murder a cup of tea.'

* * *

Back in the farmhouse kitchen, Uncle Tom popped his head round the front door to say a proper hello to me. 'How are things, Maddy, darling?'

'Oh, you know, I'm getting there gradually. Just need to sort out my finances and work out what I'm going to do with the apartment.'

'Why's that? I thought you loved your lakeside space.'

'I did, but I don't any more and to be totally honest, I'm really not sure it's wise to be spending the sort of money I do on rental there every month now I'm not working. My redundancy money is going to run out eventually and I really need to find a job.'

'Well, hopefully now Beth's back home and we don't have to keep nipping out to the hospital, we can work out some proper structured hours here for you, instead of doing a few hours here and there, but only if you want to, of course. Beth's critical illness insurance has given us a bit of breathing space over at doggy daycare and we just need to sort out the other farm jobs and work out what needs doing. Perhaps we could sit down later and do that. The other thing I wanted to mention was that the couple renting the barn conversion are moving out on Friday and I need to find some new tenants. You don't know anyone who might be interested, do you?'

'It would be great to sort out proper hours and get some structure back into my life. I feel like I've been floating around aimlessly for the last few weeks. It's been really strange after years of working every single day. I'll mention the barn to Mum. I blooming love that barn. I remember when you renovated it. So beautiful. She might know someone who's interested. She's more aware of what's going on in the community than me.' I handed him a cuppa and went back upstairs with our drinks and a packet of biscuits tucked under my arm. 'I'll pop over later and give you a hand settling the dogs down for the evening if you like.'

'I need to show you what we do with the chickens too. You are wonderful, darling. We have missed you being around the place. See you in a while. Don't rush, it's not busy and I know that Beth loves having you sit with her.'

* * *

When I got back to the flat that evening, I rang and spoke to Hayley, who was the activities co-ordinator at Meadow View.

'Oh, Madison, I'm so pleased to hear from you. We can't wait for your performance on Saturday. Now, I believe you'll be singing songs from across the decades for our residents. They are going to love that so much. Is it OK if we aim for two half-hour slots and see how it goes, with a cup of tea and a bit of cake in the middle? That way it's not too much for the older residents.'

My heart sank; I hadn't sung in public since I'd left the choir all those years ago. I knew she said it would only be to a few people, but what on earth was Beth making me do? She really was pushing me way outside my comfort zones just lately. She knew that I'd got myself into such a tizzy years ago, before I went on a stage to sing at school, mainly because they used to give me the solo parts, whereas when I was in the choir, I was just one amongst many people who loved to sing. I knew there probably wouldn't be a stage at this venue, but it was still a massive thing for me to do. I'd be drinking a whole bucketful of Rescue Remedy before I stepped foot inside that care home on Saturday.

'Just let me know if you'd like the piano at all, or whether you'll just bring an amplifier and CD player with you, if you would, please, so we can organise it all for you. You'll be singing in the day room and there will be a few of the residents and the staff.'

'The piano would be fabulous, thank you. And I'll bring some backing tracks with me to play on my laptop too. I'll judge it on the day and see what they prefer and I'll alternate between the two if that's OK.'

That also gave me a bit of breathing space to see whether I was more comfortable with one more than the other, but I didn't share that. I'd checked out some Facebook groups and it had been recommended that I bought a cheap amp and microphone, and as someone was selling one for a great price, I snapped it up. If it sold that easily, I was sure I could put it back out for sale if I didn't use it again.

'Perfect, well in that case, we'll see you on Saturday. Thank you again. We're very much looking forward to it.'

She rang off. I was glad. She could probably have heard my heart thumping from where she was.

I popped the CD into the CD player in my lounge. The dulcet melody of 'Moon River' started to play and a smile spread across my face as my heart warmed and memories of times gone by came flooding back. I remembered Mum singing this when I was not much older than five or six. I adored the film *Breakfast at Tiffany's*. It was still one of my favourite films, although I hadn't watched it for years.

Mum taught me everything I knew about music when we used to sing around the piano in the dining room. She had a beautiful voice and as a child I was fascinated by the way her fingers danced across the keyboard. Thank goodness I inherited her musical genes and also became a competent pianist. I used to wonder from time to time about my father and whether he was musical too. It was strange – I hadn't thought about him for years but he seemed to be on my mind a lot lately.

It had been ages though since I'd played properly. I wondered if Mum still played. I hadn't heard her for years. If not, perhaps she'd loan me her old piano so I could start to play again. Although I had no idea how we'd get it up the stairs of the flat. Like the singing, I only really gave up playing when I became busy with work and hadn't had time to be at Mum's. And busy was something that I absolutely was not these days. Perhaps that was why I'd been thinking about my father a lot too.

Flicking through the backing tracks, I noticed 'Que Sera Sera' by Doris Day, 'Getting to Know You' from *The King and I*, 'Singin' in the Rain' and 'My Favourite Things' from *The Sound of Music*. Some of my favourite songs that we used to sing in the school choir that Beth had clearly picked to remind me of a time when music was everything to me. Thinking about them now brought back such fond memories. There were a few that I could probably still play but I'd have to rehearse first. I counted the days till Saturday. I needed to pull my finger out and start practising.

Beth's note said that she'd picked some songs to start me off, but that it was up to me to find some more, so I set the rest of that afternoon's task, as I had nothing else planned, to search for more tracks that everyone would know and hopefully get them foot-tapping and singing along to. Now I'd listened to the tracks and sung along to the ones I knew the words to, I was actually starting to look forward to this project. I found it bizarre that I could remember the words to songs I knew from years ago, but not what I had for tea yesterday.

Uncle Tom had given me the afternoon off as Russell was working, so I spent a wonderful afternoon listening to songs and singing along, trying to pick some that I knew people would know and might like to sing along to, before deciding on 'Fly Me to the

Moon', 'Over the Rainbow', 'When You're Smiling' and 'Unforgettable'. I'd see how long they took me to play out before I decided whether I needed any more. The more I played and listened to these songs, the more I was actually starting to look forward to my afternoon at the care home and not feeling quite so anxious after all.

* * *

The rest of the weekend and the following week flew by. I was helping out at Growlers as often as they needed me; we'd worked out a nice little rota so everyone knew what they were doing and when. When I was there, lovely little Baxter followed me around like a shadow. I was still amazed that none of my old friends from work had contacted me. Clearly I'd been totally forgotten. The evenings were full of me browsing the internet for houses to rent and permanent jobs, but there was nothing that was really pulling on me at all.

I popped over to Mum's as often as I could in that week too and threw myself into rehearsing with gusto, adding more songs to the playlist, tinkling away on her piano that needed a good tuning, as it hadn't been played for years. Mum sang along to most of the songs as she pottered around in the house looking as pleased as punch with herself. 'I love having you around, darling, it feels like the heart and soul is back in our home when you are here. Do you know, I'm sure there are a load of music books up in the loft. There might be something you can use.'

'Ah, that would be fab, Mum. Can I go up and have a look?'

'Of course! I'll go and make a start on some dinner while you pull the loft ladder down and have a look around.'

I crawled through the hatch and made my way on my knees over to a big old chest in the corner, where Mum said she thought the books were, making sure that I only knelt on the joists. I'd always had a fear of lofts and falling through since Uncle Tom put his foot through their ceiling once. Aunty Jen was fuming at him for weeks because they'd had to have the whole of the bedroom ceiling re-plastered because he'd tried to patch it up and it never looked the same as the rest of it. She was probably fuming even more because Beth and I were rolling around the floor laughing hysterically at the sight of one of Uncle Tom's legs dangling precariously from a hole in the ceiling, and she'd shouted at us to stop being silly, which just made us laugh even more.

As I reached the chest, my sleeve caught on the edge of a flat, rusty tin box around the size of a shoebox that I'd never seen before. Curiosity got the better of me and I tried to open it to have a nosey at what was inside but it was locked. By this point Mum was standing at the foot of the ladder asking me if I'd found anything.

'Mum, what's this red tin box up here? I've never seen it before. It's locked though.'

'Mmm, what's that, Madison? I can't hear you very well.' Stalling for time was the equivalent of Mum's poker face when she didn't want to answer a question. *How strange,* I thought, giving the box a shake to see if I could work out what was inside.

'There's a red tin box, sounds like it's got papers and some other bits and bobs rattling around in it. I've tried to open it but it's locked. Any ideas?'

'I'm not sure, love. I'll have a think,' she said, brushing my question away in a voice which was an octave higher than normal. She didn't seem to have any problem hearing me that time, even though I hadn't spoken any louder.

Intuition was telling me she wasn't being totally honest with me here. I ran my fingers across the top of the box, making the trail of a question mark in the dust, wondering what Mum wasn't telling me. I was sure she had her reasons for wanting to keep it to herself, so I placed it to one side carefully, grabbed the books and passed them down to Mum through the loft hatch, hoping I'd remember to ask Mum about the box later.

* * *

Stuffed after one of Mum's fabulous pie and mash dinners, we were sitting in front of the fireplace. The time felt perfect, so I asked Mum *the* question I hadn't asked her for years.

'Mum, will you tell me about Dad, please?'

Her shoulders visibly tensed but then relaxed and she exhaled a deep breath. She patted the space next to her on the settee. I moved from the fireside chair across the room and she picked up my hand and kissed it. She held it tight as she started her story.

'I probably owe you an apology first,' she said, choking back tears. 'You have asked me many times over the years and I've never really answered you. I've always found it difficult to talk about. I've felt so guilty that you had to grow up without your father around and because I was trying so hard to be your mum and your dad, I was always too busy to explain and too embarrassed. Then it seemed too late and I didn't know when would be the right time to bring it up... and then you stopped asking. I suppose at that point I felt relieved because I didn't have to go through it all again.

'Your father was a lovely man. I met him at work, and I fell in love with him the moment I clapped eyes on him. He was tall and dark-haired, very handsome, with big brown eyes that I just lost myself in. He worked in the accounts office and kept himself very much to himself. No one really knew much about him and I worked on the reception so we didn't really mix at work. He was five years older than me and seemed so much more mature and, I suppose, sophisticated. We became really good friends at first, and we used to meet up at break times in the canteen at work, but when he asked me out to dinner I was so excited. I *really* liked him. We got on like a house on fire and he made me feel a million dollars, showering me with gifts and affection over the next few weeks. He was perfect and charming and wonderful and we were so in love.

'After three months of seeing him, I found out I was pregnant. I'll skip over the how-it-happened bit. I'm sure you don't need to know every detail. I had arranged to see him that evening and was going to tell him. I was scared stiff, because I was only twenty-three, and because we'd not been together for long, but once I'd got used to the idea, I was so excited. We were going to be a family! But when I told him, his face dropped and he kept thumping his head with the balls of his fists, saying "No! No!" I didn't understand. He got really angry with me. It was then that he dropped his bombshell.

'He was married. He told me that his wife had ME and suffered from severe depression, so he couldn't possibly ever consider leaving her. He said that he loved what we'd had together but that there was no way we could bring a child into the world together. He said that we had no alternative but to "deal with it".'

Tears streamed down Mum's cheeks as she relived what must have been such an emotional time for her even though she was recalling something that happened such a long time ago. I put my arm around her shoulders and she leaned into me.

'I'm sorry that you have to learn this, darling. I thought that he was the love of my life, and I was devastated at this turn of events. But then the moment you were born, I knew that you were the love of my life and not him.

'He never came back into work after that night. At first they said he was off sick, but then I was told that he'd left the company, a week after I'd told him about the pregnancy.'

'Did you ever contact him again?' I had so many questions I'd been wanting to ask for so long but didn't want to push her too hard, yet I was so very angry with someone I'd never met, that he'd hurt her in this way. How dare he have carried on with Mum when he was already married?

'I sent him a letter when you were born with a photograph of you. I took his address from the files at work before I left to have you. I know it was wrong of me to take confidential information, but I had to try to make him realise what he was giving up. If not for me, then for you. I never heard anything and that knocked me back more and more. It was such a tough time for me; I was so happy to have this little miracle growing inside of me, but so very sad that he'd left me and I was having to do it on my own. I bumped into someone years later who I used to work with and nonchalantly asked whether they'd ever heard what happened to him, and I was told that he and his wife had moved out of the area and that was that. How on earth could I have been so stupid as to think that I meant more to him? But it was clear that I was never enough for him, and therefore you and I were on our own in life. He obviously wasn't the man I thought he was.' She stroked my cheek. 'I'm so sorry, and I'm so sorry that we've never had this conversation before.'

'I'm sorry that I came between you and him, Mum.'

'Darling, you have absolutely nothing to be sorry for. From the moment I knew you were in my tummy, you were all I ever needed. You were my everything. I knew that you and I could get through anything, and we did alright, didn't we? I know you didn't have everything that other children had, but Uncle Tom and Aunty Jen were so very good to us. I owe them both such gratitude. If it wasn't for them, looking after you so much, I wouldn't have been able to work and earn money for the things we did have. And your childhood wasn't so bad, was it?'

My mum was the most amazing mum ever. When I started at nursery and primary school, she spoke to them in advance and made sure that when there were occasions when fathers were spoken about, I wasn't made to feel like an outcast. I didn't understand when I was a toddler why all the other children had daddies and I didn't, but Mum told me that I was special and didn't need a daddy and that families came in all shapes and sizes and ours was just a small but perfectly formed family of two. These days, there were so many versions of families – children with two mums, or two dads, some with foster parents, some with stepparents and siblings – that now, no one would bat an eyelid about a single-parent family, but in those days, things were very different and it would have been frowned upon.

'It was great, Mum, thank you. I've not always shown you how much I appreciate everything you've done for me and how hard you worked. I suppose as a child you just take for granted that that's what your parents do. But thank you, Mum. I really do love you, and I'm loving spending time with you, learning to get to know you all over again.'

'I know you'll have lots more things to ask me, but do you mind if we leave it there for now, darling? Let's talk again soon and I might even be able to lay my hands on a photograph of your father if you'd like to see it.'

My mind wandered back to the red tin box that I'd stumbled across in the attic and I wondered whether it held the answers to a million questions that I'd had stored up for years.

Mum smiled at me through shimmering eyes and I'd never loved her more than I did right now. It was only when I was driving home that night that I realised I still didn't even know my father's name.

* * *

Saturday soon came round. Parking up outside the palatial-looking building, which looked more like a hotel than a care home, and taking a deep breath and a huge swig of Rescue Remedy for my nerves, I headed for the double front doors with my arms full of kit. Walking in backwards, pushing open the first set of doors with my considerable arse, which was getting increasingly lardy now I wasn't working and was eating all the time, I pressed the bell with my nose and announced my arrival on the door system. God, I hoped they didn't have cameras and weren't all watching me on CCTV. They'd wonder who on earth was visiting them.

Hayley came to meet me and helped me with my baggage and showed me through to the communal area, where they'd very kindly arranged for a beautiful old upright piano to be wheeled through for me to play, alongside a table where I could put my computer, amplifier and microphone. With fumbling fingers, I set everything up and decided to take a moment to see how the piano sounded so I could decide which I'd rather do.

The sweet, mellow tone of the piano was just beautiful and I knew that I had to do as much as I could on that, so I bent the microphone accordingly so that I could still be heard. I didn't want it so loud that I might blow up hearing aids, but I did want the hard-of-hearing to be able to enjoy the words and music too. I played the intro to 'Fly Me to the Moon' and when I stopped, there was a round of applause and I noticed that there were three care workers standing in the doorway, listening. A little embarrassed, I began tidying up my music and fumbling in my handbag. Hayley came over and said that she'd heard me from her office and couldn't wait for me to get started.

My audience was arriving and there were lots of people. Shit! *Lots of people!* Was I really doing this? *Beth Millington,* I muttered under my breath, *if this doesn't work out, I might have to kill you.*

The next time I looked up, more than sixty faces were staring at me, and you could have heard a pin drop. Hayley introduced me as that afternoon's entertainment and explained that I'd sing for a while, then we'd have tea and cake and then I'd sing for a little bit longer, then they could all go and have a lie down to recover. There were a few polite laughs around the room but I thought for the first time that they could be quite a tough audience. This was so bloody scary. How on earth had I managed to let Beth talk me into this?

For my first song, I channelled my inner Audrey Hepburn and chose 'Moon River', something gentle to ease them in, and I practically hid behind the piano. I spent the first verse looking at the keys, nervous but lost in the melody. When I had the courage to look up, there were smiles all around me. Two of the ladies who were sat at the front were humming and swaying along with me, and then a few more joined in along the way. One little old lady was making up her own words and singing, but she was still joining in and enjoying herself and that was all that mattered. My heart lifted and filled with joy to know that I had made these people smile. When I finished the last note, there was a gentle clap from most of the audience, but my posse in the front row gave me a rapturous applause. I was thrilled to bits.

I was feeling a little more confident now so I decided to go with 'Unforgettable'. I noticed that another of the ladies from the front row had got up, I presumed because she didn't like it and was leaving the room, and I was horrified, but then to my surprise she sauntered over to one of the gentlemen who was sitting by the window and whispered to him. He got up to join her and to my great surprise, they started to waltz on the carpet beside where I was playing. Others started to applaud them, and another couple got up and joined them. This was delightful. Their faces were an absolute picture; they looked so happy. This was better than an evening watching *Strictly* anytime! I relaxed and could feel my voice sounding more confident and stronger. I was really getting into my stride.

'Getting to Know You' was my next choice for something a little more upbeat, and this time there was foot-tapping aplenty, and the sounds of hands clapping along warmed the cockles of my heart. Seeing something pink and white heading towards my face, I reached out and realised, to my absolute horror, that I had caught a pair of false teeth in my hands. I looked over and one of the old ladies in the front row was laughing her head off! I screamed and dropped them, which made her cackle some more. Hayley came over and apologised, saying that she should perhaps have warned me that Betty had a habit of laughing so much that her teeth flew out.

There was so much laughter in the room at this point that was a pure delight to hear. We decided to calm ourselves down with another more mellow song, so I introduced 'Singin' in the Rain' and thought that might do the trick. I should have known better really when one of the residents came in swinging a brolly around and started doing what I can only describe as twerking. I could not stop laughing. I thought I was going to have a coronary, let alone these old folks. They clearly knew how to enjoy themselves. Tears of laughter streamed down my face as I tried so very hard to compose myself and carry on singing.

Hayley announced that it was definitely time for a cup of tea and I went round the room talking to the residents in the break, balancing my cup and saucer while chatting. It was so lovely to be thanked by them and told they were having such a lovely time.

I didn't realise how much of myself I'd lost over the years of working at Ronington's. Work was all I'd got into the habit of doing. When I was younger, singing used to be like a drug to me. If I didn't sing, I missed it. I felt so light and happy singing again and

I'd almost forgotten just how much I loved it and how it made me feel. Beth had been right all along. She knew me so well.

The ringing of the dinner bell signified that the second half was about to start and I prepared myself as the residents took their seats. Ethel and Beryl from the front row, who I'd met properly in the interval, got up and danced along to 'Twist and Shout', even though we had to help Beryl back up again when she twisted down and only shouted because she couldn't get back up again and roared hilariously. We shared the microphone for the chorus of 'Que Sera, Sera' when they became my backing singers.

I'm sure Abba wouldn't have been too insulted when my backing singers sang 'Fandango' instead of 'Fernando', and Lord only knew what they were singing when we did 'Jambalaya' by The Carpenters, but what they lacked in tone and the correct words they made up for in enthusiasm and volume.

At least half of the residents were out of their seats and having a dance, and the others who could raise their arms up in the air were waving along when I sang 'Sweet Caroline', which was my pièce de résistance, and totally brought the house down with nearly everyone singing along. They loved the choices I'd made to the playlist and I was so happy that they were the right ones for the occasion. Their joy was intoxicating. My face literally ached from smiling so much. Who would have thought that I, who hadn't sung publicly for literally years, would have spent one of the most enjoyable afternoons of my life entertaining old folks in this way?

Cries of 'More! More!' came from my audience. I looked to Hayley and she held two fingers up at me. As she was smiling, I hoped she meant that I could play another two songs rather than anything else, so I fired up 'Daydream Believer' and we ended with 'Love Changes Everything', which I played on the piano to rapturous applause. I thought I'd better calm them all down a bit before I buggered off leaving the care workers with a whole load of people with high blood pressure and irregular heartbeats.

'Oh, Maddy, what a joy to see my darlings having so much fun. You picked exactly the right type of tracks. Everyone knew them all and even though they got a tad over excited, you seemed to know when to tone it down a bit. And I thought I was going to wet myself when Betty's teeth flew out at you. I really should have warned you that might happen.'

'I'm so happy that you're so pleased. It's meant the world to me to come and do this today. I was really nervous but when I saw those smiles, I knew it was the right thing to do.'

I couldn't stop grinning as the residents came and took my hands in theirs and thanked me for a wonderful time, and they sang and kicked their legs and danced their way back down the corridors to their rooms with the carers. What a picture to treasure in my mind. What memories I'd made this afternoon.

'Will you come back, Maddy, please? We'll have you anytime. It has truly been a wonderful afternoon. You'd be doing us a huge favour. We don't have a huge budget for entertainment, but if you could come back some time, I know they'd love it. And perhaps we can invite their families along too so they can see the pleasure they got. In fact, I'd definitely like to book you for our Summer Fayre. We'll be doing a family day and it would be wonderful to have you at that. Now, let me get you your payment. I'm sorry it's not much.'

'Me doing *you* a favour, Hayley? Seriously, experiencing this afternoon has done *me* the biggest favour ever. It's been *delightful.* I'd come just for the fun of it, I don't want payment. Thank you so much for having me. I'll give you a call when I've got my diary and put another date and your summer event in. After this afternoon, I wouldn't miss it for the world.'

As I drove away from Meadow View Care Home, the sun came out from behind a fluffy cotton wool cloud and I realised that this afternoon had given me another one of the most uplifting experiences of my life. It made me think that the life I'd been living had been one of having the best of possessions, and I wanted to be a better person in the future, making memories that filled my heart with joy. My whole thought process had changed and I just wanted to be the best that I could be.

10

On Sunday morning, I was lying in bed contemplating life, when a ping signified the arrival of a text and my heart annoyingly skipped a beat when I saw who it was from.

> Morning, Mad. On the farm, there are a number of allotment plots that we rent out. The couple who left the barn on Friday had one and Beth has allocated it to you to keep it ticking over. She asked me to tell you so you wouldn't kill her and to tell you that it needs a bit of tender loving care. Please come and pick up keys when you can.
> Alex x

An allotment! What the flipping heck was I supposed to do with an allotment? I wouldn't even know where to start.

The sound of another text pinged through.

> P.S. Beth said that you wouldn't know where to start so has got you some books to help you and said that Ivan Jenkins in the village is your man if you get stuck.

I grinned. Not much chance of getting out of this one then, it seemed. I loved that Alex was using his childhood nickname for me. Most people called me Maddy or Mads, but Alex was the only one who said I was mad so should be called Mad. Ivan Jenkins had lived in the village as long as I'd been alive, and rumour had it he could normally be found in the Dog and Duck most afternoons after a hard day's work down on the fields. I made a mental note to pop in and have a chat with him when I had some free time.

Why Beth had chosen this route for me I had absolutely no idea, but I was sure it'd become obvious in time. I was actually starting to quite like these little challenges she'd been putting my way and wondering what was next. She never ceased to surprise me. Everything so far had given me quite a lot of anxiety to start with, but it soon disappeared and was never as bad as I thought it was going to be. Somehow I managed to find an inner strength to cope and it was actually fun pushing outside of my comfort zone. Maybe she was just making her point.

I texted Alex back to say I'd pop in for the books and the keys later that morning (no time like the present) before I went to Sunday lunch at Mum's, if that was OK, and was just a tad disappointed when I got a short sharp 'Fine' in return. I was spending more and more time at Mum's. I didn't want to be at the flat; it felt cold and emptier every time I was there, and I was loving being back in the village. The apartment complex was only a twenty-minute drive away but at times it seemed like it was much further.

Giddywell Grange's farmhouse kitchen was one of my favourite places in the world and was the whole hub of the house. There was a huge pine table in the centre of the room where we'd eaten many meals and spent hours poring over our homework and studying for our exams. When Aunty Jen was alive, there was always the smell of freshly baked bread from the moment you walked through the door, and our treat when we got home from school each day was a piece of warm, fresh bread and butter. Aunty Jen's bread was the best I'd ever tasted. Perhaps that was something else I could do with my time these days. I hadn't baked for years. Maybe I could bake some cakes for the next time I saw Stuart and the Darbys. Perhaps if the allotment took off, I could share some of the produce from there too. I noticed that I was actually finding things to do with my time these days and I was looking forward to getting up each day and having a new adventure discovering what Beth's life was all about.

Alex hadn't even noticed that I'd walked in, and I watched him as he sat at the head of the table, paperwork spread across it in a haphazard manner. He pushed his glasses up as they slid down to the end of his perfectly shaped nose and he was frowning. Our eyes met as he looked up and he stood to greet me. As we moved towards each other, he reached over and kissed my cheek. Inhaling his scent, I tried to pinpoint what it was but then realised it was just Alex. A mixture of deodorant, aftershave and a smell that was – just Alex. A smell I would never forget in a million years.

'How are you doing?' he asked. 'How's unemployment?'

'It's not so bad, to be honest, thanks to your lovely sister. She's got me running round on these little missions of hers but I've nothing else to do so I'm pleased to have something to focus on.'

'Ah, yes, the allotment. The books! I nearly forgot why you'd come.' He reached up to the top shelf of the vintage Welsh dresser at the far end of the kitchen, to which Beth had given the shabby chic treatment in her youth, and the back of his t-shirt rode up and showed me the waistband of what I'd like to think were snug-fitting boxers. It suddenly felt rather warm.

'Here you go, Mad. Are you stopping for a cuppa, or do you have to get off?' I always felt tongue-tied around him, so I declined his offer and asked if he knew where on the farm the allotments were.

'Come on, I'll show you.' He grabbed a pair of wellies from the boot rack in the porch and pulled an anorak off the coat pegs. I hadn't seen him in an anorak since we were growing up and the memories of us playing around the farm made me smile. He looked dead cute. We headed behind one of the barns at the far end of the farm; a place I never really knew existed.

In my mind, based on what I'd seen on TV, I thought of allotments as being places of beauty, full of stunning blooms, blossoming fruit trees and rows and rows of thriving vegetable patches, so I presumed that seeing my allotment plot for the first time would be really exciting. I was looking forward to imagining what it would look like all planted up with a small herb garden, some lovely flowers and maybe a strawberry plant or potato tub or two.

As we walked through the allotment gate, I passed perfect rows of vegetables, beautifully neat weed-free plots, garden sheds that looked more like Swiss chalets and summerhouses, and I was really getting quite excited.

Sadly the reality was very different, so I was bitterly disappointed when we got to the very end of the field and the only thing left to look at was a rectangular, large piece of scruffy, overgrown land that could only be described as derelict. It looked like it needed levelling with a bulldozer and was arid and almost empty, except for a flimsy shed at the far end that looked as though it would topple over if you blew on it.

'Tell me that's not mine!'

'Now, I know what you're thinking.' Alex grinned. 'But with a little hard work and determination, this plot will soon be looking like the others, and will be something that you can be dead proud of and show off to your friends and family and they can all reap the benefits from your homegrown fruit and veg.'

The thought of what lay ahead, and just how much hard work would have to be done here, made me literally want to weep.

'And I can help you for the odd hour or two when I have a chance. Maybe?' he questioned.

For a moment my mind drifted as I imagined me and Alex working wonders together on a plot of land, which was full of flourishing fruit and veg, Alex looking hot and sweaty as he leant on his hoe and wiped his perspiring brow.

I was aware of my own increasing heartbeat and pulled myself together. This was Alex, for goodness' sake. I needed to calm the hell down.

'How long are you over here for, Alex?' I asked, trying to change the subject, and willing him to say he was back for good.

'I suppose I'll have to go back sooner rather than later to sort some things out, but who knows what the future holds? It's great being back, to be honest. I've missed this old place.' He looked deep into my eyes and I gulped, not knowing what to say. Eventually, I was the first to break eye contact and I looked over at the plot again, hoping that it would look totally different.

'Is this a joke, Alex? Go on, please tell me it's a joke,' I asked. 'I've never been a gardener in my life. I don't have the patience for gardening. And this looks like an army of people wouldn't be able to clear it in a lifetime.'

'No joke, sweets. It's all yours. And Beth tells me that a little gentle gardening in your time off from doggy daycare will do you the world of good and put some colour back into your cheeks. And maybe it'll help you to chill a bit and not be so impatient.' He held his hands up in surrender. 'Her words, not mine. Don't shoot the messenger. I'm heading back to the house and will be putting the kettle on shortly. If you'd like to join me, you'd be most welcome.

In the meantime, I'll leave you to appreciate your, erm, kingdom then.'

He stomped off across the farmyard, leaving me staring at my 'erm, kingdom'. I'd done a bit of research on the internet last night and it seemed that this was a good time of year to be attacking an allotment and it definitely looked like this one needed attacking – with a bulldozer. I wasn't sure what the couple who'd had it beforehand had been doing with it. Bugger all, by the look of it. I decided that I'd pop into the pub later and see if Ivan was around and ask for his advice in exchange for a pint or two.

I pulled a notebook and pen from my coat pocket and made a list of what was there. Picking up a bamboo cane from the ground, I gingerly prodded at the shed door, trying to open it, which was rather difficult as it was practically hanging off with only one hinge joined to the structure. I poked my way through some major cobwebs (all too aware of what was also around when there were cobwebs) and shuddered before making a note of the tools that I could see propped up against the work surface. There were actually quite a few and I took a picture on my phone of some of them, as they looked more like torturing tools than something you'd garden with. I'd definitely be needing some help from Ivan to find out what they were used for. A rusty old wheelbarrow, which looked like it had seen better days, sat in the corner containing loads of plant pots, which looked like they might come in handy at some point. When I walked back outside, I noticed a small greenhouse at the side of the shed with a couple of broken panes of glass, but there was a metal shelf rack inside with yet more plant pots and what I seemed to remember were seed trays. They might come in handy too. I jotted that in my book too to tell Ivan. I was absolutely needing some advice.

I headed back over to the farmyard. Uncle Tom and Alex were

sat looking at some figures and Uncle Tom was scratching his head but looked up as I walked in.

'We were just talking about you, Maddy. I have a little proposition for you. As you know, it's important for us here to have someone who lives in for doggy daycare and I just happen to have an empty barn conversion. You said to me the other day that you weren't feeling particularly fond of your apartment and more than that, that you didn't think you could afford to keep it. How about you move in? Your rent could be a nominal amount and part of your employment package. You'd also be close at hand to help out looking after Beth, which again would be really helpful, and you'd be right back in the heart of the village. It's a win-win situation for us all. You don't have to decide now, but please would you just think about it.'

'You mean the barn conversion that I've loved ever since you renovated it?' I laughed. 'And in the village that I used to hate but now long to live back in? I don't need to think about it. It's a yes from me, Uncle Tom.' I paced across the kitchen and flung my arms around him and kissed his cheek. 'Thank you.'

'Well, you can thank young Alex here, it was his idea. It's probably him you should be kissing. I think he likes the thought of being able to keep an eye on you.'

Alex reddened and turned away and I smirked.

I felt a surge of excitement. Recently it was as if all my senses were being woken up. I hadn't been excited about life for so long; I'd actually been just existing. And the feeling I was getting right now told me that there was a huge difference.

11

The door to the Dog and Duck clearly needed a good spray of WD40 as it creaked open, alerting everyone inside to a new customer, although 'everyone' in this particular instance consisted of just the young girl behind the bar and Ivan, who was sat on a bar stool with a pint of mild.

'Good Lord, is that you, Madison Young? Haven't you got that high falutin' job in the city? It's not often we see you around this neck of the woods. I didn't recognise you at first. What are you doing in here on a Sunday afternoon?'

'Hello, Ivan, you're looking well. Sadly, I don't have that job any more. In fact, I don't have a job at all right now. I'm helping up at Giddywell Grange for the moment while Beth is recovering from an operation.'

Patting the stool beside him, he invited me to join him. 'Come on, lass, sit with me. What's your poison?'

Not really used to drinking in the afternoon, I wasn't sure what to have, so I asked for a gin and tonic. It was a long drink, not too strong, and it would last me a while. As it was being prepared, we started to chat about life. After he'd told me all about his bunions and I'd managed to stop myself from heaving when he offered to show me one – which I obviously declined – I finally got round to telling him about my good fortune at suddenly becoming the not-so-proud owner of a plot in the allotments.

Once I got Ivan talking about his favourite topic, he was in his element and I couldn't shut him up. Another two pints of mild and two gin and tonics later, I had written down three lists: one of things that I needed to do, one of things that I could grow and the final one of things I needed to get. Apparently I needed a rototiller, which would enable me to till an entire area of soil in minutes (whatever that meant) but he had one that I could borrow to keep the costs down. He also told me that I'd get hung, drawn and quartered by the other owners if I put weeds in the wrong compost bin because they'd take root, and that a water butt was a must.

When I showed Ivan the pictures on my phone, he said that I'd got nearly everything I would need right there in my shed. The big metal bin was a compost bin and the huge thing I had been unable to identify had turned out to be a water butt. Big necessities, which were already in situ. Ivan was getting more excited about my allotment plot than I was and promised to come over in the next day or two to have a look and offer me his expert advice on the land and what order to tackle it. He also said that he'd try to introduce me to a friend of his son's called Vinnie who was a landscape gardener and who lived in one of the neighbouring villages, Little Ollington, and had studied horticulture at university. Apparently Vinnie was amazing at anything to do with gardening and landscaping and had helped Ivan a few times with his allotment, and he might also be able to help me out with some hints and tips.

I decided that I needed to pay a visit to the ladies', and when I moved, I wobbled and nearly fell off my stool. Ivan grabbed my arm to right me, laughing that I probably wasn't used to drinking doubles in the afternoon. Bloody hell, doubles? That meant I'd had six! I wasn't used to drinking in the day at all. No wonder I felt totally squiffy.

When I came back from the loo, there was my hero, standing at the bar. 'I had a feeling I'd find you here.' Alex grinned at me across the room. 'Ivan, I do hope you haven't been getting this young lady drunk, have you?'

'Me? Never!' Ivan grinned and glanced at his watch. 'Bugger me; I'd better be going. Marjorie will batter me with a frying pan if I miss my dinner.' He patted me on the arm as he jumped off his stool really sprightly for an older gent who had been on the mild all afternoon. 'Always around for you, me darlin', I'll be over to check out your patch very soon,' he said, and he winked at me on his way out. I giggled, thinking how funny it was that an eighty-year-old man could make a double entendre out of talking about allotments.

'Come on, you. You'd better leave your car here and fetch it tomorrow. I'll take you home.' Years ago I would have longed to hear him say that. Alex offered me his arm and a spark of electricity ran through me as I tucked my arm into his and we meandered out to the car park. I thought I could get used to this. But then I told myself that lovely as Alex was, I didn't need a man in my life to depend on. I was perfectly capable of looking after myself. Just like Mum had been capable of looking after us both. And I certainly didn't need one that was in a relationship.

I talked complete nonsense in the car all the way back to my riverside apartment, the combination of the gin and his presence making me feel a tad giddy. Alex walked me up to the door and made sure I got in safely. He hovered on the doorstep and I thought about inviting him in, but I'd had way too much to drink to behave sensibly and there was a little bit of me that wanted to throw caution to the wind and just chuck him on the sofa. But then I remembered that he was not mine. That thought sobered me up, and I kissed him on the cheek, thanking him politely for making sure I got home OK, and when he shut the door on his way out, I stumbled over to the sofa and conked out.

12

Swallowing two tablets down with a huge gulp of water to stop my banging headache wasn't the ideal way to start the day at Growlers. While the filter coffee machine was creating the liquid fuel that I craved and the aroma of fresh coffee permeated through to the bathroom, I stood under the shower for what seemed like an hour but was probably only ten minutes. It did the trick perfectly and woke me up. Feeling much more refreshed and sure that the tablets were working their magic, I wrapped myself in my towelling dressing gown and flicked on the radio. As I poured myself another strong black coffee, I was starting to perk up and found myself singing along and dancing around the kitchen to the radio while waiting for my toast to pop up. When was the last time I had done that? This was a complete contrast to my working life at Ronington's. I'd been constantly stressed to the max, checking emails, answering calls and rushing around all over the country whilst all the time portraying professionalism. I felt that some of the stuffiness of the old me was being gradually cast aside and a new me was starting to shine through, and to be honest, I quite liked this new Maddy.

Walking into my bedroom with a piece of toast hanging out of my mouth, I grabbed the pair of jeans I had taken off last night from the chaise longue in the corner, as my guess was that a clean pair wasn't going to stay clean for very long, along with an old sweatshirt that I found at the back of my wardrobe and hadn't worn for years. That'd do. It wasn't like I was on the pull or anything. Well, obviously Alex would be there, but he'd seen me look way worse than this over the years. And it wasn't like I was trying to pull him. Firstly, I'd be punching *way* above my weight and secondly, he was married to bloody perfect Sophie, so it wasn't like it really mattered anyway.

I pulled my hair back into a ponytail, swirled some bronzer over my cheeks, gave my lashes a quick lick of mascara and swept a natural-coloured lip gloss on. Looking in the mirror, I thought I looked reasonably presentable considering the state I had come home in, and I headed over to Giddywell Grange where Uncle Tom was waiting at the gate.

* * *

Russell was telling me that he was desperate to become a vet in the long term. If he failed his vet's exams, he said he would 'downgrade and be a doctor', which I found bizarre. If you were not good enough to become a vet you could become a doctor?

We took the dogs back through to the main kennel yard and put them back in the indoor barn where they all went for a lie down in various corners. To be honest, I could have done with one myself. That was the most exercise I'd had for ages. It was so much fun watching them chase the toys. Such a simple game to us meant the world to them. Dogs didn't ask for much, did they? Just love and food, a bit of company and a play from time to time.

Russell and I chatted about him popping round to the Darbys' house and he said he'd be delighted to. Every bit of extra cash helped his uni fund build nicely and he was really grateful for any additional work.

I went back into reception to see Uncle Tom and we sat and pondered over another rota to keep the business ticking over nicely, slotting in times so that someone was always nearby and able to check in on Beth from time to time and make sure she was fed and watered at mealtimes, as well as the dogs.

'So how long is Alex over for, then?' I asked casually. 'Do we work him into the rota too?' I thought it was a good way to satisfy my curiosity.

'Not too sure, to be honest. He and Sophie have got some stuff that they need to sort out over the next few months or so, so I know he's definitely going back, but I also know that he wants to be around for Beth too, so who knows? I think we should leave him off the rota, and then any time he can do is a bonus. Russell is prepared to work some extra hours too, so hopefully we've got it all covered.' He covered my hand with his. 'Thank you, darling, for helping us out like this. I really don't know what we'd have done without you right now.'

'Well, like Beth said, perhaps the universe was conspiring and made me redundant just at the right time. At least I'm able to help out here, while I'm looking to get back into the world of PR.'

As the words left my mouth, I already couldn't imagine myself back in that world. It was as if that life belonged to another person, even though it wasn't that long ago. The fact that it was all I knew made me quite honestly feel really low and I was struggling to find any excitement about searching for work in that field again. Perhaps the best thing I could do would be to put the feelers out as soon as I could before I took too much time out of the corporate workplace. That would also be frowned upon by future employers. But working here would keep me busy in the meantime anyway. More than that, it was fun, which was something that had been missing from my life until recently.

* * *

Lunchtime soon came around, so I walked across the yard, noticing that Alex's hire car wasn't there any more, to the farmhouse kitchen, to make us all a sandwich. It seemed that I'd quickly morphed into Beth's role and I was actually loving it – loving being needed for something other than facts and figures for a change.

I wandered up to Beth's room and poked my head around the door and noticed that she was sitting up in bed, reading.

'Hello, gorgeous, how are you feeling today? I've brought lunch and a pot of tea.'

'Bloody tea! Drinking tea is all I seem to do these days. I don't feel very hungry either but I suppose that's because I'm in bed all day and not doing anything.'

'Oh, you're a bit bad tempered today. Has someone upset you?'

'No, I just wish I could do something from here. I feel so useless sat here with you guys all doing the work. I can see you all rushing round the yard from my bedroom window and I feel really miserable. I'm bored to bloody tears!'

'Make the most of it, lady, because when your new physio starts working on you, you'll be back to work in no time, I bet.'

She smiled but looked so fed-up and weary. A spark of an idea began to form in my mind. 'Do you have a laptop, Beth?'

'Yes, it's over there on the dressing table. Why, what are you up to?'

'Well, I know you're poorly, but maybe throughout the day when you're feeling up to it, you could set up a Facebook page for Growlers. I know you said it was something you wanted to do but hadn't had the time. This is something you can do as and when you feel up to it. There are no deadlines at all. We can send you pictures throughout the day, and the people who have dogs boarding here or in daycare can check the Facebook page to see what their pets have been up to while they're away. How cool would it be for Alice, for example, over in Australia, to be able to see what her lovely little pal Baxter is up to and how much he's enjoying himself?'

Her face lit up. 'What a great idea. You're a genius!'

'Not a genius, darling, just utilising my amazing PR and social media skills as no one else seems to want them, and also I want to stop having to look at that mardy face every time I bring your lunch up!' I winked at her and she threw a cushion at me.

'Just because you're in bed doesn't mean you can sit on your arse and read books all day, you know. You've still got two hands so you can type, can't you?'

She grinned at me. I loved that we had fallen back into this easy, teasing relationship that we'd always had which had been missing over the last few years. I didn't realise how much I had missed Beth. 'I jest, babe, but maybe you could do short little bursts when you are feeling up to it.'

'I love it, Maddy. And it'll feel like I'm still contributing. I feel so guilty that you're all running around because of me. Hopefully it won't be for too long. But this is such a good idea.' She took my hand in hers and squeezed it. 'Thank you. Not just for this but for being my proper friend again. I love having you around. And I feel like I've got the old Maddy back. You changed, you know, when you were working at the old place. You were still lovely, but stiff and no fun. And you never seemed to have any time for any of us. When Mum died, it took me a while before I could cope better with the grief, but it taught me that life is short and you have to make the most of it while you're here. And enjoy it! Find something you love to do and do it. We just need to find you your thing!'

'I thought I knew what my thing was, but now I'm not so sure. I feel like in time, it'll come to me. Until then, I'll keep looking out for another corporate role to get back into and help out here for as long as you need me. And on that note, I'd better go back and take over so Uncle Tom can have lunch too.'

* * *

Being on my own for a while over lunchtime got my mind working overtime. What would I do if I could do anything in the world? What floated my boat these days? What did I feel passionate about? It was really quite upsetting to realise that I had no idea of the answers to these questions, but I really wanted to find out. Out came a notebook and each of these questions were written on the top of a new page. I'd keep them in my mind and surely the answers would come to me.

Uncle Tom interrupted my thoughts when he returned from lunch and asked me when I'd like to move into the barn. I said that I'd put in my notice on the flat straight away, but I could move in as soon as possible, so we agreed that there was no time like the present and that Friday would be a great day, so I could have the weekend to get settled. We only had a few dogs over the weekend so it wouldn't be too busy.

Living just over the yard would make life so much easier for us all as I could pop in and see Beth and sort the dogs out at any time without a twenty-minute drive over. Uncle Tom said I may as well have the keys straight away in case I wanted to do any measuring up, so I wandered over when I had a break to remind myself of what it was like. It had been a while since I'd been there.

Light flooded into the open plan lounge-dining area from the dual aspect double doors and there was a back door at one end of the modern kitchen and round a corner, a cupboard and a downstairs loo. It was very simply furnished, but classy too, with two chocolate-brown leather settees either side of a coffee table, with a bookcase in one corner and a Mexican pine dresser on the back wall next to a matching dining room table with matching leather chairs. The cream stone-tiled floors made it look really clean and fresh and easy to look after. A wooden staircase led to the first floor where I had to duck under a beam to go along the landing to the beautiful main bedroom with a half-moon window, which overlooked the fields. It was an incredible view – you could see for miles. There was also an interlinking bathroom which led through to another smaller bedroom. I remembered coming in here when it was first refurbished. Beth showed me round and I totally adored it. I could hardly believe that I was going to live here. I did a little jump up and down on the spot with excitement and then stopped in case anyone could see me through the window.

The simplicity of the décor didn't detract from it being full of character and I couldn't wait to get my own things in here. I wouldn't be bringing much. The flat was fully furnished and so was the barn, so I didn't have anything major to bring, just my belongings really. And Mum had said that I could have the piano too if I wanted it. She rarely played it these days and said how lovely it would be if I got use out of it. It was strange that I'd lived in that flat for seven years yet already the barn felt more like home.

Mid afternoon, I took a break and walked into the village. I thought I'd pop in and see if Rebecca was around at all, as I knew she alternated between the village and Stafford Library, to see if she needed me to get involved in any more projects for her. Having an afternoon break every day left me with time on my hands and I wanted to make sure I was using it effectively and trying to help someone. Rebecca was just about to finish her shift for the day, so she invited me to go and have a cuppa with her in the Copper Kettle café in the village before she picked her younger children up from school. She was really easy to sit and chat to and I asked her how she came to be working in the library, and I wasn't expecting the answer that I got.

'Well, I know you are a friend of Beth's and if she trusts you, then so do I,' she said, looking over her shoulder fleetingly to make sure no one else was listening. 'I was given the job at the library after I left my husband. I was a victim of domestic violence, you see, Madison, and I needed to change my life.'

I could never have pre-empted that. I was surprised she didn't tell me to shut my mouth because I was doing a really good impression of a goldfish. Rebecca seemed really put together; it just wasn't what I had been expecting. I supposed it just went to show that you really didn't know what people went through in their lives.

'My husband was abusive, both mentally and physically. I protected my children from it and let him hit me instead of hitting them. He was a man who everyone thought was bloody wonderful when they first met him. He charmed the pants off everyone, but the minute the door was shut he was moody and he drank. He had severe depression, we discovered years later, but it doesn't condone what he did to me. One night he hit me once too often, and I'd just had enough. He was making us all desperately unhappy and it was no life to bring children up in.' Rebecca took a deep breath. 'You are very easy to talk to, Maddy. I feel like I'm burdening you here.'

I smiled at her. 'It sounds like you need to talk about it. It's not always good to bottle things up.'

'Thank you, Maddy. I've not told many people our background

and it's actually quite cathartic to say it out loud.' She breathed deeply before she continued.

'His behaviour was getting worse with each episode. I should have got out years ago, but I couldn't. I wasn't mentally ready. I had amazing help from my local Women's Aid support unit, and they put me in touch with Beth up here. I lived over a hundred miles away. She helped to set up a new home for the children and me without him knowing, and then one night I laced his hot chocolate with sleeping tablets so he didn't wake for a while and I grabbed the children from their beds, and we just scarpered. Poor lambs; they didn't have a clue what was happening. They put coats on over the top of their pyjamas, and we left with literally nothing but what we were wearing.

'Thanks to Beth, we were able to start a new life. There was a local charity who gave us support and clothes and furniture, and when I was ready, I started working at the library, just around school hours so I can take the children to school and pick them up, and I help out where I can at the local women's refuge, helping women just like me. It's really important to me that I help others realise that they don't have to live that way and that there are options. Without the help I had, I'd still be there. It's also really important to me that I'm around for those school times for the younger ones, and then we go and shut ourselves away in our house where we feel safe and secure.

'I suppose I want to make it up to them. Make them realise how much I love them and how sorry I am that they had to go through everything that they did. And it's so wonderful to see them enjoying life now that the look of fear has left them. So that's my story, basically, Madison. So what's yours?'

To be honest, I was speechless. I really hadn't realised before just what victims of domestic violence went through, yet here I was, feeling sorry for myself because I had been made redundant and couldn't afford the latest Michael Kors handbag. Learning more about Beth's life was really opening up my eyes to what other people were going through.

I told Rebecca a little of my background and that I'd recently moved to the farm. I suggested that she brought the children over one day and I could show them around. She said that her and Beth had talked about this before, but they were both so busy that they hadn't got round to it yet, but she said that she would make the time because she knew the children would love it. It would be more fun next spring when the ewes had their little lambs dancing about, but they could come over soon and help me to feed them and help me to find the eggs in the chicken coops. I always found it really fulfilling to eat poached eggs on toast when I'd had to find those eggs for myself. I bet the children would love it too.

Somehow, the chickens over the last few days had become my responsibility and my first job of the morning was to spend a good while rummaging around in the bedding hay to see what delights we'd been left from the night before. And my evening job was to lock them away, which was easier said than done when you had to find and persuade twenty chickens and one gobby cockerel to go into their coop all at the same time, locking them away so the foxes didn't get them in the night.

The children could come and look round the allotment too and maybe we could find them their own little patch with their own jobs to do, and maybe they could grow some fruit and veg and watch the food literally go from farm to fork. Even though she realised that it would be a long-term project, Rebecca loved this idea and said that they'd never done anything like this, so we arranged for them to come over one evening after school and see how they enjoyed it.

We parted with Rebecca also promising to see if there were any other projects in the community that I could get involved with or whether the women's refuge needed any help at all. If nothing else, I was sure there was stuff I wouldn't need any more that I could pass their way while I was moving out. I'd gone from not having anything to do to filling my days quite easily, and I felt that the things I was doing these days, although simpler, were way more fulfilling. I gave her a hug as we left. I'd turned into a right hugger these last few weeks and I felt good that I'd made a new friend.

13

As the rest of the week passed we fell into an easy routine at the farm, which suited us all, with me going home each evening and packing my old life away.

Friday soon rolled round. Uncle Tom very kindly let me have the afternoon off and Alex offered to come over with me to give me a hand with all the lifting for which I was extremely grateful. It was great living in a flat until you moved in or out, or had tons of shopping to carry.

I'd learned to calm down a bit more around Alex over the last week and to stop blushing every time he looked at me. He was going to be grabbing a flight back to the US soon, so there was no point getting too attached to him again even just as friends.

Mum was coming over later; I was really looking forward to seeing her. She was going to bring a measuring tape and jot down anything that we needed and we were going shopping the next morning. There wasn't much I needed but there were a few ornamental things that I wanted to pop around the place to make it feel more like mine than a temporary let. I was hoping to catch Mum in a good mood too as I wanted to ask her more about my father.

It seemed like she'd got the same idea as me though, because as soon as she arrived that evening, she was looking pretty serious and said that she'd got something on her mind that she wanted to discuss. I held up the bottle of wine that she'd brought over, and she nodded, so I poured us both half a glass. I wasn't sure if wine glasses were getting bigger or wine bottles were getting smaller but you could easily lose a bottle in a couple of glasses these days.

As I sat opposite Mum, I noticed her handbag at the side of the coffee table, and there sat on the top was the mysterious red tin box. She clocked that I'd seen it and passed it to me.

'I'm sorry, darling, I wasn't quite truthful with you when you asked about this box before but I really feel that the time is right to give it to you now. I'm going to pop to the loo and leave you to look through it. Hopefully it'll start to make sense as you go through it.'

I had no real idea what to expect, but as I opened the box, there on the top was one of those photo booth strips of four black and white pictures of Mum when she was younger with a very handsome man. I turned the pictures over, and it said 'Josie and Theo, Blackpool, 1981'. Oh my bloody God! Was this my father? I stared at him, devouring every single detail of his face. I couldn't see much, but I could see that he had a neck scarf on top of a collarless white shirt and he looked like he should be a member of Duran Duran. He had strawberry blond hair, which flopped over to one side. In one photo, he was kissing Mum's cheek and she was laughing, and in another they were staring at each other and looked very much in love. I gulped as I took in every tiny detail of his face. His eyes, his nose. Oh my! I put my hand up to touch his nose on the photograph. He also had a freckle right on the end of his nose. It was just like mine. Or should I say, mine was just like his? Touching his face on the photograph made me feel like I was reaching out and touching him in person.

A cough brought me back to my senses and I noticed Mum standing beside me.

'Is this him?'

'Yes, darling. Your father. This is Theo.' She rested her hand on my shoulder and I just looked up at her. I couldn't speak. Nothing would come out. I was thirty-seven years old and this was the very first time that I'd seen my dad. In my head he was becoming 'Dad' now, because I'd seen him and his features were familiar to me. I was gobsmacked.

'OK, darling, I can see that you are totally stunned, so pass me the box back and I'll give you things one by one and explain what they are. That might help. They're all things that really meant something to me from the time that Theo and I spent together.

'Theo normally left work after me, but one night we were on the same bus and he sat by me and we chatted like old friends. He asked me if he could take me to watch a film. This is a cinema ticket from our very first date. We went to see *Raiders of the Lost Ark*. How romantic!' She giggled at the memory. 'It was such a lovely evening; I didn't want it to end. We went for a drink in a late-night café and they had to throw us out because they were desperate to close but we just didn't want to part company. We walked around talking until around one a.m. when he walked me home to the flat I lived in above a florist shop.

'I'll never forget that first kiss as long as I live.' As Mum spoke, I could see just how painful it was for her to relive this memory, and a tear trickled down her cheek as I held her hand in mine.

She wiped away the tear and delved back into the box. She laughed as she passed another ticket across to me. 'Adam and the Ants at the Odeon in Birmingham. It was our next date and the first pop concert I had ever been to. I had never seen anything like it. Girls were screaming and crying and there was one girl at the front who passed out when Adam Ant touched her hand. It was brilliant. The bass vibrated through your body, it was so loud and so fantastic. One of the most exciting moments of my life.'

A menu was the next thing that she passed over. I couldn't bring myself to speak. I was mesmerised by these mementoes that my Mum had kept for over thirty-eight years.

'This was from the first meal we ever had at Romano Italiano in Birmingham. Not sure why I kept the menu; I just wanted to treasure the memories, I suppose. They all meant such a lot to me.'

Taking a sip of her wine, she passed me another keepsake, and I was surprised to see that it was a handwritten note. My breath caught in my throat when I realised that I was looking at my father's writing. This was such a weird feeling.

My darling Josie, I'm trying to work, but cannot think of anything but you and our kisses. Meet me at the bus stop after work. I just cannot wait to feel you in my arms and your lips upon mine once more. Just four more hours to go. Theo xxx

'This was a note that was on my desk when I got back from lunch one day. He took a risk putting it there, but I suppose it was in an envelope, so no one could read it. I remember slipping it into my handbag and then when I met him that night he said that being able to see me but not touch me at work was driving him crazy. It was strange because he was so quiet at work, didn't say boo to a goose, just got on with his job and very rarely came out of his office. But then there was this passionate side to him too. That was the first time in the short few months we'd been together that he told me he loved me. We were sat on the top deck of the bus holding hands and he just blurted it out. I couldn't believe it. It seemed so soon, but then again, it seemed so right, too.'

Mum's cheeks started to flush as more memories came flooding back to her. 'We caught the bus back to the shop and we stumbled through the front door, and, well, you can probably guess what happened next.'

At this point, I was torn between wanting to know what happened next as it sounded so romantic and wanting to hold my hands over my ears and shout 'la la la!' This was my mum after all and there are some things you really don't need to know about what your mother gets up to in the bedroom department.

'Don't worry. I'm not going to go into detail, darling.'

Thank God for that! She was sparing me the intimate details. I was thankful for small mercies.

'This is a birthday card from the one and only birthday of mine that we spent together.' She passed over a beautiful card with 'To the One I Love' on the front, and once again, seeing his writing on the inside, declaring his undying love, made my stomach lurch.

A baby scan picture was passed across our knees. 'I was so happy to know I was having Theo's baby after the initial shock wore off. I thought he'd feel the same way. The rest you know.'

Mum looked sad but unburdened at the same time. 'Darling, I'm so sorry that I've never shown you these things before. The last time I looked at them was just after you were born. I was so ecstatic to have my beautiful baby daughter that I loved with all my heart, but so immensely sad to be without Theo. My emotions were all over the place. My hormones, too! I really thought that my parents would have been there for me. I know I haven't told you this before, because I was not only hurt but also totally mortified by what they did, but they disowned me the moment I told them I was pregnant. I know they were disappointed in me, understandably, and horrified, as was I, that Theo was married and was not going to be able to make an honest woman of me. They were embarrassed and didn't want their friends to find out. At the time when I really needed them the most, they weren't there for me.' Her voice wobbled.

'He should have been there with me. To see his beautiful daughter.' She banged her hand on her knee and raised her voice. 'He should have been there for you, for us.' Then all her anger dissipated as she whispered, 'He should have been there for us,' once more. Tears streamed down her cheeks as those feelings of betrayal from the people she thought cared about her came flooding back to her and the hurt came tumbling back into her life. She took a deep breath to steady her nerves.

'This is why I packed everything away in a box and hid it in the loft. I couldn't bear to look at them and think about how quickly it all went wrong. Obviously I didn't hide it well enough though, Miss Eagle Eyes.' She smiled at me through her tears. 'Can you ever forgive me? I was just trying to protect you.'

'Mum, there is nothing to forgive you for. You can only ever do what you feel is right at the time. You dedicated your whole life to me and to making it the best it could be. You gave me more love than any other child I know. You worked around the clock so we could have a nice life. I couldn't have asked for a more dedicated, perfect, wonderful mother.'

Mum ran her thumb down my cheek. 'My beautiful, kind, sweet girl. You are beautiful inside and out. He has missed out on so much. I'm so proud of you and love you so very much. There was a point in my life where I wished nothing more than that one day, before my time was up, we would meet again, and I could hold my head high and tell him that we never needed him. That we did OK.'

'We did more than OK, Mum, we – well, mainly you – did brilliant. But can I ask you one more thing?'

'Anything, darling, anything at all.'

'What was his surname?'

Mum took in the deepest of breaths and time stood still for what seemed like minutes because she knew that the words she would say next would be life-changing. She breathed out and whispered, 'Knight. Theo Knight.'

14

Once she realised that I'd got over the initial shock, Mum said that she was going and that she'd be back the following day after she'd given me some time to think. She kissed my head as she left. 'Sleep tight, darling. I love you.'

* * *

I sat for ages just staring into space, completely bowled over by the fact that I now had a name. I rolled it around my tongue. Theo. Knight. It was a good strong name, and I wondered what a name said about a person. Once I started to come to my senses, I grabbed my phone from my handbag and started to look online for my father.

However, Theo Knight was nowhere to be found. I tried to cyber stalk him by looking for him on Google, Facebook, Twitter and Instagram. But I kept drawing a blank. In hindsight, if he was older than Mum by five years, and Mum was sixty this year, that would make him sixty-four or sixty-five, so maybe that made it less likely that he would be on social media? I thought there was a chance that I might track him down but even before I'd really started I'd hit a dead end. What now?

I thought Beth might have some suggestions when I'd pop in to see her tomorrow. I could get her on the case while she was resting. It would give her something to do.

My sleep was fitful that night; I was tossing and turning with my mind whirling in all directions, but in the middle of the night everything always seemed a million times worse, and the harder I tried to go back to sleep, the less able I became. As the sun rose across the orchard, I trudged downstairs in my 'jamas and slippers and made some coffee. I desperately needed a caffeine boost to start the day. As I boiled the kettle, I remembered that Mum was coming over mid-morning to go shopping and it gave me the kick up the bum I needed to drag myself out of this daze.

* * *

Around 9 a.m. the post thudded onto the front door mat and made me jump from my daydream. Looking at my watch, I realised it had been a while since I'd moved from my book and it was about time I got myself another drink to liven me up. I was waking up early these days and really enjoying having a coffee and reading to start the day. I flicked the switch to reboil the kettle and picked up the post which had been directed from the apartment, rifling through to see if anything looked interesting. One A4 manila envelope had the Ronington's franking stamp and I opened it to find some final paperwork from the HR department. My heart thudded as I recognised the sweeping handwriting on one of the other envelopes that was also included. Propping that particular bit of post next to the kettle, with my hands shaking, I made a drink but was definitely really out of sorts because of it. I sat back down on the sofa and tried to ignore it, but it was staring at me, calling me to open it.

How could something like this have got me so worked up? It was no good; I decided I may as well get it over and done with, like ripping off a sticking plaster. I stomped over to the envelope, counted to five and opened it. A sheet of A4 paper dropped from my shaking hands onto the floor.

Maddy, it's been a while. How are you?

Cheeky bastard. 'It's been a while!' It had only 'been a while' because the last time I saw him, he was literally in the middle of shagging one of his clients, and that was on top of the fact that I'd been devastated about what had recently happened too. My blood was beginning to boil.

Over the last couple of years I've spent time with other people, but none of them are like you. They don't make me laugh like you do, they don't turn me on like you do, and they don't work as hard as you do. They're just not you. I miss you, Maddy.

I know about the redundancy and it doesn't matter to me. What I want, Maddy, is for you and me to be together again. I want us to work together again and be a couple again. A team. You and me against the world, just like we used to be.

I'd love to chat to you, to see if you'll forgive me and take me back. I need you and would love to hold you in my arms again. Please get in touch and say we can try again. I have always and will always love you, J x

OMG! What the hell was this? It was so totally and utterly out of the blue, I literally did not know what to make of it. This was what I'd longed for so many times after we split up. I wanted him to apologise and tell me it meant nothing to him. To beg me to reconsider and take him back. That I was all he ever wanted and needed and that he'd been stupid and given in to ridiculous primal urges. If he'd done that, I'm sure we could have got through his dalliance if that were the only issue.

It had taken me a long time to get rid of the image of his arse pumping up and down while Alisa smirked at me over his shoulder as I stood in stunned silence. It took far too long for him to even realise that I was there and jump up and have the decency to cover himself up, whilst at the same time exposing Alisa to the elements so that she flashed her snatch right at me! Bloody hell, there are some things you really just can't unsee!

I couldn't believe he'd done that to me and especially not then. I thought that my heart would literally never recover from such a betrayal. I wondered if it was my fault. Whether it was because of what had happened...

Three weeks beforehand, I'd found out I was pregnant. I was on the pill, but it must have happened when I'd had a bad stomach after a dodgy curry so the pill wasn't effective. I'd realised recently that my period was late, which was very unusual for me, and I'd worried about it for days until I decided one day, without saying anything to anyone, that I should probably do a test. I knew there was a pretty remote chance that I was pregnant but thought that perhaps stressing about it was making it worse, so I decided it was time to find out once and for all and put my mind at rest.

With shaking hands, I picked up the test after the required two minutes and read the word *pregnant*! I was shocked. I had no idea what to do. Should I tell Jamie yet? I felt I needed a bit of time to get my own head around it before I told him. For two days, I'd worked late, gone in early and tried to avoid him as much as possible. I made a doctor's appointment and it was confirmed that I was definitely pregnant. Over that time it had started to sink in. I was going to be a mum. At first, it was scary. I worried about whether I could be a good enough mum, like my wonderful mum. I'd never really thought about being a parent. Jamie and I had never really talked about it, even though we'd been together for years. I didn't think he particularly liked children, to be honest. He was always commenting about people he worked with putting their kids before work and he couldn't understand it. But once it had started to sink in, I began to think about a future as a family. Jamie, our baby and me. And I liked what the future had in store for us. We'd already committed to living together and being together forever; we often talked about growing old together. This way there'd just be more of us in our family unit. The more I thought about it, the more excited I became. I pictured walking down the street pushing a pram, with our baby inside it. Once I'd got used to it, I loved the idea and I wanted to share it with Jamie, sure that he'd feel the same way.

I realised that I was just prolonging something that I really needed to tell him, so I made him his favourite meal of steak and chips, opened a good bottle of red and plucked up the courage to say that I couldn't drink when he went to pour a glass for me.

'Are you having to take antibiotics for something, babe?'

'No Jamie, I'm… I'm…' I struggled to put the sentence together.

'Spit it out, babe. The football is on in a bit.'

'I'm pregnant!' I blurted.

Jamie laughed.

'Nice one! But you can't fool me!' But when I didn't smile, his grin dropped and he became deadly serious.

'Tell me you're joking,' he whispered.

'I'm not joking, Jamie. I'm pregnant.' I was so relieved the words were out. It was amazing how just one short sentence was so life changing.

He stood and paced the room, holding his head. I stood up and tried to comfort him, but he gently pushed me away.

'But you're on the pill,' he said.

I explained that it must have happened when I was ill.

'This is just the worst news ever!'

That sentence hit me like a ton of bricks. He slammed out of the flat. I sat up until 2 a.m. waiting for him to come back but by then I was shattered and fell into bed, exhaustion taking over my body. He still hadn't returned by the time I had to go to work the next day.

Worried sick, I sent a text first thing which he replied to later that morning to say that he was staying with a friend for a few days and that he'd be in touch soon.

For the next few days, my emotions were on a rollercoaster, one minute seeing us playing happy families together once Jamie had got round to the idea of it, and then seeing me on my own with our baby. But in every picture, I was a mum. And I was a great mum and I loved my baby totally and unconditionally. Well, I'd had a wonderful teacher.

Being pregnant in those early days was exhausting, morning sickness lasting nearly all day and totally wearing me out, so I took as many opportunities as I could to nap. I was told that at ten weeks pregnant, it hopefully shouldn't last too much longer, maybe a couple more weeks, all being well.

One morning, I woke to griping pains low down in my belly and I knew immediately that something was not right. As I looked down, the pure white Egyptian cotton sheets were a contrast to the red pool that was forming between my legs. I dragged myself to the toilet and wiped myself as much as I could. As I did this, I knew that there was something terribly wrong and I rang an ambulance. Once admitted to A&E, I was taken for a scan and told that it had gone. My baby had gone. But it wasn't just my baby that had gone. It was all my dreams of the future. Our family.

I texted Jamie from the hospital and he arrived two hours later to take me home. He was quiet when he arrived. He didn't comfort me. He kept his distance. The doctors and nurses reassured me that there was all probability that I could get pregnant again and that miscarriages were a natural part of life and that it happened to lots of ladies.

Once home, he changed the sheets on the bed and I couldn't wait to sleep. To shut everything away. Jamie brought me a cup of tea later that evening and he sat on the bed and held my hand.

'It's probably for the best, Madison.'

Snatching my hand away, I turned over, my back now facing him. Tears streamed down my face. Something so precious to me had been lost. How could he possibly say that it was for the best? I'd lost something that I'd never be able to replace. My future with my baby.

Celine had been told that I had flu and was keeping away from the office. Refusing to get up for two days, I could tell that Jamie was starting to get pissed off with me, but I couldn't seem to shake it off. I was overwhelmed by the sadness that I felt. On the third day, I realised that Jamie's life was going on as normal and that he'd already forgotten why I was feeling so bad. It was almost like I'd just got a cold, in his eyes, and I'd be over it in a day or two. He clearly didn't realise that this was something I would never get over. I made the effort to get dressed, and oh boy, was it an effort. He dropped me off at work on his way into town and I said that I'd see him later. We'd hardly spoken for days and as I got out of the car, he leaned over to me and called me back.

'Madison. You really do have to pull yourself together, you know. It's happened and it's over. You have to move on.'

How could this man that I loved so deeply have no regard at all for my feelings? How could he tell me to just move on?

This wasn't just a baby that hadn't been born. This was a life that wasn't going to be lived. My toddler not taking its first steps. Not reading to my child at bedtime. Not being able to take them to nursery and then to school. Not watching them go to their prom, not watching them get married.

Every magical moment that a parent goes through with their child had been stolen from me. Our future together, wiped out, and I couldn't just forget that the way he obviously could.

I couldn't concentrate on a thing at work and at lunchtime Celine said she thought it would be better if she sent me home in a taxi as I'd messed up the three tasks she'd asked me to do in the morning, and I still looked so dreadful. She said it was clearly the flu and she didn't want everyone else to get it too.

When I arrived home, Jamie's car was in his parking space. I decided that I'd go up and ask him to hold me in his arms. I knew that once he realised how I was feeling, now he was getting over the shock of the last few days, he'd be there for me. He would be my rock, to support me.

But when I got into the flat, I found him with Alisa.

* * *

As I ran out of the flat, he'd tried to follow me but got the sheet wrapped around his leg and fell over the coffee table, and the last words I heard leave his mouth were, 'Ouch! Fucking fuck, bollocks, fuck, shit!' Charming. No: 'Sorry, Maddy.' No: 'Maddy, don't go.' No: 'It's not what you think' (although it would have been pretty hard to get out of that one). No explanation; nothing. And not one bit of sympathy for what had happened over the last few days. All those words that could have possibly repaired the damage to our lives, yet he couldn't find a single one.

Giddywell would always be my home and Mum welcomed me with open arms when she saw me standing on her doorstep with tears streaming down my face. She knew what it took for me to trust someone in my life and how devastated I was. I knew that I would never be the same again and the impact of first the miscarriage and then his infidelity would affect me forever. I went through a stage of not wanting to leave the house, didn't want to bump into people. I just wanted my mum to look after me. She seemed to know how I felt.

A quick text from me to Jamie telling him to pack his things and leave was the only contact we'd had. And I hadn't heard a word since. Until this.

Part of me wanted to meet him because I was intrigued and wondered why the hell he was getting in touch now. Part of me wanted to go to just punch him in the face then leave. But that wouldn't be very dignified of me, even though it would be quite satisfying. And the other part of me wanted to screw the note up into a little ball and throw it onto an open fire and pretend I'd never seen it. I hadn't a clue what to do. I needed to talk to Beth and see what she said, although I could probably imagine. I knew it was early, but when I looked out of my window, her bedroom curtains were open so I knew she was awake and I grabbed my fleece off the back of a dining room chair, popped my shoes on and headed over to the farmhouse.

As I walked into the kitchen, my shoes click-clacked across the old stone floor. This house was amazing, so cosy and simply furnished in a mishmash of styles, which all perfectly blended with the décor. It had beautiful cast iron open fireplaces in every room, which in winter were all lit permanently, making it a place you never wanted to leave. There wasn't a soul around and I breathed in the familiarity of this big old beautiful house. The long, wood-panelled hallway led to the most stunning sweeping staircase that I had always loved and a curved polished wooden banister that we all used to slide down as kids and come to a flying stop just before we hit the huge sideboard at the bottom. I used to imagine myself gracefully gliding down the stairs, channelling my inner Scarlet O'Hara, in a stunning ball gown and elbow-length white silk gloves, ready to meet my beau (Alex, it was always Alex in my dreams) who would be anticipating my arrival at the foot of the stairs, dressed in a frockcoat, tails and boots, to whisk me away in his arms, to dance elegantly in the ballroom, unable to tear his eyes away from me.

Pushing these silly teenage fairy tale notions away, I went straight up to Beth's room, knocked and entered to find her propped up in bed, reading. I threw the letter at her, and she frowned as she read it. 'What the fucking fuck?'

'I know! That was exactly my reaction too.'

'Well, please tell me that there's not even one tiny bit of you that wants to actually go.' She passed me the letter back.

'I'm not sure.'

'*Not sure?* You are kidding, right?'

'Well, I thought perhaps I'd just go and see what he's got to say. There's just a little bit of me that's curious about why he's getting in touch now.'

'Clearly, he's after something. Where's he been for the last three years? Shagging his way round Europe by the look of his Facebook page, which I've always got my eye on.'

'OK, so you don't think I should go then?' I smiled at her.

'No, I bloody well don't. I don't even want to discuss it any more. He cheated on you at a time when he should have been supporting you. He left you broken and devastated. How can you even think of it? I'll not speak about it again, Maddy. That's the end of the conversation. OK?'

'Oh, OK, you'd better tell me how you are then.'

Beth talked to me for the next ten minutes, but to tell the truth, I had absolutely no idea what she said. I was finding it difficult to process anything she was saying. I was just thinking about the fact that despite Beth's good intentions and advice, the half of me that was telling me to get dressed up, show him what he was missing and see what it was all about was overtaking the half of me that thought I shouldn't go.

* * *

Excusing myself by saying I had the beginnings of a headache, I went back over to the barn and put the TV on to fill the time before Mum arrived. There was a cooking programme on, and I was watching it but not taking any of it in. My mind was all over the place, dredging up memories both good and bad about how Jamie had changed my life for what I thought was the better, then stolen it all away.

But he was also the man who I had given everything to and had loved with all my heart. The man I'd met at a cocktail party I'd gone along to on behalf of Ronington's. The man who had seen me standing alone and come over to talk to me, saying that I looked beautiful but alone. The man who worked for a rival PR company and knew all about me and my work life. He'd obviously done his research. The man who had then wooed me for weeks, gently edging his way into my life, making himself so indispensable that in the end I couldn't bear to live without him. The man who knew I had relationship issues and one Christmas gave me a box with a key to his house and a toothbrush to leave there. The man who eventually asked me to move in, saying surely that was proof of his commitment to me. The man who, if he got home from work first, and I'd had a long and stressful day, would run me a bath, light candles and welcome me at the front door with a rum and Coke and let me luxuriate in a long soak while he cooked dinner.

He was the man I had given my whole heart to. I loved our life and it was no hardship to me to put everything on hold and devote my whole life to him, to the detriment of my friends and Mum, I realised later, although I didn't see it at the time. I loved him so intensely and really thought that he was the love of my life and the centre of my world.

We had an amazing life together. With two fantastic salaries coming in, we had the best of everything. We went on the most exotic holidays; the two weeks we spent in the Maldives were the best of my life, just him and me in a stunning water bungalow, overlooking the sparkling turquoise sea, with tropical fish swimming around our ankles as we dangled our feet over the decking. I felt so incredibly loved at that time, walking around the island, holding hands and drinking cocktails, gazing at the most glorious sunsets from the Sundowner bar.

Just a normal weekend for us was filled with shopping and hospitality. We'd walk into the local town and share a bottle of wine, chatting about everything and nothing. We had designer everything. For me, it was handbags and sunglasses. For him, it was suits and ties. Sometimes he was just a little flash and cocky though. I remembered the day that he bought his Tag Heuer watch and flashed it around in the pub. When the bar guy admired it, he said that he had paid more for his watch than the bar guy would earn in a month and laughed. I laughed along with him but then afterwards realised that what he'd said was cruel and crass. Money was no object to either of us, but it wasn't until afterwards that I realised these were just things.

When I didn't have Jamie any more, my Dolce and Gabbana handbag didn't seem to hold the same appeal. In fact, it was my birthday the week before I found him with Alisa and he bought me a star, which was the most romantic thing that he had ever done. I was so touched to read the dedication on the certificate, which said '*This star will last as long as my love for you.*' Just the week then, tosser!

What I remembered vividly now was how my whole world came crashing down around me just a week later. Just thinking about it reminded me of how it made me feel at the time, and made my heart thump a million beats per minute. I would never have said I was an anxious person, but this was the start of a very long period of not being able to cope with anything at all. A couple of months off work, with Mum looking after me, really helped, but I knew that I would never be the same again. I was totally gutted. I clearly didn't mean as much to him as he did to me or he would never have betrayed me in this way. And I hadn't heard a word from him till now. So why would he get in touch suddenly?

There was a little voice on one shoulder saying, 'Don't you bloody dare go and see that scumbag,' and the other voice, which needed closure, which was yelling way, way louder: 'Go on, go and meet him and see what he has to say.'

15

Mum knocked on the door and walked straight in around ten thirty and I was still sat in my jimjams. 'Come on, lady, shake a leg! We can talk more as we drive into town.'

Grabbing the quickest shower I'd ever had and throwing on jeans, a t-shirt and a hoody, which seemed to be my style these days, I ran back downstairs to see Mum gazing out of the barn window across the farmland. Putting my arm around her, I rested my head on her shoulder and we stood for a moment or two, no words needed, both of us in our own thoughts.

I broke the silence. 'We should make a move, Mum.'

We jumped into my classic sports car, Mum moaning at how low it was. 'You're only nearly sixty, you know, not eighty! I had to have something different to my company car, Mum, to make it OK and to help me to move on.' The day they drove my company car away was just another kick in the teeth for me and it really hurt. Silly really to get upset over a car, but it wasn't just the car I was gutted about, it was symbolic of the whole situation.

'I know, lovely, but these knees are getting on a bit, and this back. Honestly...' She grinned at me but I found it hard this morning to smile back.

* * *

Sometimes life drifted by with not much going on at all, but right now I felt like I just couldn't take any more. I'd got Mum telling me about Theo, and Beth was ill. I'd moved into a new home and was trying to get used to a new temporary job and fulfil all of Beth's community obligations and now, on top of everything, there was Jamie. They do say that life doesn't throw at you more than you can take, but I didn't feel like I could take much more right now.

We drove out to the local retail centre just outside Stafford, which was around twenty minutes away, and I picked up some lovely bright cushions, a couple of Moroccan lantern-type table lamps, and some mohair throws to make the lounge more cosy. Since I'd become a reader, I loved nothing more than getting comfy on the sofa, with a throw over me, immersing myself in my latest novel. I also treated myself to a new duvet set, which I unpacked and threw in the washing machine the minute I got home, just after lunchtime, so that I could get it dried on the line and on the bed. There was nothing nicer than the smell of fresh air on your bedclothes, although living on a farm, the fresh air here had a distinct whiff of 'eau de cow shit'. Ridiculous as it was, I'd missed having a washing line. In the flat, everything got tumble-dried, but here I was looking forward to putting up the rotary washing line and pegging my washing out. It was the simple things in life that seemed to make me happy these days.

I made Mum and me a sandwich, but to be honest, now I had nothing to do, I couldn't stop thinking about my father and wondering about him. I wasn't much company and told Mum I had a headache and was going to have a lie down. I was sure she knew that I just needed some time to myself as she didn't question a thing, and she looked at me sadly as she said goodbye and that she'd text me later to see how I was feeling.

I didn't even know how I was feeling myself. Russell was on shift over at Growlers, so I made the most of a quiet afternoon and picked up the latest thriller I was reading to give me something else to think about. Last night's lack of sleep meant that I was shattered and two hours later I woke up with the book face down on my chest. I felt a little groggy at first but after a cup of tea, I was glad I'd had the chance to catch up on some sleep. I spent hours poring over the allotment gardening books that Alex had given me, which up till now had been sat on the coffee table in the lounge. I couldn't allow myself to think right now, so I needed to occupy myself. Throwing a pizza in the oven, as I really couldn't be bothered to cook a proper meal, I sat down and started making notes about the allotment. One thing I had really missed since I'd been living alone was cooking for someone. There never seemed much point when I was on my own, but at least I'd be eating a lot more healthily once I'd started to harvest the fruits of my allotment. There wasn't much on the TV, so I half-heartedly watched a film with Rebel Wilson in it. She normally made me smile and it definitely did brighten my mood throughout the evening. A sharing bag of Maltesers to myself helped too. Share? Not tonight!

The week ahead was quite uneventful and I managed to avoid most people as much as I could. My mood wasn't the best. I was confused and couldn't stop thinking about my dad, and I couldn't stop thinking about Jamie either and wondering what the right thing to do was. I was getting into a routine of getting up at six and making myself a cuppa and sitting around before working at Growlers. I'd made a lovely little seating area in the garden with lots of cushions, and I took a throw out with me and snuggled under it reading. Not having to commute made a huge difference to the time I had, and I was still showered and ready for work at seven thirty when the first dogs arrived for the day.

Uncle Tom attended to the ones who had stayed overnight and let them out for their early morning ablutions before he headed off for some food, when I took over and sorted out their breakfast routines. I had a few hours off each afternoon after lunch, due to the early start, and spent that mostly planning the allotment or working the community slots that Rebecca had given me. I'd been back to see the Darbys and Stuart once again and was going to be making them a regular call until Beth was driving and fully back, when Rebecca would sort some other tasks out for me.

Rebecca had been over to the farm with her younger children, and I'd left her chatting to Uncle Tom a few times while I took the children to see their big brother at work in the kennels. They found eggs in the chicken coop and seeing their delighted faces was very entertaining.

I'd spend most of my evenings thinking about my future and working out what it looked like in my head. And who was in it.

But today was Saturday. A whole week had gone by without me contacting Jamie, although I had picked the phone up a time or two and then stopped myself. Mum had always taught me that if you are in a situation and are not sure what to do, then it was best to do nothing... But goodness me, it was hard. I decided to walk into Giddywell and get some air into my lungs. I needed a change of scenery and to pick up a few bits and bobs from a couple of the shops in the village. Now I wasn't working all hours, and needed to fill my spare time, I thought I'd do some baking. I hadn't baked for years but decided to give it a whirl. As I walked past the Copper Kettle café, I couldn't believe my eyes when I saw Mum sat at a table with a really handsome grey-haired man, laughing and touching his arm. In all my years of being alive, I had never known Mum date anyone. Trying to persuade her to sign up to a dating website was a mission of mine and Jamie's at one point, but she was having none of it and said that she had everything she ever wanted in her world and that she'd never let anyone else hurt her again.

I didn't know what to do. Should I just walk on past, or should I go in and say hello? But then, if she didn't see me – and there was a chance that she wouldn't as she looked so comfortable chatting and flirting with this man – I could possibly get away unnoticed. But then, I'd have to say that I'd seen her, because curiosity would be eating away at me, and I was actually dying to know who he was.

Just as I was dithering as to what to do, old Mrs Craddock who lived just up the road from my mum crashed into me with her shopping trolley, and all her shopping tumbled out over the ground and into the road. I yelped from the pain in my ankle as she'd caught me right on the bony bit at the side.

'Oh my dear, I'm so sorry. I didn't see you there.'

I helped her to pick everything up and when we put it all back in the trolley, I turned back to the café to see Mum staring at me with a look of pure panic on her face. If bloody Mrs Craddock hadn't made all that commotion I could have just sloped off but she'd seen me now. There was nothing else for it but to front it out and go and say hello. I limped across to them.

'Hello, how lovely to see you.' I bent to kiss her cheek, noticing that she smelled beautiful. I turned to her companion and smiled. 'Hi there, I'm Maddy.' I didn't say I was her daughter, just in case she hadn't broken the news yet that she had one.

Mum looked like she wanted to crawl up her own backside. Her face had gone from frowning to grimacing. She realised that the only thing she could do was introduce us.

'Edward, meet Maddy. My daughter. Maddy, this is Edward. He's... er, a friend of mine.'

I could clearly see that! I leant across to shake his hand.

'Hello, Edward. It's so nice to meet a friend of my mother's. You never said you were meeting anyone today, Mum. Do you live around here? Actually, have we met before?' Now that I could see him close up, there was something about him that seemed incredibly familiar. He was even more handsome close up, with his salt-and-pepper hair framing a healthily tanned face sprinkled with freckles. He was casually dressed in smart jeans, a white shirt and a beige suede jacket. He was quite a looker for an old 'un.

'I'm just visiting. Not sure how long I'll be sticking around for. I've been living in Spain for a good few years now and have popped back for an extended visit to see some family and decided to look your mother up. We used to go to school together. I think I just have one of those faces, you know how it is.' He laughed nervously.

Mum was fidgeting really badly and I wondered whether it was because she actually really liked this man and was a little embarrassed to have been caught out with him. She certainly looked like she had been enjoying his company earlier when I was watching her through the window, but now there was something really not sitting right with her. She must be mortified at being caught out. I didn't want to see her being uncomfortable, so I decided to excuse myself on the pretence that I'd got to get back to work; always a good alibi to keep up your sleeve.

Edward stood up as I left and gave me a quick hug, which was rather unexpected but not at all unpleasant. I could tell by Mum's face that she was a bit spooked by his familiarity too because her eyebrows nearly shot out of her head. He seemed like a really nice man from the few minutes I had met him. He had a kind face which seemed to be full of character and his eyes wrinkled as he smiled broadly at me.

Walking away from the café with a grin on my face, I was

thinking how much of a dark horse my mum was and how it was actually about blooming time that she'd found a man to spend time with. She was such a lovely kind soul who had always put me first all her life, and she deserved in her later years to meet someone just as lovely to be a companion to her, if not yet a lover. But I did hope that something more might come of it than friendship.

* * *

Once I got home, and packed away my bits of shopping, I thought that instead of procrastinating, which I seemed to be quite good at these days, particularly since I found out that I had a reasonable redundancy payout and didn't need to get a job instantly, I should crack on with the baking that I'd been planning. Beth had leant me a cookery book – one she'd been given years ago which was full of basics and loads of Aunty Jen's scribbled notes. It felt like there was a bit of Aunty Jen beside me, guiding me. Beth loved a cake and was great at baking, and I knew she was finding it hard being so incapacitated, so I decided to do what she'd do for me and make her favourite chocolate brownies. Rock cakes were easy enough too, surely. I'd make some of those as well. I bet Mr and Mrs Darby would like a rock cake. I was going to see them again later this week, and Stuart too. It felt good to do things for other people and lifted my spirits. I was ready to face the world again.

I'd spent so long doing things for myself, spending hours having my nails and hair done, making myself look respectable for Jamie really, not even for me, to be a proper trophy girlfriend to him, which now seemed selfish and pretty egotistical. I'd discovered that I was really loving working with the dogs and being around Uncle Tom and Beth. But I was worried that I was wasting valuable time, when I should be looking to get back into the world of PR, although the thought didn't lift my soul in any way.

I put the radio on and danced around the kitchen, singing along. I wasn't a good cook; I could get by, but there never seemed much point cooking just for one. But baking for others, I almost felt that I was pouring love into the cakes I was making, knowing that my food might bring people joy. Being here at Giddywell Grange had made me realise all the things I'd been missing out on: spending time with friends and family again, and having animals around me who wanted nothing more from me than food, exercise and love, who didn't care what I looked or smelt like, was comforting and liberating, even. I loved being part of a community and helping others more than I ever would have thought possible.

16

My cakes didn't turn out too bad at all for a first attempt and I was pretty proud of myself. While they were cooling, I decided to go over to the allotment and make a start of some sort, as it wasn't going to do itself. I'd bought some seeds and wanted to put them in the shed. I felt like it needed a good clean before I went in there – it was full of cobwebs when I'd popped in before, and I wasn't a huge fan of spiders so I went armed with a long broom. But when I arrived, and went to open the shed padlock, I noticed that it wasn't locked. I must have forgotten to close it properly when I was here with Alex. So I was really surprised when I poked my head through the door and it looked completely different to the last time I'd been in there. The door was now attached to the shed frame by some new hinges. There was already a broom right by the door and it had definitely been swept out. All the cobwebs had gone and it was looking clean and tidy. The pots had been put in one corner and there were a few packets of seeds on the side. There was a huge bag of potting compost by the door and I picked up the packets of seeds and noticed that there was a note propped up against a small radio which hadn't been there before either. I turned to the light to read it.

I know how much you hate spiders and I couldn't risk being doused in another hot coffee, so I got rid of them all for you! Hope you feel better about your new kingdom now it's a bit tidier and you have something to listen to while you work! Alex x

Oh wow! How thoughtful. He knew about my fear of spiders because once when we were teenagers, he had pretended he had something in his hands and I told him not to come near me. He kept on teasing me and I told him if he came any closer, I'd throw the hot cup of coffee I was holding over him. He didn't believe me and came that one step closer. I had warned him though and he squealed like a girl when I threw it. I'd told him I would though. He ran off into the farm fuming and yelled, 'There was nothing in my bloody hand anyway, you daft cow!' Clearing out the shed for me was such a lovely, kind gesture that made me realise what a bloody lovely bloke he was and I loved him just a little bit more than before. As a brother figure, of course.

In the past, my Saturday afternoons were filled with shopping and working, yet I found spending time on the allotment today was so much more fulfilling. The sun was starting to go down so I decided to stop working. I'd been there for hours and as I stood and surveyed my surroundings, I was actually starting to see a difference. There was now a small but whole square of land that hadn't got any weeds on it at all, but my shoulders ached liked hell and when I got up I felt like an old lady. Nothing that a soak in a hot bath wouldn't sort out, I was sure. I couldn't wait for the days when I could come here to pick some veg for tea. I'd be so proud of actually growing my own produce. I never thought it would be something that would appeal to me but it really did. Everyone needed a hobby. When I worked I didn't think I needed one. I just seemed to work all the time and didn't really do much else. It had been years since I'd sung, and I'd practically given up music, because Jamie didn't approve.

I was really enjoying myself these days just doing simple stuff that I would never have thought was my cup of tea. Perhaps when my veggies were ready I could take some to Mr and Mrs Darby, and Stuart too. And I could share them with Mum... I hoped I would have a good crop! I smiled as I wandered back over to the barn and watched the full sunset from the arched window of my bedroom while I waited for the bath to fill. It was absolutely stunning and I felt so very peaceful. What a difference to my life just a few weeks ago, which was packed full of events, work and constantly being on the go. I warned myself not to get too comfortable though; it was only temporary until I found something else back in that corporate world. Weirdly, that thought didn't fill me with as much joy as it once would have.

While soaking in the bath, I pondered on just how much my life had changed over the last few weeks. That chain of thought brought Jamie back to mind. Was I going to meet him or not? I still hadn't made up my mind. But I knew that I was curious. I suppose it helped that when we were together Jamie and I were the same and we never minded working all the time because we were both doing it. We even used to sit in bed on a Saturday morning, drinking coffee and reading trade magazines. But now I'd started doing other things, I felt like I'd been really missing out.

The things I was doing now, that Beth had always done, I'd always felt were completely boring and dull, yet these small tasks that Beth had got me to cover for her had fulfilled me more than my previous work role ever did. I was a little embarrassed if truth be told, as even though I didn't mean to, I must have shown my disdain to Beth on the rare occasions that we met up or spoke.

I even thought that I was happy on my own. Because I felt that my father had let me down before I was even born, it had taken me a while to trust in a relationship, but I met and fell head over heels in love with Jamie and I did put my trust in him... only for him to prove me right about my fears. After Jamie had let me down, I vowed that I'd never trust anyone in a romantic relationship again. I'd put him and the thought of anyone else to the back of my mind. So why was I constantly thinking about Jamie since he'd been in touch? I decided that there might be only one way to get him out of my system once and for all.

* * *

I always thought that arriving early to a meeting gave me an advantage over walking in last, so I arrived at the pub early before the Monday after-work rush started and got myself a prime seating position so I would be able to see him when he approached the entrance. Now I was here though, I was really not sure if this had been the best idea after all, because I could hear my stomach gurgling with trepidation. I was really nervous. Oh God! He was here and about to walk through the door.

The bell above the door tinkled, and I pretended to be on my phone, but before I knew it, he strode across the room and was standing literally two feet from me. I looked straight into those baby blue eyes, which crinkled up in that oh-so-familiar way as a smile spread across his face. I stood and hesitated, a little unsure of how to greet him, but before I could decide, he grabbed both my elbows, leant forward and kissed me on both cheeks before I had the chance to back away.

'God, you look gorgeous, Madison. Even better than before. You have a healthy glow about you, absolutely stunning. What are you drinking?'

In shock over how familiar he was, I said that I'd already got a coffee, so he went off to the bar to get himself a drink. It gave me time to study him. He looked well too. He'd lost a bit of weight and was looking lean and fit, his clothes fitting him well, especially his trousers. He turned and saw me looking at his backside and grinned and I excused myself to go to the ladies' as soon as he returned to our table. I stood with my back against the toilet door, my heart thumping so loud it felt like it was on the outside of my body. My hands were shaking and I knew I really needed to get a grip before I went back out there.

It was time for my superhero pose. I always felt like a complete twat when I did it, but apparently scientific studies had proven that if you stood with your hands on your hips and your head tilted upwards, in a superhero stance, before either a job interview or a big presentation or a really hard task, then not only would you feel significantly more confident, you would perform measurably better. Well, that's what it said once on *Grey's Anatomy* and I'd never forgotten it! And it worked too. Every single time.

My breathing began to slow right down and after a minute or two it returned to normal, and right now I felt like I could take on the world. So I was certainly ready to take on Jamie.

* * *

'It really is good to see you, Maddy, you've been on my mind so much and I've wanted to get in touch so many times but didn't know whether to or not. But then I thought, what's the worst that could happen if I did? And the worst thing was that you might have said no, so I'd be in exactly the same position. So, I bit the bullet and wrote you that note. I've never stopped thinking about you and wishing that things had been different between us before I fucked it all up.' He did actually look ashamed, I was glad to see, as he blurted all this out. I sat in silence and just looked at him. In the past, I would have started to fill the silence with words reassuring him that it was OK, when it wasn't, just to make him feel better, but I needed him to know not just how much he'd hurt me but also how much I'd changed.

'I know it was entirely my fault. You were such a good influence in my life and I know it's all down to me that we're not together any more. I miss you, Maddy. I've missed you since the day I left. Things have never been the same since.'

Saying nothing seemed way more powerful than saying anything that could have been misconstrued. I gave him a stare that Paddington Bear would have been proud of.

'I suppose what I'm trying to say is that I'm, erm... I'm sorry.'

There they were. The words that I'd waited to hear for so long. The words that I had felt would be life-changing. The words that were coming three years later than they should have. And the words that actually, now I was hearing them, meant nothing at all. And there was nothing about the pregnancy. My baby. It was almost like he'd completely forgotten about something that I would never be able to forget.

'Jamie, three years ago, those words may have been much nicer to hear. Now, they mean nothing. Why did you want to meet me? Shall we get to the point?'

'I wanted to meet you because I wanted you to forgive me. I've been feeling bad about how things ended between us and wanted to put things right. And I love you, Maddy, I have missed you more than I could ever tell you. I've never stopped loving you, Maddy, even though we've been apart. I'd love us to be friends again and maybe eventually even become a couple again. I know that won't be for a while, and that I have to earn the right to have you back, but I'd really like us to try.'

He seemed totally genuine, but I could just imagine what Beth would be saying if she were sitting here right now.

I looked deep into his beautiful big blue eyes. Eyes in which I used to get lost forever, and I could feel myself falling deep into them once more. He smiled at me and his eyes twinkled as he reached across the table with his hands.

Hesitating at first, my hands joined his as if they had a will of their own. Those big, smooth, powerful hands that I knew so well, that had caressed my body so many times, were intertwined with mine and it felt familiar and it felt right. It was bringing back lots of warm fuzzy feelings, and my heart was starting to thaw as I remembered just how much this beautiful man sat before me had meant to me in the past. An ache deep in the pit of my stomach reminded me of just how much I'd loved him, and it made me wonder whether I could possibly love him again. Looking deep into those eyes, even though my head was saying *no, don't do it*, my heart was saying that I really wanted to try.

More confused than I had ever been before, I told Jamie that I had to go as I had an appointment to get to. I just needed some space to think, to put everything into perspective and try to work out what I really wanted. When we parted, he hugged me close to his chest.

'There's never been anyone that's come close to you, Maddy. Never!'

I had no idea how to answer that. How do you respond to someone who has let you down so badly, but who you loved with everything you had? Did second chances ever really work? There was only one way to find out, but was that a route I wanted to go down? I hadn't a clue what I wanted right now.

* * *

Early on Tuesday morning, I could hear Skype ringing on my iPad. I clicked on the icon and Alice's face came into view. She didn't look happy.

'Is everything OK, Alice? You look sad. How's Australia?'

'Oh, Madison.' She burst into tears. 'I have a huge decision to make. Emily and I have had a wonderful time and she's asked me to come and live with her.'

'Wow! What an offer! And how do you feel about it?'

'I love it here, Madison. I've never felt more comfortable. Here, I'm Alice, Emily's sister. I'm not Alice who lost her husband and who everyone feels sorry for. And it feels so very different. I know Des would be encouraging me to stay and have an adventure. But what about my Baxter? I don't think it would be fair to put him through the trauma of having him flown out here. He'd be so scared and alone, I couldn't bear to think of him that way. Yet it breaks my heart to think that I'd have to put him up for adoption just for me to have my dream. I love my Baxter so much and I really don't know what to do. I knew that you'd be a good person to talk all this through with. Emily has never had a dog so she doesn't understand why this isn't an easy decision to make. She keeps saying that Baxter is "just a dog!" but he's not. He's been my friend and my listening ear. He's sat by me while my heart has been breaking and he's helped me to heal. I know he's only a dog to some people, but he's the one who came and licked my tears away when he could see I was so desperately sad. He's the one who sat close to me, giving me comfort when I needed it most. What do I do, Madison? What do I do?

'And I wanted to ask you whether you might help me to do this if, and it's a big if, I did decide to do it. There are things that need doing in the house. It'll need clearing and boxing up. And I wondered whether this is something that you could help me with at all. That way, I wouldn't have to come back at all. I think it would be worse if I saw Baxter. It would make me feel so guilty and sad. One minute I've made up my mind, and the next I'm all of a dither again.'

'Of course I'll help if you need me to. It would be my pleasure.'

The pitter-patter of paws could be heard crossing the office floor and two feet followed by another two and a fluffy backside plonked itself onto my lap. As if he had heard his name, Baxter moved towards the screen and sniffed it. I tickled him behind his ears and he gave a little contented doggy groan.

'Oh my Baxter, my darling beautiful boy. How could I consider doing this?' Alice was now openly sobbing. Baxter turned round and licked my face and snuggled into my shoulder. God I'd miss this little dude if I had to rehome him. I really would. We'd formed a lovely bond since he'd been staying with me.

An idea was beginning to form in my mind.

'Alice, you could take this one step at a time, you know.'

She looked at me, puzzled.

'You could commit to a short period of time, maybe three months or so, and then if it was something you felt you'd made the wrong call on, you could still hop on a plane and come back. You could even rent your house out, instead of selling up; that way you'd always have somewhere to come home to, and it might feel less dramatic than committing to it for ever.'

'That seems like a good option, I hadn't even thought of that. In my emotional state all I could really think about was either doing it or not.'

'Alice, what sort of home do you want for Baxter?' I asked her as I stroked his head.

'I just want him to be with someone who has time for him and loves him and will look after him. If I took your suggestion and only went for three months at first, perhaps I could get someone to foster him for me, so I would still have options in the future.'

'And what if I knew someone who I think would be perfect to foster him? Would you trust my judgement?'

'I would, Madison. I know we've not known each other long, but you know that I believe that people come into your life for a reason. I was there for you when you had your bad redundancy news and needed a friend, and you were able to help me to find a kennel for my boy and now I think you might be the person to help me again. I'll repay you, my love, I'm so grateful for anything you can do to help. Having no kids means I have no one really to ask. It's one of the main considerations for coming to live here. I have my sister here. At home, I don't really have anyone. So do you think you might have someone in mind that might be good for Baxter?'

'I do! You're looking at her.'

'No! You are kidding me. Really? Do you really mean that? You'd have Baxter for me?'

'I do mean it. If I was to tell you that I have fallen head over heels in love with this furry little fella, would you believe me? He's my little shadow. I turn around and he's there all the time. I absolute adore him, Alice. I was getting worried at the thought of you coming back and taking him home, to be honest. I knew how upset I'd be not having him around.'

'Oh, Maddy, you are my guardian angel! You really are. It breaks my heart to leave him behind, but it wouldn't be fair to ship him out here on his own. He would hate that, yet this is an offer too good to be true. The weather is fabulous and my gnarly old hands and my achy old joints feel better just for being in the warmth. And I've so enjoyed spending time with my sister – it's made us realise that we don't want to be apart any longer. She's got a job here and a life, and I have Baxter and my memories. And I can bring my memories with me. And if you were to have Baxter, it would be absolutely wonderful.'

'Honestly, Alice, it would be my absolute pleasure. He's no trouble at all. He's been such great company for me. Saves me talking to myself. He's adorable. I've always wanted a dog, but it's never been the right time for me to have one, and I'd always been worried about what would be the right dog for me. I've never wanted a puppy, I don't think I could cope with that, but the time is right now. And I couldn't be better placed. I'm working at a kennels and I live on a farm. It's perfect.'

'Oh, Madison, you've taken such a weight off my shoulders, you really have. I was dreading the thought of him going to a family that I didn't know and never knowing if he was happy, but this way I could still find out how he is.'

'Of course you can. You can Skype him any time you like. And I promise you that I already do and will continue to love him and will take good care of him. The situation is perfect for us both. And we can talk more in time about the house and the best way to progress that, too. I can keep an eye on things for you from here. Take the pressure off you.'

'Oh, I'm so happy, Madison. You are amazing. Thank you so very much. I must go and tell Emily this amazing news. Would it be OK if I slept on it for a day or two and let you know for definite? It's such a huge decision to make and I need to make sure it's the right one... but you have made all the difference. It seems to me to be the perfect solution. The thought that Baxter could be living with you makes me feel very different about things. Not quite so sad. I know you think the world of him and I know that he loves you too! Thank you, thank you, my sweet girl. Speak very soon.' The screen went blank and as I closed my laptop, I turned to my little furry friend and stroked his head. His big brown soulful eyes looked deeply into mine and my heart filled with love and excitement at the possibility of having him around permanently.

* * *

Much as I wanted to play it cool and make him suffer a little longer, when Jamie texted me and asked if he could take me out for a meal on Thursday evening, I agreed. However, when Thursday came around, I was in a right old tizzy about what to wear. Did I dress up for him, did I dress up to make myself feel better, or should I just go in my new casual wardrobe? I hadn't dressed up for a while.

There were two reasons why I'd agreed to meet him at the restaurant that he'd suggested rather than let him pick me up. The first was so that he didn't come to my home – I was still surprised at how much the barn already felt like home; far more than my flat ever had, and I wasn't ready to have him in my personal space. The second was so that if I realised that I'd made a bad decision, I could make my excuses and leave. All I had to remember was not to get drunk! I really needed to keep my wits about me and not do anything stupid, so it just seemed like a good idea all round to make my own way there.

Part of me was kicking myself for getting butterflies just knowing that I was going to meet him, and the other half was trying to tell myself to pipe down and stop being ridiculous. It was Jamie and he was the man who had let me down so badly and broke my heart into smithereens. And I'd never forgive him. The only reason I was going was to find out what else he had to say for himself.

So, my decision had been to dress up, but to do it not for him, but for me, to give me the confidence I needed. The dogs didn't appreciate me making an effort so I didn't bother much these days and lived in jeans and hoodies, with my hair up in a clip and rarely any make-up, but to my surprise, I was feeling more comfortable in my own skin than ever before without all the decoration that I used to need.

I chose my favourite navy-blue wrap dress that pulled me in and pushed me out in all the right places, along with a pair of red high heels which hurt like hell but looked good, and a linen short jacket. I'd spent hours with my hair in curlers, and I carefully applied my make-up, and my bright crimson lipstick gave the perfect finishing touch and that extra boost of va va voom! It felt good to get dressed up, yet a little fake, considering how I normally spent my days right now. To be totally honest, I felt more comfy in my scruffy clothes and flat shoes, and I never thought for one minute that I'd admit to that. But right now, I needed to feel confident, to make sure I had the upper hand and wasn't a pushover. As the taxi driver beeped his arrival, I practically fell over in my high heels. It had been weeks since I'd worn this type of shoe, and I felt like I'd already forgotten how to wear them despite, not very long ago, wearing them every single day.

Walking into the restaurant, early of course, I noticed heads turn in my direction, and I smiled coyly at a group of businessmen that I had to walk past to get to the table. When I sat down and flicked my hair seductively, smiling at the men, I felt something that didn't feel quite right hit me in the side of my face and was completely horrified to discover three fluorescent self-gripping rollers still in my hair and one stuck on the back of my coat. Oh fuck! I was such an idiot.

The waitress came over, noticing my distress, and blocked the way so that I could adjust myself and pull the rollers out. She was so kind and helpful. It brought to mind that saying: 'Be the woman who fixes another woman's crown without telling the world that it was crooked', and I vowed there and then that I wanted to be that woman too and that the next time I saw someone in a position like this, I would do everything I could to help them.

'Thank you so much...' I looked at her name badge. 'Lou. I cannot tell you how much I appreciate this.'

'You're grand, hun. You were looking a little flustered there.' Her gentle, quiet Irish lilt was so calming and I found myself blurting out that I was meeting an ex and was incredibly nervous. I'd been holding it in for so long. I couldn't tell Beth; she'd kill me. And so would Mum. And to be honest, who knew if anything was going to come of it anyway, so I just felt it was better not to say anything to anyone. Thank goodness Lou let me pour my heart out. 'Oh god, he's here!'

'Hey, I'm just a yell away if you need to escape and I'm very good at accidental-on-purpose spillages, you know!' She winked as she walked away and Jamie approached the table. I stood to greet him and once more he went for the continental kiss on both cheeks, but I was ready for him this time.

His eyes looked me up and down to make sure I met with his approval and it was as if the years in between had never passed as I remembered that he used to do this all the time.

'Looking good, babe. Are you having your usual? Glass of bubbly for the lady, please?' He clicked his fingers at Lou and she raised her eyebrows and looked at me as if to say, *Really?*

I was also actually a bit annoyed with him for getting straight back into this familiarity, but I breathed deeply and replied, 'Oh no! That's not been my usual for a long time. I'll have a gin and tonic please. Double!'

His eyebrows were the ones that raised this time as Lou came over to take our order. He looked her up and down, appraising her body. I'd forgotten that he did that too. It made me feel really belittled that he didn't respect me enough to even pretend he wasn't looking at other women. Perhaps he'd been up to no good behind my back all along and I just hadn't seen it.

For the first fifteen minutes, he talked about his day, his week, his job, his home and generally his life. Then he mentioned a client that I used to work with who had apparently been asking about me and saying how much they had loved working with me.

The evening went well in the end; the setting was sophisticated and the meal was divine, although a little rich compared to what I was eating these days. I'd have preferred Uncle Tom's good old pie, homemade chips and gravy to be truthful, and even though the conversation was a bit stilted at first, eventually it became really natural and it felt right to be back in his company once more. He'd been telling me how he'd set up a rival company to Celine's and that they had a healthy competition going on.

He must have realised that I was quiet while he dominated the conversation, so he asked me what I'd been up to since I'd been made redundant. He'd heard the news from Celine. We caught up on family news and it all started to feel very natural and comfortable, although that could have been the two double gins I'd had working their magic. I made a mental note to make sure I didn't drink any more! I did notice that Jamie turned his nose up when I told him that I was working at Growlers, helping on the farm and with some of the community.

'I think if I was you, Maddy, I'd be getting straight back into the PR scene before people turn you away because you've been out of it too long. It's all very well and good wanting to help the "locals" but is that going to keep you in the manner you've been living?' I wondered whether he had a point, even though I was living a much more minimalist life these days and enjoying it.

Looking at my watch, I realised that it was now nearly eleven o'clock and I had to be up and at work at seven thirty the next morning, so I excused myself, thanked him for a lovely evening, kissed him on the cheek and left. As I walked away, I could still smell the same aftershave that he always wore. Whenever I'd smelled that aftershave over the years, it had always made me think of Jamie. The taxi ride home only took fifteen minutes and I think I must have been in a bit of a daydream because I don't remember an awful lot of the journey. As the taxi pulled up in the farmyard, I looked up at the Grange and noticed a shadow in one of the upstairs spare bedrooms just before the curtains closed. Alex.

I wondered whether he was purposely looking out for me or whether he just happened to be looking out and closing the curtains at that time. Maybe it was wishful thinking on my part, thinking how nice it would have been to have someone looking out for me after being on my own for such a long time. It wouldn't be long now before he went back to his beautiful girlfriend and his wonderful life in the US, and that thought made me sad.

* * *

The following morning, I couldn't concentrate on a thing at work. At one point, Uncle Tom really shouted at me to get my attention as I'd been in a deep daydream imagining being back together with Jamie, lying on a beach in the Caribbean, holding hands.

Uncle Tom and I were trying to move all the kennel space around because we'd had another enquiry from someone who had to go into hospital as an emergency, but much as we tried to accommodate everyone, when we worked out all the comings and goings, it couldn't be done. We already had ten dogs and we only had ten kennels. We couldn't double up; it wouldn't be fair on anyone. Then an idea came to me.

'Uncle Tom, how about if Baxter came to stay with me now in the barn while we're waiting for Alice to make her decision? He could come over here with me in the daytime and I could take him home in the evenings. He's hardly in his kennel in the daytime anyway when I'm in the office as he just comes to sit under my feet, and he always wants to come out to the field when I take the dogs out too. And that way, it would cut down on costs for Alice but you wouldn't be losing out because you have the new dog.'

'What a brilliant idea, Maddy. Why didn't I think of that? It's perfect and he'd be lovely company for you over there. I know you're OK but I'd love you to have someone to chat to, even if he is a big furry daftie. And it'll give you a proper test run as a dog owner too. It's a huge commitment and I know that you're keen, but in reality it might not be all it's cracked up to be for you.'

But it felt like a really good decision. I immediately messaged Alice just to double check that it was OK with her. She came straight back to say that she couldn't be happier and that although she knew Baxter was well looked after in the kennels, she also knew that he'd be much happier in a proper home with me. I was also really excited. I'd always wanted a dog but it was a huge commitment to take on and Jamie had never allowed it, in our pristine apartment with its clinical white furniture. I had thought about it after Jamie moved out, but decided against it. Not quite so daunting I suppose, if you were a family and there were more of you to take on the walking and feeding and looking after, and to juggle everything, but when there was just you, it was literally just all down to you. This way, perhaps it would give me a taste of how having a dog would fit into my life.

Baxter seemed very happy when I brought his bed over to the barn after work and had a good old sniff around before weeing up one of the kitchen cupboards. I'd half expected it as Uncle Tom said that male dogs did this sometimes, so I disinfected and hoped it would be the only time he did it.

My phone pinged and my heart did a little flip when I saw that there was a text from the man himself.

Babe, really enjoyed last night. What are you doing next Tuesday night? Remember I told you that Geoff from Faith and Co had been asking about you? Well you'll never believe it, but I bumped into him this morning in town and I said that we were back in touch and he asked whether we'd both like to go out for a meal with him. I'd love you to come, Maddy. What do you think? x

Playing it cool, I left it for over an hour and thirty minutes to respond, not wanting to play into his hands and reply straight away. A whole hour and thirty minutes.

I'll have to check my diary later, but if I'm free, that would be nice. Let me know where and when and I'll let you know as soon as I'm able to get to my diary.

Obviously, I knew I was free. I was always free these days. And if not, I was at Mum's or sat propped up in bed next to Beth watching TV or out and about being a do-gooder in the local community. How had my life changed so much in the space of just a few weeks? Life up until recently was full of trendy bar and restaurant launches, theatre performances to review, goody bags galore full of the latest anti-ageing beauty and make-up products, which promised to knock years off you but never actually worked, and fragrances to make you irresistible to the opposite sex. My bathroom cabinet was stocked to the brim with so much stuff that I'd never use.

It was hard to see at the time that these were all work events and that if it wasn't for work I wouldn't have had a social life at all, or any friends. I thought the people I worked with were friends, but when it came down to it, they were just colleagues who didn't care about me at all once I'd gone. Not like Beth; she was a true friend.

I hated to see her so down at the moment. I knew it wouldn't be forever but she was so fed up with not being able to get up and about as much as she could before without the use of crutches. Hopefully when she started her physio sessions soon, it would see her on the mend and recuperating fully. I decided that perhaps I should pop over and see her later; even if we just watched TV together, it was company for her.

Although I lived on a farm, it was still nice to get out and about, so I decided to take Baxter for a walk in the forest. The rattle of his lead alerted him to the fact that he was going out for a walk and he bounced up and down on his back legs in excitement. Dogs were simple creatures and just wanted to be fed, loved and walked. Maybe a belly rub every now and again. I didn't think I wanted much more than that these days, to tell the truth.

I chatted along to Baxter as we drove along. I was sure people might think I was loopy, however I presumed other dog parents did this too. It was a beautifully sunny day, although still a little nippy out of the sun, and I was glad that these days I always left a lightweight body warmer in the back of the car. I was constantly in jeans and hoody tops these days instead of smart suits, and I was never caught out without one pocket full of dog treats and the other full of poo bags. Oh the glamour!

The forest was quiet as we got out of the car and we walked for miles. As we headed up an incline, deep into the forest, I stopped to take photos on my phone every so often so that I could show Alice just how fine Baxter was. The light was shining through the tall trees and the photos looked gorgeous. I chatted away to him, inane rubbish, taking in the stunning countryside around me; something I'd not really noticed for a long time.

From the higher ground, you could see for miles. I supposed when you worked all the time and had a company car, there was no need to walk anywhere so you missed out on lots of beautiful things along the way. I'd not been a good sleeper for years but I already knew that the fresh air I was getting from playing with the dogs at work, and getting out into the allotment when I could, was definitely helping me sleep better at night.

There was a memorial bench at the end of a tree-lined avenue, so I decided to take a break and got a bottle of water out of my rucksack with a pop-up bowl and gave Baxter a drink. He was panting like crazy.

The bench had an inscription on it. I ran my hands over the brass plate as I read the words:

Christine Robinson 1936–2006
Beloved mother and wife.
Missed every day. Forever in our hearts.

I wondered about Christine Robinson, who she was and what sort of a person she'd been. It sounded like her family adored her and I felt quite sad thinking that I'd lost a chance at being a mum and might never get the chance again.

I closed my eyes and lifted my head to the sun while I thought about her. Footsteps brought me back to the present and Baxter started to bark lightly. A pretty thirty-something lady and her dog were walking over to the bench.

'May I join you?'

'Of course.' I shuffled across to make some room, and I stroked Baxter who went up to the lovely Labradoodle and sniffed his bum.

'Beautiful day, isn't it?' She smiled at the dogs. 'Good job people don't behave like that, isn't it?'

'It sure is. Breaks the ice though, I suppose.' We both laughed.

'I was just sitting here wondering about the lady who the bench is dedicated to.'

'Well, I might be able to clear that up for you. Christine Robinson was the loveliest lady you could ever imagine.'

'Oh wow! You knew her?' Madison asked.

'My mum.'

I really didn't know what to say, and there was a long pause before she spoke again. 'I like to walk my dog Becks and come and sit on this bench and chat away to her when I need to be close to her.'

'Oh, I'm so sorry. Let me go and leave you to it.'

'No, please don't. Do stay. We had a bench put here so that other people could enjoy it too. I'm a big believer in everything happening for a reason, and there must be a reason why you are here on the bench today, and you look a bit sad, if you don't mind me saying. Sorry, I'm very forward, aren't I? My ex-husband always used to say that I'm way too overfamiliar with people I've just met. Good job my second husband doesn't feel the same way. I'm Grace, by the way. And this is Becks.'

'Maddy, and my buddy Baxter. It's nice to meet you, Grace.'

'You too, Maddy, and I do hope I haven't offended you by saying that you looked sad.'

'No, not at all. I just have a lot on my mind, to be honest.'

'Want to talk about it? Or would you rather not?'

'I've met up with my ex recently, and he wants us to get back together, both at work and at home.'

'And what is your heart telling you to do?'

Breathing deeply, I sighed. 'I really don't know.'

'Well, my lovely mum always used to say that if you weren't sure of what to do, then you should do nothing and eventually the answer would come to you. When it feels right. If it doesn't feel right, don't do it. She always said that anything you have to wait for is worth waiting for, if it's meant to be.'

'My mum said exactly the same thing. Sounds like your mum was a very wise lady, Grace. I'm sorry she's not around any more.'

'Oh, she's always around me, Maddy. In the whispering trees, in the fragrance that comes from nowhere, in the smile of my boy Archie, the twinkle of my daughter Meredith's eyes. I know she's always around me and that's such a comfort.'

'Well, I think that's just beautiful, Grace. What a lovely way to remember her. And what you said before about doing nothing until you have the answer that feels right is exactly what I needed to hear right now. You sound like you have experience in making decisions like this.'

'Oh, I do, indeed. I had to choose between going back to my cheating ex-husband, which would have rebuilt our family and made my son happy, or making a new life with someone I didn't know very well. As I mentioned earlier, I'm married to my second husband now, and we have a daughter, so you know how that worked out – although it was a really hard decision. I am of the opinion, though, that leopards don't change their spots. But that's just me. Who knows what your future holds? All I know is that everyone deserves to be happy in what they do and who they are with. I'm not sure if that's helped or not.' She laughed.

'It's certainly given me more to think about. Thank you, Grace. I'm going to leave you in peace now to chat to your mum. Thank you for your help.'

'See, I told you; there's always a reason that people meet. I wish you well in making your decision, Maddy. If you are ever over in Little Ollington, perhaps we'll bump into each other.'

'Little Ollington! That's the second time recently I've heard someone mention that village. A friend of mine who is helping me with my allotment mentioned a friend of his who lives there who studied horticulture and said he might be able to help too.'

'Little Ollington is only small. And I just happen to be married to a landscape gardener who studied horticulture.'

'He wouldn't be called Vinnie by any chance, would he?'

She laughed. 'He would, indeed!'

'Wow, isn't it a small world? What a coincidence.'

'You could say that. To be honest, I'm a big believer that there's no such thing as a coincidence in life. I told you, everything happens for a reason.' She reached in her back pocket and pulled out a business card with her husband's business details on it and handed it to me. 'Give him a call. If you tell him that you met me here, I'm sure he'll come over and do a free consultation for you. If he does, perhaps I can pop over with him too and you can update me on your situation.'

'That would be so fab, Grace. I have a feeling you and I would never stop talking! I'll give him a call and sort something out. Thank you so much. Now I really am going. Enjoy your chat with your mum.'

Grace smiled at me kindly, and Baxter and I made our way back into the forest.

As I walked back along the forest path, I realised that since I'd left work, I'd made more new friends than I had for years. I used to call the people I worked with my friends, but were they really? Drinks in the pub after work, and me being the one who was always relied on to do a birthday whip round, but where were they when I was desperately low after I'd been made redundant? I didn't even get a measly card, and not one of them had picked up the phone to see how I was. The people I'd met since I'd left had been way more genuine; Rebecca and now Grace. Caring people that I could see myself being friends with, in time. How lovely.

Baxter was properly frolicking in the long grass, alternating between jumping over the heather, which was starting to flower, and stooping low to stalk a bird. I stopped to take lots more photos. I had decided that I was going to put a book together to send over to Alice in Australia as a surprise, and to keep Baxter in her thoughts so that she could rest assured, knowing that he was having such fun.

Suddenly I realised something really important. I could feel myself grinning and my heart felt full. Which meant that I was happy. What I was doing now was so simple but it was absolutely filling my heart with joy. I'd put thoughts of Jamie to one side for now. Like Grace's mum said, I now felt sure that it would sort itself and worrying about it constantly wasn't helping my state of mind at all.

When Beth was in hospital and she had asked me what made me happy, at that time, I'd had no idea. But now I felt like I was really coming into my own.

Once more, it made me realise that it was the simple things in life that made me happy, like being surrounded by stunning countryside views, enjoying the warm sun on my face and watching squirrels chasing each other, scampering up and down the tree trunks, Baxter barking his head off at them in the hope that he might catch one, not realising that they were way too fast for him. It was watching him having fun, and seeing the other people in my life enjoying themselves that brought me joy. Working at doggy daycare was wonderful. And I was loving spending small pockets of time here and there on the allotment too. I was enjoying my life.

Chatting with Grace today had really helped me to find some clarity in my life. It was time to stop stressing and let life take its course. There was no need to rush, to find another job in the corporate world for a while until I was really sure that was what I wanted to do. My redundancy money would see me through for a bit and the doggy daycare wages helped too.

For the first time in a very long time, I felt at peace.

* * *

After tramping around the countryside for a good hour and a half, we headed home to the barn. The fresh air must have worn us out as Baxter curled up beside me on the sofa and we both had a little snooze.

When I woke, I decided that I couldn't sit lazing around for the rest of the day, so I grabbed my shopping list from the noticeboard on the side of the fridge and decided to take off to the retail park. There were some bits and pieces I needed to get and I wanted some new pictures to go on the walls. The wall art I had brought from the flat wasn't right for here and I was looking forward to making it even more homely. I left some treats for Baxter and patted him on the head, telling him I wouldn't be too long. He curled up in his basket and looked sad, which made me feel really guilty. He had a real gift for making me feel bad when I went out without him. Those big brown eyes were so sad at times.

Wandering around the aisles of the big hardware store, looking for something to hang pictures with, I banged into a shopping trolley. A smile greeted me and I grinned back as I realised my trolley sparring partner was my mother's new acquaintance.

'Hi, Edward, nice to see you. How are you?'

'Hello, my dear. I'm great thanks, how about you? How's your day been?'

'Well, it's been OK, so far. I was at work this morning, then we went for a big walk in the forest, then had a little snooze and I thought I'd better make an effort to get some stuff for my new home.'

'Ah, that's good to hear. Have you managed to get what you wanted?'

'I've bought some lovely pictures and need some things to hang them with now, but I'm at a bit of a loss, to be honest. I've always been the type to just bang a nail in a wall and hang a picture precariously, and move it around until it looks straight enough, but I'm told that they need to be done properly because the walls are so old. All suggestions most welcome.' I laughed.

'Now this is an area I do know about. I'm a little bit obsessive about things like this, so I can definitely point you in the right direction. I'm presuming you have a small hammer in your toolbox? And a spirit level, obviously?'

I looked at him blankly and then laughed. 'Erm... toolbox? What's one of those?'

'Oh, goodness me, Madison.' He shook his head, grinning at me, dumped his trolley and linked his arm in mine. 'Come on. We need to start right at the beginning, don't we?'

Edward and I wandered around the store, chattering away comfortably to each other. He was so easy to pass the time of day with and he advised me on the best things to get to start myself off with a small toolbox and with hanging hooks and wire, and he told me exactly what to do to put my pictures up.

'You know, if you're struggling, I could always pop over with your mum one day and help you.'

'Oh, that's so kind of you, Edward. I'll see how I get on, and if I'm struggling, I'll put an emergency call out to you. I'll bake you a cake to say thank you.'

'Ooh, I'll do anything for a Victoria sponge these days.' He patted his belly gently. 'Although I probably shouldn't.'

I grinned at him. A month ago, I hadn't baked a cake for years, and now apparently I felt confident offering my culinary efforts as a thank you. How times had changed.

We walked out to the car park together and he helped me to load my shopping into the car.

'How lovely to bump into you, my dear. I do hope to see you

soon, and remember that offer. I'll do anything for cake!' He winked and kissed my cheek as he walked back towards his car.

As I drove back to the barn, I thought about how well matched he and my mum were, and I hoped so much that this was going to work out for them and be something really special. She certainly deserved some love in her life and he was perfect for her. I really liked him and hoped that after everything that had happened with my father – and with Mum choosing to wait until someone really exceptional came into her life – Edward was everything that he appeared to be.

17

After playing it cool for a few days, I now found myself on a Tuesday evening, after a busy day at Growlers, sitting across a table from Geoff from Faith and Co, and his wife Libby, next to Jamie, who was looking deliciously dapper this evening in a dark suit and a black open-necked shirt, and who smelled divine. He had booked a table in the same restaurant we went to last week on the outskirts of Birmingham, and I saw Lou, the waitress from the other evening, behind the bar. Jamie had arranged for a car to pick me up from home; I'd given in and told him where I was living but as he was sending a car rather than coming to pick me up himself, I didn't see it as a problem.

It was actually really nice to see Geoff; he and I had always got on like a house on fire, and after lots of general chit chat he asked me my opinion about how working with a PR agency could help him to get more exposure. I'd had a couple of huge glasses of Pinot Grigio by this stage and the drink must have loosened my tongue and my brain, and I came out with a ton of PR and marketing ideas. Once I started, the ideas wouldn't stop coming, and Jamie seemed delighted and had even been making notes on a napkin.

'I bet you've missed all this brainstorming, haven't you, Madison? You're so good at it! Do you know, Jamie, you should be offering her a job with your company. Celine was a fool to let her go.'

'I'd take her on tomorrow if she'd consider it, but I don't think she's in the right place at the moment. I'd love to be working alongside her. We'd make an awesome team both at work and at home. Maybe one day soon she'll consider that.' He took my hand and intertwined his fingers with mine. It was a little embarrassing to be honest, so I pulled my hand away and lifted my wine glass.

My mind started working overtime and I wondered whether this was the real reason that he'd got back in touch with me. If he offered me a job, then I'd be able to stop thinking twice every time I spent any money. I had what was left of my redundancy money after I'd bought the necessities I needed, but I'd put that in a savings account, not knowing how long I was going to be out of work for, and was being particularly frugal at every opportunity. But was he doing it because he loved me, like he said, or because he needed me in his business and was trying to butter me up?

I suddenly sobered up and became a little guarded with what I was saying. My intuition was telling me something here; I just needed to work out what.

I excused myself to go to the ladies', and to have a moment to myself to think. I was trying to work out whether he would stoop this low. When I came out, Lou was standing waiting for me.

'I hate to tell you this, and I'm only telling you because my ex-husband was a serial cheater, but your ex has just slipped me his card and told me to give him a call if I'm ever at a loose end. You seem like a really nice lady and I hate to see people being taken advantage of. I really hope you don't mind that I've told you.'

'Bloody bastard! I should have known. What do I do now?'

'Why don't you wait here a little bit, then go back and tell him you've been sick and have to go? You could say you've eaten something dodgy. Come back in here tomorrow and have a coffee with me if you like and we can have a chat and see how we can pay him back. I could be a honey trap for you.' She laughed but I thought that it might not be such a crazy idea after all.

When I got back to the table, Jamie couldn't have been more attentive and I found it hard to believe what Lou had told me. Perhaps she wasn't the lovely lady that I thought she was and was just one of those people who caused trouble, and just wanted him for herself, so I stayed until the end of the meal and avoided making eye contact with Lou for the rest of the evening. She must have been completely wrong about him.

Geoff was quizzing me towards the end of the evening, asking how much I missed my old job, and how much it would take for someone to poach me back into that old world. Whilst I was loving working at Growlers, I knew I couldn't stay forever, as Beth would soon be on the mend.

'Yes, it's about time you stopped fannying around at that daft doggy daycare and with your little community projects and started doing something worthwhile, darling. We need to get you a proper job again, back in the real world. We could get you booked back into that hairdressers and beauty parlour and get you looking like yourself again, get some of that glamour back.' Jamie laughed and Geoff joined in.

'How does £50k a year and a company Jag sound to you, Madison? Something to get you thinking, maybe?' Geoff passed me his card and it certainly did sound appealing. 'Make sure you call me if you like the sound of that deal. OK, that's enough work talk for tonight, folks, let me tell you about the fabulous holiday to Bali that we're going on next week.'

The rest of the evening was lovely and the meal and wine had made me feel mellow, so when Jamie called up his driver and asked him to drop me off first, I didn't even think about the fact that he'd be coming in the car to the farm. I didn't make eye contact with Lou as we left. Jamie put his arm around me in the back of the car and I snuggled into him. We had always been a perfect fit and it felt so right to be back in his arms. I must have dozed off, because the driver coughed and brought me back to the present as we pulled up outside the Grange.

Jamie walked me to the front door. 'Shall I tell the driver to come back later, or maybe even tomorrow?'

Above his head, the stars looked like a net of fairy lights, and above the farmhouse shone the brightest star in the sky. We always said that the brightest star was Aunty Jen keeping watch over her family, and I still believed it now. At the front of the farm-house was a duck pond, and not long after Aunty Jen had passed away, Uncle Tom had bought a bench and placed it next to the pond. It was where he said he could go and chat to Aunty Jen when he needed to feel close to her and when he missed her most. It made me think of that lovely lady Grace who I'd met on my walk in the forest and her mum.

I shivered as I had the feeling that I was being watched. My eye was drawn to that upstairs window where, once again, I saw a shadow step back from the curtains, but it was definitely there. Was it Alex again?

'I'm tired, Jamie, so I'm going to say goodnight.'

'Oh, babe. My poor wounded heart.'

I swallowed down the words that I wanted to say. It was *my* heart that had been wounded by *him*, and it was still very delicate and I was treating it with kid gloves.

'Goodnight, Jamie, thank you for a lovely evening. See you soon.' I leaned forward to kiss his cheek, but he moved his head and before I knew it, his soft lips touched mine. I melted into his arms, and as he kissed me, his tongue flicked across my lips, which I kept tightly closed. I wasn't quite ready for that.

'I can't tell you how much I've missed you, Maddy; it feels so right to be with you again. Please tell me that you'll consider us getting back together. I want us to be a couple again. I want that more than anything and I hope you do too.' His hands wound their way into my hair and began to stroke my neck. I leaned into his hand, that familiar touch that he knew I loved. 'I could stay with you tonight. We don't have to do anything. I could just hold you.' That old chestnut; I'd definitely heard that before.

My eyes were drawn to the curtains in that upstairs window which swiftly shut and brought me back to my senses.

'Goodnight, Jamie.' It took all the willpower in the world to walk through my front door that night and not look back.

* * *

Being greeted at the door by Baxter that night I think was one of the best things in the world. He was so uncomplicated, adorable and fussy. He loved me for who I was. He didn't care about anything apart from me. When I headed up to bed, he was right by my side, even sitting at the bathroom door while I went to the loo and brushed my teeth. He seemed to sense that I needed some calm in my life right now and when I got under the duvet, he snuggled right into me and I was soon hearing sweet little doggy snores.

* * *

It seemed like there was only Russell and me at work the following morning. Uncle Tom and Alex were nowhere to be seen and we were rushed off our feet with viewings as it was getting to the end of the summer and people were booking last-minute holidays and wanted to check out where they were leaving their precious furry friends. Just before midday, Uncle Tom came over with two steaming mugs of coffee for us and told us to take a breather.

'So sorry to leave you in the lurch this morning, guys. Had to drop Alex off at the airport. Not sure why, but he decided to book a flight back to America late last night and he left this morning. Something must have rattled his cage but he wouldn't say what. He must have had a call from Sophie or something last night.'

Alex leaving made me feel incredibly sad. I loved being around him. Even now I'd got my head round the fact that he'd never be mine, I still loved being in his company. Bloody Sophie didn't realise how lucky she was.

* * *

My phone pinged two days later with a text from Jamie asking if I'd like to go out for dinner again soon. I knew that I needed cheering up, and he may as well be the one to do it. Alex and I would never be together, but it didn't stop me missing him being around.

I was in two minds about another night out with Jamie. Up until recently, it had been a while since I'd been wined and dined at posh restaurants like we used to visit all the time, and even though I didn't think I was missing that old life, it was nice to be spoiled when we went out recently. Yet there was also a little niggle in the back of my mind about what Lou said to me at the restaurant. Would I ever be able to trust Jamie again? I suppose there was really only one way to find out.

* * *

I was flicking through the channels on the TV and there wasn't a fat lot that I fancied watching, so I snuggled up on the sofa with a book. I really had become a big bookworm since my visit to the library and Amazon's biggest customer of late. Even the local delivery guy knew me by my first name now and found it highly amusing when he delivered yet another book-shaped parcel. Two seconds later, I felt a warm, furry body press itself into mine and Baxter had climbed onto the settee commando-style without me even noticing and had snuggled up against me. He couldn't have got closer if he'd tried. I stroked his head and we settled down, and within seconds he was snoring gently. He seemed quite content. The next time I looked round at him, he was lying upside down with his tongue hanging out and his dangly bits on display for all the world to see. I rubbed his tummy and I'm sure he smiled at me. He really was a delight and I could see that we were going to be the best of friends. When it came to bedtime, he looked at me sadly as I left him in the kitchen, telling him to be a good boy and go to sleep. I woke in the middle of the night to whining and padded downstairs in my slippers and dressing gown to see if he was OK. Letting him out for a wee seemed to do the trick but before I could turn the key in the lock afterwards, he'd shot up the stairs and had plonked himself on the corner of the bed by the time I got up there. 'You are a funny little thing, aren't you?' I said to him as I stroked his head, and I'm sure he winked at me. We both settled down to sleep and the next thing I knew it was eight o'clock the following morning and I'd slept longer than I'd slept for weeks. Good job it was Saturday.

A text came in from Jamie asking if he could come over as he had a proposition for me and it couldn't wait until we met for dinner. Mmmm! This really got me wondering what on earth he wanted to talk to me about that he couldn't have brought up at dinner. I was still mulling over Geoff's job offer too. Although I realised Jamie was being deliberately vague so I would agree to see him to find out what he meant, I was intrigued, despite myself. I told him that I could be free at twelve thirty, once the dogs were all settled for a lunchtime nap.

Jamie pulled up into the yard in his perfectly polished dark green Aston Martin DB9, and I stood at the door and waited for him. As he walked towards me, he was looking suave, in smart jeans and a blazer, clean-shaven and as handsome as ever. Baxter tried to jump up at him as he came in and he turned his nose up and shoved him away. I understood that he probably didn't want dog hairs all over his nice clothes and explained that I was just looking after him for a friend when Jamie questioned why I'd been stupid enough to get a dog. I'm not sure why I'd slipped back into my old ways of making him hear what he wanted to hear, instead of just admitting the truth.

Baxter barked as if to get our attention, and as we turned to look at him, the little monkey ran over to Jamie's car and seemed to grin at us as he cocked his leg up the passenger side front wheel. I couldn't help but smirk when Jamie tried unsuccessfully to shoo him away – nothing was putting Baxter off the longest wee I think he'd ever had.

After much cajoling to get Baxter back to me, we retreated to the barn. It felt a bit weird having Jamie in my personal space, which was strange, as I hadn't felt that at all when Baxter moved in.

I invited him to take a seat at the dining room table, not wanting to be too informal and certainly not wanting to end up sitting on a settee next to him. Curious as to what he was going to say, I purposely asked him if he preferred tea or coffee and how he took it when he chose tea. I didn't want him to think that I still remembered every little thing about him. I cupped my hands around my steaming mug of coffee as they were shaking.

'Madison. I'm just going to say what's on my mind, if that's OK.' He started before I'd even acknowledged with a yes or a no, as usual so confident that I wouldn't question a word that he said. 'When Geoff offered you a job the other night, it was like a light bulb went off in my brain. I know I'd joked about it earlier in the evening, but it made me realise that you and I *should* be working together. We are awesome together, we always have been, and just the ideas that you were coming up with when we were chatting were amazing and I've not been able to stop thinking about it since. I'll match what Geoff offered you financially, and you can come back when you're ready and even do some work here part-time in the meantime if you want to until Beth is ready to come back full time.

'We can get you booked into the hairdressers and get that dreadful hair sorted out.'

I put my hand up to my hair. These days, I let it dry naturally and it went quite wavy, but I actually liked it. It probably did look a mess compared with how it used to be. When I was with Jamie, it was permanently pulled back into a tidy but severe bun, which actually used to give me a headache and I couldn't wait to shake it loose at the end of the day.

'Then we'll book you into a beautician and get your hands and feet sorted out. I've never seen you before without polish on your nails. I can't see your feet when you are in those clodhoppy boots, but the Maddy standing before me today is just not the Maddy I know and love. We definitely need to get that sorted out before we put you in front of customers. And the clothes. Er... wow! Where to start? Obviously, we need to get you back into wearing those smart suits that you used to wear. I presume you still have them. You might think you are rocking the wax dungarees babe' – he looked me up and down and shook his head – 'but I have to honest with you – they really need to go.'

For once, I was speechless. He was on a roll and he wasn't stopping now.

'You don't have to give me an answer straight away, but all I will ask is that you promise me you'll seriously think about it. Imagine, darling, we could work hard and play hard but we'd be doing it together. You could even work on Geoff's account, that would soften the blow for him and I'm sure he'd be fine with that. And we could have all our wonderful things again.'

He waved his arms around at my surroundings and smirked. 'You wouldn't have to live in this dingy place on a smelly farm. We could get another swanky apartment in town together and we could have all of those amazing holidays that we used to have too. Please, Maddy, just think about it. Promise me that much.'

Totally stunned by his offer in many ways, I really didn't know what to say. He was criticising me, yet giving me a backhanded compliment at the same time. He'd also still not mentioned the miscarriage. It was almost like he'd completely forgotten it had ever happened, but it was something that would stay with me forever. I really wasn't sure what to think, and more than that, what to do. Jamie stood and walked around the table. Standing over me, he reached out to put his finger on my lips.

'I know! Exciting, isn't it!' He obviously took my silence for excitement. 'Don't say a word, just think about it. You know I'm right and all you have to do is say the word and we can get you out of this dreadful place and this dead-end job and back where you belong, in a life of luxury.' He kissed the top of my head and left as quickly as he had arrived, not even touching the drink I'd made him. He sneered at Baxter, who uncharacteristically growled at him, and then snapped at his ankles as he walked past him. Jamie kicked out at him, missing him by mere inches, and Baxter whimpered and ran off to his basket. 'That's how you teach dogs who the boss is.' He grinned as he walked towards his car, got in and then drove off without a backward glance. I couldn't believe that hour had just happened.

I was stunned by his offer. I hadn't seen it coming and my thoughts were all over the place. I didn't know what would happen between Jamie and me on a personal basis yet, let alone if we worked together. It could be inviting trouble. I supposed there was no harm in thinking about it, like he said. And we did have a lovely life together... and lovely holidays. Seeing him after all this time had confused me even more. I didn't know how I felt about him; did I really want to go back to that life?

Could I ever forgive him? Could I ever forget what he'd done and how he had just seemed to cast aside one of the most important things in my life? And it wasn't until now that I realised that he was really rather critical of me and seemed to want to turn me into someone that I'm not.

There was also the fact that I was really loving my life these days, even though I was on my own. I adored working at Growlers, so much more than I had ever thought I would. I was really enjoying looking after Baxter and having a dog in my home, and Rebecca and I had made arrangements to cover Beth's shifts for the next few weeks and then to get some of my own when she was back, because she knew how much I'd enjoyed that whole sense of community spirit.

When I'd explained that I was also looking after Baxter, she said that I might be able to take him along to some of the visits I did because animals, particularly dogs, were excellent therapy for the elderly and for less able-bodied people that they had signed up to their projects. There were also families that had been rehomed and troubled children using the programmes. Rebecca said that sometimes children reacted better to animals than they did to adults and might open up more if they were comforting a dog. Apparently studies had shown that stroking a dog was good for lowering blood pressure, lowering stress levels and helping your body to release a relaxation hormone.

She thought it would be a great idea to trial doggy visits and we arranged for her to pop over and meet Baxter. I was really excited by this thought and couldn't wait to start experimenting with my little fur buddy. Even though I was really excited about all of this, I would really need to think hard about Jamie's proposition and my future.

* * *

Thinking about nothing else but Jamie's proposition, I was unable to sleep properly for the next three days and had a constant headache. Without Alex around, I was doing full time at Growlers, and with Uncle Tom so busy on the farm, we were rushed off our feet. I hadn't even seen Beth for two days. If truth be told, I was a bit scared that she'd see straight through me and know that there was something on my mind. Jamie was taking me out again tomorrow night and I knew he'd want to talk about his offer.

It was typical; just as I was starting to get my life together again after the awful redundancy shock and things had started to settle down, Jamie was back in my life, turning everything upside down again. I needed to talk things through with someone, but that person couldn't be Beth because I knew that in the past she had such fixed ideas about Jamie; I didn't feel that she was the right person to go to now. I needed to pop to the village store for a few bits and pieces so I'd do that and then pop in to surprise Mum on the way back and see whether she could offer me some good old impartial Mum advice. She didn't dislike Jamie when we were together, but she did once tell me that she thought he had taken me away from spending time with her, because he wanted me all to himself.

A silver Mercedes C-Class was parked on her drive, and as I walked through the front door and down the hallway, I could hear laughter coming from the kitchen.

'Hellooooo!' I called ahead loudly to make sure they knew I was there. If it was who I had a feeling it might be, I'd hate to walk in on anything untoward.

Poking my head gingerly round the kitchen door, I was delighted to see my mother fully clothed sitting with Edward at the kitchen table, also dressed, with his hands cradling a mug.

'Hello, dear, what a surprise to see you. Are you OK?'

Mum did actually look a little flushed, but I presumed that was down to the fact that I'd caught her with her man friend again.

'What are you doing here, darling? Anything in particular, or just a pop in?'

'Well, I had a couple of things that I wanted to chat to you about, but I can come back another time. It's not urgent. I'll head off and ring you later.'

'Oh, I'll go, shall I? Leave you ladies to talk.'

'No, Edward, you were here before me, I'm sorry to interrupt.'

'Not interrupting anything, my dear, come and sit. Your mother talks about you constantly and I'd love to get to know you a little better.' He patted the seat beside him. I looked over at Mum and she was rubbing her neck, a habit of hers that she had when she was feeling nervous. I did exactly the same too and we'd always had the nature/nurture debate about it and whether it was because I'd seen her do it so many times, so had naturally learned to do it too, or whether it was part of my genes.

'I'll put the kettle on again then, shall I?' she questioned.

'If you're sure – it's not a problem to come back.'

'No, you're here now, so you may as well stay. Is everything OK?'

A single tear rolled down my cheek.

Mum was at my side immediately, her arm around my shoulders. 'Darling, what on earth is it?'

'Jamie's back, Mum.'

'Oh dear!' She looked across at Edward and pulled a face, and he excused himself to go to the toilet. I'm sure he was just giving us a little bit of time.

'And what has he said to you to get you in this state?'

'He says he loves me and he's missed me and that he's sorry and that he wants me back. And I don't know what to do.'

She wrapped her arms around me. Whenever I was upset, she made everything feel a million times better just with one of her hugs.

She broke away as Edward came back into the room. 'Perhaps we need something a little stronger than tea!' She reached to the top shelf of the Welsh dresser by the back door and pulled down a bottle of gin and grinned at me.

'Edward, you'll join us for a little one? Madison has man problems.'

He walked past me, gently resting his hands on my shoulders for just a short moment. It was a very reassuring, kind gesture and I felt a little of the pressure leave my body through his hands. 'Just a very small one for me, as I'm driving later.' He smiled at Mum.

'Oh gosh yes, me too, I have to drive home. Perhaps I'd better not.'

'Nonsense, darling, you can get a taxi back to the farm or walk, or you can stop here. You know that we've always had the biggest discussions in our life over a gin and tonic. There's nothing that a good chat with your old mum and a gin and tonic can't sort out. Isn't that right?'

'You're right. I'm so sorry, I wasn't planning on spoiling your afternoon though, Edward.'

'Honestly, Madison, you're not spoiling anything as far as I'm concerned. We were only sitting chatting. You never know, maybe I could give you the man's perspective on the situation. And I can even be a taxi driver later and run you home if you fancy another G&T after that one.' He really was a kind man and I liked him very much. His smile reached his eyes, which were all twinkly, and he was very handsome. He really reminded me of someone but I still couldn't put my finger on who. I was sure it would come to me one day. I was so glad that this lovely man was in my mum's life.

'Oh go on then, Mum.'

She patted my hand and grabbed some tall crystal cut glasses out of the dresser.

'Crikey, Edward, you can come again. She's using the best glasses.'

Mum grinned. 'I'm getting too old to save things for best these days. And we're worth the best all the time, don't you think?'

Edward seemed really good for Mum. She was generally brighter, if possible, as if she was happier. She was also looking really lovely today and had obviously made an effort, knowing that she had a visitor. A cornflower blue cashmere jumper really brought out the colour of her eyes and I spotted that she was wearing mascara, a natural-coloured lipstick and possibly a bit of bronzer, which really complemented her beautiful face. She always said that her hair was grey, but today, it looked like shimmering silver, glossy and sleek. She looked like Helen Mirren, and I saw her for the first time as a really attractive, striking older woman. My lovely mum!

'So come on then, spit it out. What's he got to say for himself?'

Mum and Edward listened attentively while I explained that Jamie had been back in touch and about his proposition. Even though I hadn't known Edward long, it felt right to be sat here discussing these things with him. I had a whole backstory to fill him in on, and he ummed and aahed in all the right places, making me like him even more.

'So what is your heart telling you?' Mum asked as she poured us another G&T. This drinking in the day was beginning to be a bit of a habit. That afternoon in the pub with Ivan had kick-started another enjoyable pastime for me. Edward shook his head and smiled at her as she offered him another.

'My heart is telling me that I used to love him. That we were really good together, and that we had lovely things, a nice flat, a great life. I never had to worry about where the next penny was coming from and we enjoyed being together.'

'Before you caught him having it off with that floozy, you mean?' Despite the fact that this was true, hearing my mum say 'having it off' was hilarious. Edward and I sniggered at each other across the table even though we were talking about one of the worst moments of my life. Maybe the combination of gin and unburdening how I felt was making me feel lighter about the whole situation.

'And what about your head, Madison?' Edward quizzed me next.

'Well, there's a part of me that's wondering why he's getting in touch now after three years. And there's another part of me wondering whether he offered me a job because his business is struggling and whether that's the only reason he wants to get back with me. And there's yet another part of me that wonders whether because he's cheated on me once, he'll do it again one day, after I've put all my trust back in him. You know, Mum, how hard it is for me to trust a man. I've never had a father in my life, you see, Edward, and it's made me really wary of getting too close to anyone. I lowered all my barriers with Jamie and then he let me down. Do people just hurt you on your way through life? And is it a case of better the devil you know?'

'If I may comment?'

I nodded at Edward's question. 'Please do. I'm so confused, any advice is welcome.'

'People can change, Madison. Perhaps giving him a chance to prove himself is the only way you'll know if he has. Your mother has obviously told me about how much you've missed having your father in your life. I'm sure that if your father was lucky enough to meet you now, he'd see the beautiful, wonderful, kind, feisty girl that you are today, despite him not being around. I'm sure he's kicked himself every day of his life for not being part of yours. Sometimes you regret things more than you ever think could be possible. But you've damaged things so much that you don't know how to start to mend them.' He caught Mum's eye and she turned away and looked out of the window to the bottom of the garden.

'Sometimes you have to go back in life to be able to move forwards. Don't let the past hold you back and stop the future being wonderful. People don't always get the chance to be with the people that they love.' I saw him quickly glance at Mum. I don't think he knew that I'd seen it. 'Sometimes you meet people again later in life and feel like you've missed out on a whole life in between. But life is too short to regret things you did and even more the things you didn't do, and you don't want to wonder "what if" for the rest of your life. You can't change anything that's happened in the past, but you can change the future. The future is in your hands. Make sure you choose wisely.'

Blimey, that was a bit deep and meaningful. I wondered what had gone on in his past for him to make this monumental speech. I wasn't even sure whether he was talking about my father here or Jamie.

Mum was looking rather glassy-eyed; perhaps she'd been a bit heavy-handed with the Bombay Sapphire. She stared at Edward as if seeing him for the first time. She couldn't take her eyes off him. I think she liked him an awful lot and I really hoped that for the first time in many years, she'd found someone that she might make a future with, someone who would spend the rest of his life making her happy. There had obviously been something between them when they were at school and it was nice that they were rekindling an old friendship, whatever it might lead to in the future.

She deserved happiness with someone after all these years of being alone. If I ever met my dad, there would always be a little bit of me that would want to wring his neck for putting my mum through what he did. In my head, I'd definitely given him a piece of my mind many a time. Shame it was only in my head.

'What do you think, Mum?'

'To be honest, darling, I was going to say stay away from him. He hurt you so much and as your mum, the last thing you want to see is your child being distressed, but perhaps Edward is right. Perhaps if you don't try, you'll never know if someone has changed, or whether you want to be with them.'

Mum somehow, in her tiddly state, managed to put some nibbles together to soak up the gin, although Edward did make her sit down at one point and took over, as she was getting a little lairy, waving a knife around as she was talking to us. I asked Edward if his offer of a lift home still stood. Even though I hadn't made any decisions about the Jamie situation, it really had helped to talk about it.

When I got in the passenger seat of his car, Edward smiled at me and we chatted amiably for the journey. He was so easy to talk to. I could definitely see why Mum liked him.

When we arrived at Giddywell Grange, he said how lovely the barn was and as he had offered to carry my shopping in with me, I invited him in to have a quick look around. He stroked Baxter as we walked into the kitchen and he started to bark and ran off excitedly. I almost died of shame when I was giving Edward a guided tour and Baxter ran into the dining room with a pair of very small, red flimsy pants and started to fling them around up in the air and brought them over to Edward to throw for him. I didn't know where to put myself as I wrestled them off him which he thought was even more fun and started doing doggy tug of war.

'You should maybe buy him some toys, you know.' Edward laughed and it eased some of my horror. 'I'll go and leave you to it. Looks like someone wants your attention.' We both laughed.

As Edward walked out of the front door, he turned to look at me. 'Your father was a complete fool, you know, Madison. A huge fool! You look just like your mum. You're both beautiful and funny and kind.'

'Ooh, you old smoothie!' I batted his arm and leant across and kissed his cheek. He raised his hand in a wave as he drove away. He definitely reminded me of someone. It must be an actor or someone off the TV. I was sure that it would come to me eventually.

* * *

Work the next day was so busy that I didn't really have much time to think about anything in particular, which was a good thing. I'd managed to avoid calls from Jamie and dropped him a brief text, saying that I needed some time to think and that I'd get in touch with him when I was ready. I didn't hear back from him so could only assume that he had accepted my need for some time.

A night in, in my PJs, was on the cards, but before that, I needed to pop into the local supermarket. I'd bought some new fairy lights at the weekend and I'd wound them round the beams in the lounge but realised when I went to plug them in that they needed batteries and weren't the plug-in kind. I needed to stock up on a few bits and bobs but I couldn't remember what I needed because I'd left my list on the dining room table, so I ended up grabbing a packet of chocolate fingers and the batteries.

When I went to the checkout till, there was a new young lad who I'd not seen before. He looked really pleasant and was chatting nicely to those in the queue before me. When my items moved up the conveyor belt, he looked at what I'd bought, winked at me and said, 'Blimey, you look like you're in for a good night!' Totally mortified, I grabbed my stuff, handed over a tenner and told him to keep the change.

18

The following day, when I went to visit Beth, I was totally gobsmacked when she told me what she'd been up to.

She'd only gone and booked a surprise holiday for me and Mum. The last time I went away with Mum was when I was fifteen. We couldn't afford many holidays in those days but Mum had been working extra shifts and had saved up enough to go on a caravan holiday to Cornwall. It was lovely, apart from the fact that I was fifteen and hormonal and a bit bored, and to add to my dismay and disappointment that we weren't spending a week in the Med, like most of the kids at school, the car broke down on the way there and we had to wait for four hours to get the rescue services out. Not the best start.

As it was a caravan holiday and I was a lazy teenager, I suppose all it really meant for Mum was that she got to cook and clean in a different place to home. I never realised this till years later and it was probably too late to apologise then. And the rain! It never stopped all week. Mum must have felt awful. Why hadn't I seen it at the time?

Since I'd been working, I'd never again planned a UK holiday.

I made sure that even if it meant scrimping and saving, I'd go abroad. I never wanted to go back to Cornwall and have a holiday like that again.

But the tickets, which Beth now handed me, showed that we were going somewhere way further than Cornwall. The tickets were for a Mediterranean cruise.

'Bloody hell, Beth. I can't accept this. This is a crazy present.' I looked at the dates. It was in three days' time. For a split second, I thought that I'd never have time to get work sorted to be ready for then. Then reality hit again. I didn't work at Ronington's any more. I could actually go on holiday not worrying about a thing, apart from having no work, no plans and wondering what the hell was going to happen in my life once Beth was better.

'It's not as generous as it looks,' she said. 'I'd booked those dates for myself and then obviously ended up having the op, so I'm not able to go. And to be honest, it was never going to work out, me not being around for the dogs. I'd miss them too much and Dad would never cope without me.'

'But Beth, it must have cost you a small fortune.'

'Actually, I haven't told anyone this, but I won it in a competition. I've been entering lots of competitions recently and couldn't believe my luck when I won this one. So it hasn't cost me a penny. I've already checked and transferred it over into your names. You just need to ring the cruise line and confirm your passport numbers and Bob's your uncle. I'm not taking no for an answer. I do hope your mum has got a passport.'

I supposed I'd better check with Mum as soon as I could.

'But what about the kennels? And what about Baxter? I can't go swanning off on a cruise.'

'Yes, you can. Alex is going to be back here for a few days because I was going anyway, and young Russell has agreed to do extra hours too. Baxter can come and stay over here at the farm with me when he's not over at the kennels. It's only for a long weekend and it's all already organised. It's just something from us here to say thank you for all that you've done for us. We couldn't have managed these last few weeks without you, and you'll need to work your backside off when you come back too. Ring your mum now and tell her, Mads. Go on, I want to be with you when you tell her.'

'Beth, this is just amazing. Are you absolutely sure?'

'I couldn't be surer, Mads.'

Maddy leaned across and gave her a hug.

'Thank you, thank you, thank you. This is just amazing. Right, I'm going to ring Mum right now.' I couldn't stop smiling.

'Hey, Mum, how are you?'

'Oh, Madison, my darling, how lovely to hear from you. It does make my day when you call.'

I smiled then realised that she couldn't see me. 'Well, I might make your day even more now, Mum. What are you doing Friday onwards for the next few days?'

'Mmm, that sounds mysterious. Now, let me check.' I could hear Mum's heels click-clacking across the tiled kitchen floor and could just imagine her checking the calendar which was – and has always been – pinned to the fridge door. 'Well, it's knit and natter tomorrow morning at the wool shop in the village, and book club on Wednesday evening at the library. Apart from that, from Thursday onwards I have no plans apart from dull stuff like food shopping. Why do you ask?'

'Because, Mother, you and I are going on a cruise.' I laughed as I heard Mum gasp.

'Whatever do you mean, Madison? A cruise? Goodness me! I haven't been on holiday for years. Ooh, hold on, dear, I think I need to sit down. I feel all discombobulated.'

I explained Beth's plans and could hear the excitement in

Mum's voice. 'Well I never. What do I need to take? Whatever do you wear on a cruise? Do I need some new clothes? Oh Lordy, imagine me on a cruise. What will my friends say! They'll think I'm getting above my station. Oh bugger, where's my passport?'

'Ah well, that answers one of my questions. I didn't know whether you had one.'

'I do. I've never used it but I had one just in case I met a millionaire sugar daddy and he whisked me off somewhere exotic on his private jet.' She giggled. 'Can you imagine? "Oh, darling, I'd love to come to the Maldives for a passionate week away on a desert island, but I don't have a passport." Doesn't sound very spontaneous, does it, if I'd have to ask him for a lift to the passport office in Liverpool first and queue all day to get one sorted out?'

I marvelled at her optimism.

'Well, there's nothing like wishful thinking. I like your style. Shall I come over later, Mum, and we can have a cuppa and a chat about what we need to do?'

'Yes please, darling, how exciting. I can't believe it! Come for dinner, I'll cook us something nice. Goodness me, I need a lie down. I'm all of a dither. Whatever do I need to pack? Where's my suitcase? What shoes should I take? Are my clothes glamorous enough for a cruise? Goodness me, what will my book club girls say when I tell them? They'll think I've won the lottery and gone all posh on them. How funny! But what will I pack? Oh, Maddy, what will I do?'

At what stage of life, I wondered, did the tables turn? When did the parent become the child and vice versa? It seemed to happen seamlessly – no apparent signs but one day, it just flipped. Now Mum was the nervous one asking questions and I was the one who had all the answers.

I arrived just before lunch and she'd made my favourite dinner of minced beef suet crust pie and mash. A list of questions had been left on the kitchen table for me that she'd been working on since we'd spoken, and we started to work our way through them and get her the answers that she needed.

Her excitement was contagious.

In the last few years, Mum had driven me mad – always calling when I was just about to go into a meeting, or when I was with someone really important at work. I was always too busy to talk and found her calls a burden. But now it was as though she was a completely different person to me. She was still my mum, who I knew and loved, but also I was really enjoying spending time with her and discovering things about her that I either hadn't known or had forgotten. I'd spent more time with her over the last few weeks than I had for years.

And the nice thing was that I felt that she needed me in her life. However, she was now looking at me nervously and I asked her what was wrong. She said that she'd already asked her friend's daughter to go to the shops with her tomorrow.

'I could take you shopping for some new stuff, Mum, if you'd like me to.'

'Oh no, Maddy, don't worry, dear. You'll be far too busy to bother yourself with me. Julie said she's really happy to come with me; she often helps me out when I need a younger person's advice about something or a helping hand.'

'But Mum, why didn't you ask me? Am I really that awful that you couldn't ask me something like that?'

'Well… erm… I… Well, yes, actually if truth be told. I may as well say it. You always made me feel like you were too busy to even speak to me, like I was an inconvenience. So I'd never even think to ask for your time in coming shopping with me.'

Sitting down on the arm of the settee, I couldn't believe that this horrible person that she was talking about was me. 'God, Mum, I'm so sorry. I didn't realise.'

'You were just so busy all the time, darling, I didn't feel like I could bother you.'

Sometimes, we hurt others more than we realise. Sometimes we don't notice a smile that fades in front of our eyes or realise that we are the reason for the sadness in someone's heart or the tears in their eyes. I was so glad that I was getting the chance to put things right with Mum. I knew that Beth had real regrets over not telling her mum things, and when she was so quickly and cruelly snatched away, she never had the chance. I had the chance and was going to make damn sure to make the most of it.

'Ring Julie, Mum, and tell her it's OK but I'm taking you.' The smile on Mum's face said everything.

'Will you stay tonight, Maddy? You could help me get my suitcase down from the loft.' Mum's face lit up again when I said, 'I'd love to.'

* * *

Feeling totally stuffed after Mum's fabulous suet crust meat pie, mash and veg, we fired up Mum's old laptop and over a glass of wine, got on the internet and looked at dress codes for cruises and videos of what went on, on a cruise. By the end of the evening, we had two lists. One list was for things that Mum already had that she could take, and the other was for things that she needed to get. I went to bed with a smile on my face, knowing that we'd got plans to go shopping the next day to get all the stuff we needed. Maybe I might even splash some of my redundancy money and treat myself, I thought. I wasn't sure my designer power suits would see me being cruise-ready. It would do me good to get away and not have to think about the future for a few days. I had some big decisions to make. I hadn't got back to Geoff yet, and I needed to make a decision about Jamie too. Perhaps some time away from home would help me to see things a little more clearly and find some resolution.

* * *

We burst through the front door and flung our bags on the hall floor; the handles had left sore red marks on our palms. We'd got quite a stash.

'Oooh, I'm gagging for a cuppa and bursting for the loo! Not sure what to do first. Put the kettle on, Madison, and we can have a look through all those bags at what we've got then, shall we?' Mum was glowing with happiness. We'd had *such* a nice day out. Grabbing the train from the local station was the best way of heading into Birmingham and we'd been spoilt for choice with the new Grand Central shopping centre and the Bull Ring when we got there.

The last time I'd been shopping with Mum was when she'd had to get an outfit for Jen's funeral, so that hadn't been the most joyous of shopping trips. But today really had been such fun. Mum had laughed as she turned this way and that, checking herself out in the mirror while working her way through a massive pile of clothes that she'd somehow persuaded the shop assistant to take in with her even though you were only meant to have four at a time. It was more like a personal shopping event. And she'd even splashed out on new make-up when someone in a department store offered to give her a free make-over, and she'd loved her glamorous new look.

And for the first time in years, I'd bought some summery maxi dresses that I could wear with either a denim jacket if it was a bit nippy in the evenings, a little cardy or even a stole or wrap. Today had been lots of fun. It gave me immense pleasure to see Mum enjoying herself. We needed to do this more often. Perhaps this was what Beth was thinking of when she said I needed to have more fun. I was beginning to think that perhaps she knew exactly what she was talking about after all. I really did need to lighten up and get out more.

The next couple of days flew by, with endless phone calls between Mum and me, chatting about our forthcoming trip, and our day of travel soon came round. The ship was sailing from Venice, so we were booked on a plane out of Birmingham and Uncle Tom was going to take us to the airport. Thank goodness he was going to use Beth's car and not his stinky old four-wheel drive.

Mum was so very excited; she'd never been on a plane before. There was me, who flew up to Scotland for work at least once a month, taking the experience for granted, and she was like a toddler, excited about this being her first time. She held my hand as we took off, and I could see the exhilaration in her face as the plane tore up the runway and lifted off the ground. She whooped with joy and the other passengers laughed kindly at her enthusiasm as she explained she was a flight virgin.

It was a really smooth flight, for which I was most grateful. I didn't want a bit of bumpy old turbulence to put her off ever doing it again. Her smile was bigger than I'd ever seen as we landed. Her delight was contagious and I found myself being more excited about this cruise than I had felt about anything for a long time. A short coach journey brought us into Venice docks.

'Bloody hell, would you look at the size of that!' Mum yelled, much to the disgust of the lady in the seat behind who tutted loudly while the other coach passengers giggled. She winked at me, smiled at the lady behind and turned back to the ship. It was blooming massive. The sheer hugeness of it surprised even me. It had sixteen floors, and I had no idea how we were going to find our way around the ship, let alone find our cabin!

The luggage check-in line moved quickly and we got through

security smoothly and very excitedly boarded the ship. The first things we noticed were the thick, plush carpet and polished stair rails as we went to find our room. We were in Suite 1404. We loved the fact that they called our cabin a 'suite', laughing at how posh it sounded as we made our way to our floor. All we could see ahead of us was one huge, long corridor as we tried to find door 1404.

But what greeted us when we opened the door with the key card left us totally stunned. It really was a suite, with a lounge area, a bathroom with a huge walk-in shower, an enormous bedroom and a balcony with two rattan sun loungers and matching deck chairs.

'This can't be right. This is amazing. I'll ring down to reception and sort it out. There's obviously been a mix up.'

'No, Miss Young,' said the receptionist when I rang. 'Suite 1404 is definitely correct for you. The competition prize was for a luxury suite for Miss Beth Millington, all confirmed a few weeks ago and gifted to Miss Madison Young just a few days ago.'

I took a few quick snaps of our amazing suite on my phone and texted them to Beth with a huge thank you message. The text that came back was a smiley face emoticon and one word – 'Enjoy!'

There was an itinerary on the bed. The ship set sail at 4.30 p.m., a formal dinner would be served at 7 p.m. in the dining room and then by the time we woke tomorrow, we would have arrived in Bari. We were free to leave the ship to explore during the day, then we set sail for Athens the following evening at 6 p.m.

'How do you fancy going to explore before we get ready for dinner, Mum?'

'I could murder a G&T,' she replied with a huge grin. 'Do you think we might find a bar?'

'I should think there's a very good chance of that. Let's go.' We linked arms as we pottered off to explore. We were just heading for the top deck when over the tannoy came an announcement to report to the dining room for the lifeboat drill. It was all very serious but Mum kept making me laugh and one of the attendants told us off for not paying attention.

Once the drill was over, we made our way to the top deck, which was now starting to fill up, and sat on two stools at the bar and found ourselves drinking Cosmopolitans. Mum wanted a G&T but the waiter, who introduced himself as Lorenzo (bronzed and tall, with floppy black hair, twinkly almost-black eyes, and a very sexy Italian accent) persuaded her to try a cocktail instead. If I had suggested it she would never have had one, but as she took the drink from him, he brushed his hand against hers, and as she sipped at it, she smiled at him and almost purred that it was the best drink she had ever had. She was such a bloody flirt. How had I never noticed this before?

Taking a leaf out of Mum's book, I fluttered my eyelashes at him seductively but when he handed me mine, he also passed me a tissue, asking me if I had something in my eye. Mum found that so hilarious she nearly fell off her chair. Cheers for that, Mum. It made me wonder how mums have the knack of making you feel like a helpless child all over again, even though you are an adult.

Lorenzo went off to serve a couple at the other end of the bar and Mum and I chatted about what we were going to wear that night to the captain's welcome dinner.

A bell rang to signify that the ship was setting sail and a huge cheer went up from the deck. Mum was like a child in a sweetshop as she ran from one side of the ship to the other, worried that she might miss something as the ship sailed through the heart of Venice along the Guidecca Canal. As we passed palazzos, churches and St Mark's Square, I realised why sailing out of Venice was regarded as one of the world's most memorable cruise experiences.

When we got back to our room, there was a mini bottle of

champagne on the dressing table in an ice bucket along with two flutes and a bowlful of chocolate-dipped strawberries. I poured us a glass each and smiled, listening to Mum in the shower singing 'It's Amore'. She asked me to put her make-up on for her and I realised that I had never spent time doing things like this with Mum and it was lovely to be doing it. Feeling warm and gushy, I vowed to myself there and then that I would make more of an effort to be friends with Mum as well as her daughter.

We were both ever so slightly tipsy as we negotiated our way to the dining room. All the floors looked the same when you were sober, let alone half sloshed on champers, and we had no idea how we managed to locate both the dining room and our table, and lo and behold, we were only on the captain's table. Mum couldn't believe her luck when she found herself sitting next to the man himself as she fell into her seat. It wasn't the most graceful entrance she'd ever made, and we both tittered like teenagers as she dropped her handbag on the floor and the clasp came open and her lipstick and a packet of indigestion tablets fell out, along with a pair of pop socks. She giggled as she gathered them back into her bag and winked at me as all the other diners stared at us. We certainly weren't subtle in our arrival. We paced ourselves with a glass of water between each glass of wine, and as we had started to eat too, we didn't feel the effects too much.

The captain introduced himself to Mum and asked her what she did for a living. She explained that she was a dinner lady at the local primary school. Mum once confessed to me that the reason she took this was because she loved being around young children. She had admitted that because I was now single and with no sign of Mr Right on the horizon, she wasn't sure if she'd ever be a grandmother, so this was her way of getting to watch school plays and be part of the school community, which she'd missed out on so much when I was a child because she was always busy working, trying to keep a roof over our heads. She was such a proud lady and wouldn't have dreamt of accepting hand-outs from anyone, and she had brought me up to be hardworking, honest and to have integrity. Back then, she worked part-time in an office during the day and then did the odd shift in the local pub. She also did a couple of cleaning jobs and took in ironing, which she could do at home, frequently standing and ironing late into the night. I never appreciated until I grew up just how hard she worked and how much she relied on Aunty Jen and Uncle Tom, who would always look after me when Mum needed them to.

Mum's parents had both died in the last few years and even though they'd disowned her when they found out she was pregnant, she'd inherited enough money to pay off her mortgage. She took the dinner lady job mainly for enjoyment but also for a little bit of pocket money. She didn't want for much in her life so it suited her just fine and the local children and parents totally adored her. They made her a guest of honour at their school plays and concerts and always saved a seat for her in the front row. She also helped with a reading group at school too. Some of the children were struggling with their reading skills and as an avid reader, it was something that was incredibly important to Mum and she loved being able to play her part in helping the local children to read.

Watching Mum charming the pants off the captain all the way through dinner made me realise that I didn't really know her at all and I was determined to find out more about her on this holiday.

* * *

Swishing curtains and blinding brightness woke me, and Mum exclaiming 'Oh my word!' made me sit up and look out of the patio doors. 'Oh my word' indeed. The sun poured through the windows and the view of white-washed buildings with blue roofs told us that we had arrived in Greece.

'Come on, Maddy, get your dressing gown on. We can drink our tea out on the balcony.' I hadn't even heard Mum making any tea; obviously the swaying of the boat had lulled me into the land of nod where I'd stayed till this time. I looked at my watch. How on earth had I slept till 8 a.m.? And despite having had a little drinkie or two... OK, three – maybe four – last night, I was feeling relatively rejuvenated.

Mum read out the tours for the day, but they all sounded a bit energetic so we agreed that once we'd docked, we'd go into Athens and have a wander around on our own, then have a late lunch before heading back to the ship. We found a wonderful restaurant hidden up a side alley that the taxi driver had recommended after giving us a whistlestop tour. Tucking into chicken kebabs, pitta bread and tzatziki, while bouzouki music played in the background, we enjoyed a glass of chilled rosé as we watched the world go by. We were making such amazing memories on this trip and I took a quick photo on my phone and WhatsApped it to Beth. She replied with a smiley face. It was so nice to be sitting, whiling away some hours with Mum, and I was finally starting to relax, and Mum and I chatted more easily than we'd ever done before.

'Can I ask you something, Mum?'

'Of course, darling.'

'How do you feel about Edward?'

'Ah, Edward. He's lovely.'

'He is lovely, Mum. Do you see a future with him?'

'Who knows what the future will hold, darling, who knows. We'll just see what happens. What's meant to be will be.'

I supposed it was better to be like that than worrying about the future. She was so wise and I felt that I had a lot to learn from her even after all these years.

* * *

Another delicious meal that evening saw us sat with a whole new group of people comprising of two married couples and a family. I'd always thought cruises were for the older age range, but clearly times had changed and now it was becoming a really popular holiday choice for families too.

Mum loved the fact that there was a full-sized theatre on board. She'd found out from the people beside her that there was what promised to be a 'totally incredible illusion show, which will blow your mind' – and it most certainly did. We were totally astonished by the trickery and magic that left us completely baffled. When they asked for some audience participation, I was so surprised when Mum raised her hand and yelled 'Me, me!' at the top of her voice. It was obviously loud enough to catch the attention of the show's main illusionist who asked her to join him on stage. Mum had no inhibitions, and I started to remember that she had been like this before when I was younger and at an age where I found it embarrassing. I had told her so, in a huge row one day, so she had toned it all down for me. Now I was older and seeing her as a person in her own right, other than just my mum, I found it enchanting, and I stood and clapped her back to her seat when she'd done her part in the show.

'You're amazing, Mum. I do love you!' She smiled and kissed me on the cheek as she sat back in her chair, her eyes sparkling and mischievous. How did I not know this side of her? How refreshing to get to know her properly after all this time.

'Come on, darling, let's hit the casino.' Determined to make the most of every minute she was on board this floating hotel, she grabbed my hand and I laughed as she led me into yet another part of the ship that we hadn't explored fully. It would appear that she'd been doing her homework. Satisfied when she ended the night a hundred euros up, we headed off to bed quite exhausted.

* * *

It was incredibly refreshing to wake up in a different place each day, and the following morning we opened the curtains to a view of mountains and cream houses with terracotta roofs clustered on the hillsides. The tannoy announced our arrival in Dubrovnik.

After breakfast was served on the decking overlooking the port, we took the shuttle bus into the Old Town. The streets of the centre looked as if someone had been up polishing them all night. It was the cleanest place I had ever seen. We spent a day wandering through the pedestrian-only streets, visiting Baroque churches and stunning palazzos, and sat people-watching in a little café where we drank freshly brewed coffee and ate pastries.

We were shattered by the time we returned to the ship and had a lie down for half an hour out on the balcony before getting ready for what turned out to be the most exquisite five-course evening meal. To be honest, I was ready for bed after that, but Mum insisted that we could sleep when we got home and should appreciate every single opportunity that we had on the cruise, so we ended up watching a cabaret singer in one of the larger bars on board. A saunter around the top deck before bed made us both really weary, but what a magical day we had had and what wonderful memories we had made.

* * *

The next day was a sailing day as we headed back to Venice, and Mum brought the itinerary out to the balcony as we drank our morning tea. She told me that she was going to pottery painting at ten thirty, and line dancing at three. She invited me to join her but I wasn't totally sure she wanted me to, so I politely declined and said that I was going to lie on deck with a book and would meet up with her for lunch. I'd brought a book away with me that was all about making lists for the future. I felt that a bit of soul-searching was in order for me to move forward, and Beth's words about what the future held for me had really hit home. I wanted to spend some time thinking about what my hopes and dreams actually were these days. Beth had given me some magazines to look through to give me some inspiration and told me that when I got back, we were going to spend some time making vision boards. I'd heard of them before but didn't really know much about them, but when she explained in a little more detail, and I googled the definition once I'd gone home, it sounded like a fabulous idea. Beth never ceased to amaze me. I would never have imagined that she would know about things like this, but she told me that she'd been on a course and how she found that it had really helped her. She was going to order us both some cork boards and we were going to make a collage of words, pictures and affirmations of our dreams and desires. Apparently, when you put all these things together and applied the law of attraction, it would give you the motivation and inspiration to make all your wishes come true. It sounded too good to be true to me, and all a bit mumbo jumbo, but I was willing to give anything a go these days.

* * *

After breakfast, Mum went off to her class and I ordered a coffee from the bar and chose a sunbed overlooking the pool and jacuzzi areas. I sat and pondered life and what I was going to do with my future.

I allowed my mind to wander, and I must have drifted off to

sleep as I felt a shake of my arm and woke to see Mum standing over me, saying that she had finished her pottery class and was starving. I couldn't believe that after another mammoth sleep in, I'd then slept again. I was supposed to be filling my lists in. Although I supposed there would be plenty of time to do that over the next few weeks. We pottered off to the self-service buffet restaurant and surprised ourselves by filling our plates and scoffing the lot. Perhaps the sea air was giving us both an appetite.

People were wandering up to Mum while we were eating and chatting and laughing with her and I'd never seen her look so happy. I was now seeing Mum as Josie, a really kind, funny friend of mine who was incredibly good company, instead of *just* my mum.

After lunch we just sat around on deck, chatting. Being in the middle of the ocean with no land in sight, with a book in one hand and a cocktail in the other, made me feel incredibly at peace with the world. Nothing was required of me; food and drink were available at every moment of every day, and there was no worrying about the challenges and chores of work, which had taken over my life for so long. And more than anything, I was having a really lovely time with my mum. While she went off to her line-dancing session, I pondered life and realised that as we were heading back, there were some very important decisions I really needed to make my mind up about.

* * *

As we sailed back into Venice, we stood side by side on deck with our arms around each other, taking in the spectacular sights as we sailed past the Piazza San Marco and the entrance to the Grand Canal before docking in port. Sadly, we hadn't seen much of Venice as we'd flown straight in and would fly straight back out again, but we made a pact there and then to come back for a weekend really soon together and properly see the sights.

After a short wait in one of the bars, we disembarked and were ushered to an awaiting coach where, after a swift journey back to the airport, we were whisked through all the airport necessities and back onto a plane returning to the heady heights of the West Midlands. Mum looked exhausted as she laid her head on my shoulder and fell asleep before we'd even taken off.

As we flew over the clouds, my mind wandered off at a million miles an hour, and my dad popped into my head again. I found myself wondering again what he looked like, whether he was still alive, whether he'd ever had children – which meant that I might have brothers and sisters – and how Mum might feel if I ever decided I wanted to contact him. So many questions that I still wanted to ask were unfolding every time I allowed myself to think about him, but I was so grateful that I had more answers now than I'd ever had before.

When we sat in the taxi back to Giddywell from the airport, and spots of warm summer rain appeared on the window of the car, I wondered if that spectacular trip had really happened or if it was all a dream.

19

My first day back after the cruise was going to be a home day consisting of cleaning, washing and ironing, so I decided to make some homemade sausage rolls and cheese pies before I got started on the housework. I still couldn't believe I was cooking and baking. I had surprised myself by finding out that I was actually pretty good at it.

Not having time before for cooking had made me think that I couldn't do it. Eating home-cooked food was healthier and I enjoyed spending time doing it. Meals were all about the convenience these days, yet some of the things that our parents used to have to do, such as peeling the potatoes and preparing veg, filled time and were relaxing and seen as downtime from work. Quite proud of my pies and rolls, I left them to cool and thought I'd pop some round to Mum's on the way to the supermarket early that evening. Daft as it sounded, after spending all that lovely time with her, I'd felt quite lonely last night and I missed her company.

As the food was cooling on the side, I went upstairs to sort and gather the washing from my suitcase. Baxter was sitting in his basket, licking his lips ecstatically and looking mighty proud of himself when I came down – and then I noticed the half-eaten sausage rolls on the side. The little bugger had only gone and helped himself. Clearly nothing was safe, and it reminded me to make sure that any food left on the side was put away before I went anywhere.

Annoyed that I'd wasted time and hadn't got anything to take to Mum's, I popped to the supermarket and grabbed the essentials I needed and a bunch of flowers for Mum. She always loved fresh flowers. I decided to get some for Beth too, to thank her for such an amazing gift.

When I arrived, raised voices could be heard from outside the front door. I knew that Edward was there because his car was on the drive. I knocked on the door, let myself in and quietly said 'Hello!' But they clearly didn't hear me, because they didn't stop shouting at each other. My first thought was surprise that things weren't hunky-dory between them, as I had imagined.

I didn't know whether to go in or not, so I stood for a moment outside the kitchen door leaning against the hall wall.

But then I heard Mum shout, 'It's not time yet. If we tell her now, it'll break her heart. You have to go by my pace here, not yours. We've waited this long. She's got enough on her plate without you bulldozing in and throwing this into the mix. She's not strong enough.'

'I've already missed thirty-seven years of her life, Josie, and I'm not prepared to miss any more.'

Mum sighed and seemed to give up all her fight, and I heard her say, 'Don't do this to Maddy! We will tell her, but not right now. Please, Theo, I beg you!'

Theo? *Theo?* Why the hell was she calling Edward Theo? My mind was whirling around. And as the realisation hit me, I felt hot and clammy and I struggled to get my breath. I grabbed onto the bookshelf for balance and as it toppled towards me, I dropped the flowers I was holding, slid to the floor and passed out.

* * *

As I came round, I spluttered. Mum had shoved smelling salts right up my nose. Bloody hell! They were strong and made my eyes water. As my head started to steady, it all came back to me. Mum had called Edward Theo which, if I had got my sums right, made Edward my father. I just looked at Mum who was crying and trying to hug me. 'Oh, Maddy, you're OK.'

'Well, I think OK is probably an overstatement, don't you, Mum? I think you two have some explaining to do.' I looked from Mum to Edward, or should I say my father, Theo.

'On second thoughts, save it. I'm not fucking interested.' I got to my feet, grabbed my handbag and practically ran to the front door. I jumped in my car and screeched off the drive, nearly reversing into a lamppost. Mum was running down the path towards me, yelling my name. I just wanted to get the hell out of there. How could she have been lying to me? The only person I'd been able to rely on all my life? The one who had never let me down, *never*! And now this – the ultimate betrayal. Could I trust anyone in my life at all?

* * *

Skidding to a halt in the farm, my heart was pounding as I jumped out the car and slammed the door behind me. Racing over to the main house, I walked in and found Uncle Tom sitting at the kitchen table.

'Just breathe and calm down, Maddy. I've just had your mum on the phone. I know what's happened. Come here, darling.' He opened his arms to me and I just melted into them and broke down. I was sobbing so hard, I couldn't get any words out.

'Darling, don't say a word and just listen to me for a minute.'

I looked up at him and nodded.

'Now, I know you've had a huge shock. Huge. But you also need to know that not telling you about your father was a decision that your mum made because she thought it was the best thing to do at the time. You know in your heart that she would never intentionally do anything to hurt you. You mean the world to her. And that's the reason she was trying to find the right time to tell you. The one thing I've learned from being a parent is that there's never really a right time. You can only do what you think is the correct thing to do at that moment. Now go and wash your face and I'll pour you a nice big gin and tonic. Your mum is on her way over to talk to you.'

'But, but... I don't want to see her. Or him.'

'Did you just butt me?' Even through my tears, this standing joke raised a smile. Years ago, the farm was home to a lovely little Billy goat, who had a tendency to butt you up the bum. Uncle Tom, to his surprise and to our amusement, once got butted and asked the goat very seriously, 'Did you just butt me?' and Beth and I fell about laughing. Since then, whenever the word 'but' was mentioned, we always asked, 'Did you just butt me?'

'That's better. Now go on, go and sort that face out. It's horrendous!' He winked at me as I headed to the downstairs loo. As I passed the hall mirror I caught sight of myself. God, I did look ghastly. Mascara had streaked down my cheeks, and I was red and blotchy from the chest up. I sounded extremely snotty and my nose resembled Rudolph with a cold. Very attractive, indeed.

'Mad, are you OK?'

Oh great! The one person I didn't want to see me right now was the one person who was stood in front of me.

I hesitated, took a deep breath and turned. 'Alex, hi!'

'I hope you don't mind but I was in the room with Dad when your mum rang so I heard what happened. You must be feeling a little confused right now.'

Feeling confused was my permanent state of mind around Alex. Just looking at him made me feel warm and fuzzy even at a time like this. I couldn't take my eyes off him, but then I remembered that I looked like crap and excused myself to go to the loo. I wiped the mascara from under my eyes and splashed cold water on my cheeks to try to get rid of the redness. I bet Sophie never looked this awful. I wish I hated her but over the years I'd discovered that she was actually really nice too. I hadn't even known Alex was here. I wondered when he had come back. I wished he never had to go back to the States.

Voices were coming from the kitchen and I knew that Mum must have arrived. Taking a deep breath, I put my hand on the handle and opened the door. Thank goodness it was just her. I didn't think I could have coped if he had been there too.

She looked at me with tears in her ears and whispered, 'I'm so very sorry that you found out that way, Madison. That was never our intention.'

'So what exactly was your intention, Mum? When were you going to tell me?'

'I don't even know.' She steadied herself on one of the kitchen chair backs. She looked a bit wobbly and Uncle Tom took her arm, guided her over to the sink and poured her a glass of water.

'Come on, Josie, come and sit down and I'll leave you two to talk. Somewhere neutral will do you good.'

'We were working out when and how to tell you. Theo contacted me a few months ago. He'd been keeping in touch with a friend of his that we used to know and he tracked me down. He found some pictures on the Facebook page and said that he had recognised me immediately. He said he'd know my face anywhere and that I'd hardly changed. We've been trying to get to know each other again and spending a bit of time together, as you know. We wanted to make sure that you finding out about him was the right thing for you. You and no one else. It didn't really matter how it affected us. It was all about you, my darling. You just happened to walk into the middle of a conversation that you shouldn't have heard. But in hindsight, perhaps it's best that it's all out in the open now. Goodness knows when we'd have got round to telling you otherwise.'

'How do you feel about him now, Mum, after everything that happened all those years ago? Can you ever forgive him?'

'Darling, I've done lots of soul-searching over the years. I missed Theo so much even though I'd only known him for a short time, and as you know, I was completely devastated when he left. I've since found out some things, which I'll let him tell you when you're ready, that made the decision for him, and I know that he's thought about you every day of his life and has never regretted anything more.'

'So you do forgive him then? I'm not sure I ever can.'

'I think I have forgiven him. I'll never forget what happened; it shaped our lives. But I think you have to forgive to move forward. Forgiving someone is not about letting them off the hook for what they did, it's about freeing yourself of all those negative emotions and the hurt that can destroy you so that you can finally find some peace in your life. Not forgiving someone makes you bitter and angry at the world and I don't want to be those things any more. I've been those things for long enough. Forgiving gives you strength to carry on and have a normal life.'

'So how do you feel about him now?'

A huge sigh escaped from her lips. 'It's like there hasn't been nearly forty years between then and now. He seems to be the same man that I fell in love with all those years ago. He still makes me laugh and he still takes my breath away every time I look at him. I wish he didn't, but he does.' A tear trickled down her cheek, and I went to sit next to her and took her hand in mine. I was still angry with her and him, but she was my mum and I loved her dearly, and I would never want to see her in pain.

'I never once thought that you'd still love him.'

'Neither did I.' Mum rested her head on my shoulder and I pulled her close as she sighed again. 'What a blinking mess, eh?'

If she had chosen to forgive Theo, perhaps I should consider forgiving them both. If I did, maybe then we could all move forward. I just wasn't sure that I could.

* * *

The need to talk things through with Beth was overwhelming. I'd stayed away for far too long, making excuses because I didn't want her to quiz me over Jamie. I knew she would work me out straight away. But right now I needed my bestie to chat to. When I knocked on her bedroom door, she yelled, 'About bloody time! Get your arse in here, bitch!' Which sure broke the ice.

'Do you know what that was like for me? All that shouting going on and I hadn't got a bloody clue why. Now get your arse over here and tell me what the fuck is going on.'

I poured out the story from start to finish, leaving nothing unsaid. The whole Jamie business came out, and I told her about Theo too. Beth was always the most practical person I'd ever known. She just got right into sorting out a problem without all the dramatics that most people generated.

'So let's start with Jamie, shall we? That's quite easy to sort out. Do you love him?'

'I like being with him.'

'But do you love him, with the whole of your heart? Do you like the person you are when you are with him? Can you forgive him for what he's done to you? May I remind you that you caught him shagging someone else in your bed? Just in case you had forgotten.'

'I hadn't forgotten, but cheers for reminding me. I don't know if I love him and whether I'll ever be able to forgive him, but I think that I want to try. Perhaps working together and being together will be the making of us.'

'OK, well, I think you are a complete fucking idiot, but you're my fucking idiot and if you want to try to make it work with him, then do it. And I'll be here if it goes tits up again, to pick you back up. Problem One sorted. Now onto the very important matter of Theo.'

I smiled at how matter-of-fact she was. She wasn't actually as mad about Jamie as I thought she'd be; perhaps she'd already got an inkling.

'So, you've always pretended you were OK without a dad in your life, and you kind of adopted mine, which helped massively, but deep down you were always sad that your dad wasn't around, weren't you?'

'I suppose so.'

'OK, so, now your dad is here and you don't know whether you want him in your life or not. Is that right?'

'Yep, I suppose so.'

'So, Mrs List-Maker. Let's make a list. Get your notebook out.' God, she was bossy! Beth knew that I always carried at least one notebook around and I got one out and a pen and she instructed me to draw up two columns. One was titled 'No Theo' and one 'Yes Theo'.

On the 'No' list I wrote:

- *Never had a dad so not really missing out on what I never had*
- *I might hate having a dad in my life*
- *I might still yearn for a dad in my life*

On the 'Yes' list was:

- *Mum and Theo might become a couple*
- *Theo could give me great advice*
- *I might LOVE having a dad in my life*
- *Theo could give me support*
- *I won't have to wonder what it's like to have a dad in my life because I'll have one*
- *I might realise what I've missed out on all these years*
- *Theo is a nice man*
- *Theo could become my friend*

So it was clear that one list was way longer than the other, and the things on that list were actually starting to excite me. This could be my chance to have a proper relationship with my father. Whatever 'proper' in our situation meant. I looked at Beth and she smiled.

'Well, that's sorted that out then, hasn't it, love?'

I leaned across and gave her a hug. 'It's about time we got you sorted out then. Isn't it time you got your lazy fat arse out of bed?'

'Cheeky bitch! I'm going to my next physio session tomorrow. But my normal physio has left so apparently there's a new man. I'm dreading it, to be honest. Apparently he's not long left the army but thinks he's still in it. I was going to ask you if you could take me at all? Alex is busy and Dad's on dog duty. I have to be there at eleven. Would you mind?'

'Only if I can stay and watch him put you through your paces. Now that's something I'd pay to see. I'll come up and fetch you about quarter past ten; that'll give us time to get you to the hospital and I can drop you off and get parked and all that malarkey. I'm shattered, babe. I'm going home and getting into bed. Thank you for talking through everything with me, I really do appreciate it. I do love you, you know.'

'Be off with you, you big girl's blouse. See you tomorrow.'

* * *

As promised, the next morning I helped her down the stairs and into the car. She looked so uncomfortable but we knew that the only way she was going to get better was to keep moving and get this physio regime underway. Pulling up as near to the hospital entrance as I could, I got her comfy on a bench while I went off to find a parking space. Spotting one in the next row, I headed for it, only to have some tosser in a BMW convertible screech into the space I was just about to drive into. I lowered my window and shouted, 'Excuse me, I was just about to park there!' to him but he just grinned and shouted over, 'You snooze, you lose! Sorry, babe, it's clearly not your day. Good luck with finding a space!' What a knob – even if he was an incredibly good-looking one. It surprised me that I could still appreciate a handsome man even if I was pissed off, but I still shouted 'Dickhead!' as loud as I could at him and he grinned again and blew a kiss at me as he swaggered off towards the hospital entrance.

I spotted an old dear wearing a big winter coat, a headscarf and slippers shuffling over to her car and I waited another ten minutes for her to do a twenty-five point turn to get out and face the right way. The thought of how competently she would actually drive the car scared me to death as she kangaroo'd out of the car park. She raised her hand in thanks and as she drove past and beeped, I noticed that she'd got a sticker on the back of her car that said *Honk if you're horny!* which really made me titter and forget all about the dickhead who had nicked my parking space.

'Bloody hell, Maddy, where've you been? We're going to be late if we don't get a move on. We need to make a dash for it.'

We both laughed at that, bearing in mind that she was on crutches, and I didn't think either of us would be going anywhere in a hurry. We headed for the physiotherapy department and were asked to wait until Beth's name was called. She didn't want to sit down again, so we stood around waiting for Mr Miller.

'Beth Millington, please.' We turned towards the voice and, oh great!

'Yes, it's me. Pleased to meet you. My name is actually Dan Miller though, not Dick Head.' His eyes twinkled and I knew that he was one of those guys who would be able to get away with murder and who you couldn't stay angry with for long.

'Come on, Beth.'

I turned to see that she couldn't take her eyes off him. I whacked her on the arm to get her attention and bring her back in the room. 'Close your mouth, love, you're dribbling!'

She grinned and we followed Mr Miller into his consulting room. He invited me to take a seat next to the bed.

'I'm just going to get your notes. I'd like you to get on the bed please, Beth.'

He closed the curtain around the bed and we giggled like teenagers as Beth said, 'I'd like *you* to get on the bed please, Mr Physio. Phwoar! Cop a load of him. What a bloody hottie!'

'Still here but thank you, that's very kind,' came his husky voice from behind the curtain. Mortified, Beth's eyes became the size of saucers and she turned the colour of beetroot. I had an uncontrollable laughing fit and had to grab a bottle of water to calm me down, which went down the wrong way and I snorted out of my nose, making us even worse.

When Mr Miller came back to us, I couldn't look at Beth without laughing again, and he suggested that it might be better for all of us if I waited outside so he could concentrate on his patient. Beth nodded, still a little flushed. I took a seat in the waiting room and had to take lots of deep breaths to get back to some sort of normality. Beth came hobbling out after about half an hour, with Mr Miller helping her along.

'I haven't worked her too hard today, but she does have some exercises to do at home too. It's going to be tough, but the more she does, the quicker she'll mend and we'll soon be able to get rid of those crutches.'

'You're a hard taskmaster, Dan,' Beth said. 'But thank you. I do want to get back to work as soon as possible and get my life back to normal.' As we walked away, we heard a shout.

'Beth, here's my card. If you need anything' – he winked at her – 'anything at all, just give me a bell.' For the first time in a very long time, her face lit up as she took his card. Their hands touched and you could feel the spark between them sizzling away, and I rather hoped that this might be the start of something special for my bestie. I couldn't remember the last time she'd had any romance in her life. Seeing my friend under the influence of love gave me a warm and fuzzy feeling in my tummy.

* * *

I had agreed to meet Theo and Mum at the garden centre at the edge of the next village. It was always better to meet on neutral territory, I thought. That way if I wanted to strop off and have a tantrum, I could. My nerves were getting the better of me and I was all of a dither as I drove there. As soon as I walked into the café, I saw them sitting together at a table at the back of the room. Theo was tucking a strand of hair behind Mum's ear and she smiled at him bashfully, then she saw me and brushed his hand away. I smiled at her, realising just how much she must still love him. It was a true love story really, come full circle. I supposed we just needed to all work out how and where – and even *if* – we fitted in.

Theo stood as I arrived and I didn't quite know what to do next. Did we nod at each other, high five, bump fists, shake hands, kiss cheeks? I hadn't a clue. He took the decision out of my hands and gently kissed my cheek.

'Hello, Theo. Hi, Mum.'

I gave Mum a hug and walked round the table to sit opposite her. Theo sat too and immediately launched into a speech that he clearly couldn't wait to get out.

'Madison, can I just apologise profusely? I, and we, never for one moment intended for you to find out about me the way you did. It was the last thing either of us would want. Josie and I were working out the best way to tell you. And we hadn't come to a conclusion. I am so, so sorry. I wouldn't hurt you for the world. I promise you that.' He looked genuinely sad when he said this, and my heart reached out to him. 'You must feel like you can't trust us, but I promise that you can if you let me make it up to you.

'Before anything else though, I do feel that I owe you an explanation. I've gone through it with Josie' – he leaned over and touched her hand – 'and now it's time for me to explain myself to you.

'When I met your mother, I was in a very dark place. I'd met my wife Jean at school and we just seemed to drift into marriage. It was never a huge passionate love affair but it was a comfortable life. But then Jean became ill and was finally diagnosed with ME after many years of us not knowing what was wrong with her. She suffered with severe depression because of it, and to be honest, I was suffering with depression too but was too busy to deal with it at the time because I was looking after her. I worked hard all day and then was her carer when I came home at night. I was extremely fond of her. We rubbed along OK.

'From the moment I laid eyes on your mum, I fell madly and passionately in love with her, and that love just grew and grew. Being with her was so very different from being with Jean. I felt so bad for not telling your mum that I was already married and I also felt so guilty for having an affair, but I was young and stupid and mixed up. I thought that Jean wouldn't realise that I wasn't in the places that I said I was. I never thought that she'd suspect I was seeing someone else, but the night that I went home after your mum told me that she was pregnant, I don't know how, but Jean knew. She offered me an escape, but I couldn't possibly leave her. By that time, she was in a wheelchair and couldn't even get herself dressed. What sort of man would I be if I left her? But then what sort of a man was I for leaving your mum in that predicament? I couldn't win whichever decision I made. But I knew that your mum had her parents, who I thought would help her. Jean had no one; her own parents had died years before, which was probably one of the reasons why I felt that we should marry in the first place. If I'd left her she would have literally been alone, and I felt like I owed it to her.

'I've never forgotten Josie, or you. I wondered about you both every single day of my life, the moment my eyes opened every morning. What had happened to you after I'd told you that we couldn't be together? Whether you hated me? What did you look like? What sort of person would you turn into? Would not having me in your life affect you? Did you ever think of me? Would I ever get the chance to put things right? Or would I die never knowing you? The questions were eating me up inside.' Tears were trickling down his cheeks and he didn't even seem to notice. I looked at Mum and she smiled through her own tears. This was so hard for us all.

'When Jean found out she was dying, she made me promise to find you once she'd gone. She never would tell me how she knew. I thought I'd protected her from finding out. But I suppose there's always the potential for secrets to come out.'

I looked at Mum, and she was biting the inside of her cheek and looking down at her hands, where she was fiddling with her bracelet. I looked back to Edward and he looked deep into my eyes. Eyes that were my own, looking back at me.

'I know I've never been a father to you and you might choose to never forgive me for that. I know that I can never make up for all of these missed years, but I would love, if you would let me, to be a part of your future, and if that's a small part, or a big part, I would love nothing more. Josie and I have already discussed things and if you want me to walk out of both of your lives then I will, though it would cut me to the core. But that decision is yours and we both respect that whatever you say goes.'

I still hated the fact that they had not told me that Edward – Theo – was my dad, but before I knew these new facts, I had thought he seemed like a really nice man and I was finding it hard to change that view now.

At this point, Beth's words came back to me. I could either be bitter about everything that had happened and the fact that he'd missed out on so much of my life and I'd missed out on having a father and be miserable, or I could make my peace with the past, and move forward with him in my future. I thought about the lists I'd made and how the pros outweighed the cons and right now, as

I looked into my father's eyes and saw love and sincerity and honesty and affection looking back at me, I made my decision.

* * *

The shrill ringing of my mobile on the bedside table later that evening woke me. I rarely had an early night but was exhausted after all the complications of the day. I looked at the time. It was 10.45 p.m. I'd only been asleep for an hour. The phone ringing at that time of the night though nearly always signified bad news. 'Maddy, Maddy, you have to come to the hospital straight away. It's Theo!'

'I'm on my way, Mum.'

'Hurry, Madison. They think he's had a heart attack.'

I'd never got dressed so quickly in my life. With hair sticking up everywhere, I threw on a tracksuit, sent Beth a quick text to tell her what had happened and drove like the clappers to the hospital, breaking every speed limit on the way. So much ran through my mind as I pulled up in the A&E car park. I ran through the double doors where Mum was waiting for me and I flung myself into her arms.

'What happened, Mum?'

'He collapsed, clutching his chest. They think he might have had a heart attack... He's being checked over now.'

My own heart was beating so fast, I thought it might burst outside my body. How ironic, if anything happened to Theo now I'd found him and that mum was finally happy. I raised my head to heaven and silently asked everyone in my family who had ever died to look after Theo and prayed that he wouldn't be taken away from me now. How I could miss something that I never had was beyond me, yet I felt it to be true.

'Ms Young?'

'Yes, that's me,' Mum replied, petrified of what this nurse was going to tell her. It was after midnight by now and we were both anxious for news.

'I just wanted to let you know that Mr Knight has been checked over fully and he's absolutely fine. It wasn't a heart attack, thank goodness, it was just indigestion. Would you like to come through and see him?' She looked at me. 'And you are...?'

'His daughter, I'm his daughter.'

Mum smiled and took my hand.

'Can I come too?'

'Of course, dear. Follow me, please. I believe Mr Knight had curry for his dinner late last night. It would appear that curry doesn't suit him at all so I would advise against it in the future.'

As we walked into one of the cubicles, there was Theo, sat, looking very sheepish. And so he bloody should. Mum threw her arms around him and looked like she never wanted to let him go. We were both so relieved that he was OK.

'Has this happened before, Theo?' Mum quizzed him.

'Erm, once or twice, to be honest.'

'You silly man! Why didn't you tell me?' She took his hand and sat by his bedside as I sat the other side and took his other hand. 'Wouldn't it have been better for me to know, rather than to get you blue-lighted in the back of an ambulance?'

'I'm sorry, darling. I didn't want to spoil anything by talking about any health problems I had. I'd have felt a bit ridiculous, talking about my dodgy digestive system at such a pivotal point in our relationship.' He turned to me. 'I'm so sorry if I gave you both a scare.'

'From this moment on, there are to be no secrets, Theo. There've been enough secrets to last us a lifetime. Please promise me, no more.'

'I promise, Josie. I promise. No more secrets ever, girls. Perhaps we need a chat about my dodgy bowels at some point.'

Mum smiled through tears and snuggled into his shoulder. 'I'd be delighted to hear all about them when you're ready. I do love you, Theo Knight,' she whispered into his hair. 'More than you'll ever know.'

I decided to leave them to have some time to themselves and went off in search of a coffee for Mum and me. As I turned away from the machine, I literally bumped into a big burly body and the hot coffee went everywhere, including all over my hand.

'Ow, shit. That's hot!' I dropped the cup and the coffee splattered all over the floor.

'Gosh, I'm so sorry. Let's get that seen to quickly.' I'd collided with Dan the physio. He walked me through to the A&E department, and when we reached the reception desk, he leant over and kissed the young nurse on the cheek tenderly.

'Maria, sweetheart, I need your help. I've managed to make a tit of myself and spill boiling hot coffee all over this lovely lady. I've not made the best impression on her recently, so could you help her out?'

'Of course, Dan, come through into a cubicle and we'll take a look. Wait here, you lummox.'

Beth would be so disappointed that he was clearly in some sort of relationship with this young lady. You didn't just call people you knew 'sweetheart'. I knew that Beth really liked him too. She hadn't stopped talking about him all the way home from hospital and I knew she was really looking forward to seeing him at her next appointment. She'd sent him a text later that day, thanking him for everything he'd done to help her in their session that morning, and he'd said how much he was looking forward to seeing her again. I did wonder whether I should say something to this Maria. Perhaps she should know that he had given his number out to Beth and I really didn't think it was for medical reasons.

'My big brother is such an oaf. He's been a clumsy bugger since we were kids.' The relief that flooded through me was immense. It was his sister. Beth was safe.

'I just need to take some details from you: your name, address and date of birth type of stuff.' When I told her that I lived at Giddywell Grange, she looked up and then looked at the form that she was filling in for me because she'd wrapped my hand in ice. 'But your name is Madison, not Beth.'

I couldn't quite work out how she would know Beth, and I looked at her inquisitively. 'That's right, I'm Madison. I live in one of the barns on the farm but Beth is my best friend.'

'Ah, that explains it. Dan told me he'd met someone he really liked. He didn't know what to do about it, because she was his patient. And he mentioned that she lived at Giddywell Grange. He probably shouldn't have been discussing things like this with GDPR these days.' She rolled her eyes. 'Bloody GDPR! The world has gone mad; we won't be able to discuss anything soon. Please don't say that I've mentioned anything, he could get into serious trouble.'

'I won't say a word, I promise. I know she really likes Dan, and she wouldn't stop talking about him all the way home from her appointment. I do hope that something develops between them. I know that she's my best friend and I've known her all my life, but she's the most lovely, kind, generous, beautiful person in the world and any man who gets her is the luckiest man alive.'

'Well, Dan is the same then, but in a male body. Again, I know he's my older bro, but he's awesome. He's come all the way out here tonight to give me a lift home because my car is in the garage. He'd do anything for anyone. I know he can come across as being a bit brash at times but it's to cover up for the fact that he's actually quite shy. His army days are behind him now and he might learn that he doesn't have to act that way. He's definitely calming down and I would absolutely love to see him settled and happy. Maybe one day he'll have a family of his own, too. He's such a wonderful uncle to my two. They love him to bits and he completely adores them and spoils them rotten. In fact, that's probably why they love him to bits.' She laughed.

I thanked her for treating me and said that I hoped to see her again and went off in search of Mum and Theo who were apparently all sorted. Theo had been discharged and they were ready for a lift home. What a day this had turned out to be. I dropped Mum and Theo off at her house, kissed them both and drove home. It was 3 a.m. and I was absolutely shattered. I let Baxter out for a wee in the garden and then we headed straight for bed where he curled up in a ball at my side, licked my hand and started doggy snoring within a minute or two, his feet twitching. I wondered if he was dreaming about running wild in a field having fun.

I'd done lots of thinking about Jamie and had finally made up my mind. I would get in touch with him soon. There was no rush. I smiled and felt that my life was pretty good as I turned out the bedside lamp.

* * *

It was a little weird, going on a 'dad date'. I think most people thought that he was my sugar daddy, which tickled us both. We wanted to spend time together and get to know each other better, so two nights ago, Mum, Theo and I all wrote ideas down on pieces of paper, folded them up, put them in a jam jar and shook them up. We agreed that we had to do what came out whether we wanted to or not. Mum pulled out the winning date. Ice-skating. It was random, I know, and I hadn't skated since I'd been at school, but oh, what fun it was. We did ask Mum to join us but she was adamant that she wanted us to spend time together without her. We needed to build a relationship of our own and there would be plenty of time, if things worked out, for us to do things as a threesome in our funny little family. The idea of being part of a family of three was so weird, after all those years of it just being me and mum. But the future was ours for the taking and we could make this into anything we wanted to. We just had to find our own way and not worry about what other people thought.

Theo held out his gloved hand and I placed mine in his as we skated cautiously to start, and then with each lap of the rink our confidence started to build. When Theo fell over, we laughed so hard that we cried. We weren't the most elegant ice skaters in the world and we were sure that Torvill and Dean weren't worried about us taking their title, but we should have definitely got eleven out of ten for effort.

We grabbed a hot chocolate from a stand outside the rink and sat on a bench outside huddled together for a bit of heat. I'd forgotten how the cold in the ice rink got right through to your bones, and we needed to warm up. We decided to walk back along the canal. It was a lovely autumn evening and Theo took my hand and tucked it snugly inside his arm as we walked, chatting easily about his life out in Spain and my life over here. What surprised me most was that he said that he'd like to ask Mum out on an official date but didn't know how she'd feel or how I'd feel.

He knew that they'd grown closer since they'd been back in touch, but he wasn't sure how she'd feel about making it more. And he also needed to know how I would feel about it, and if I had any doubts about it at all then he would take a step back and wouldn't ask. He said that he wouldn't do anything that I wasn't happy about and that the most important thing in the world to him right now was to have a relationship with me. Knowing Mum like I did, I could clearly see that she was besotted by him, and I liked the person that she was around him. She was light-hearted, fun and flirty, and it was good to see her letting herself go.

It was with my blessing that I told him to go ahead and ask her. I was pretty sure what her answer would be. I knew that it would take time to find our way in our funny little three-way relationship, but we'd get there somehow and there was no rush. We'd waited this long.

When Theo dropped me back at the barn, he jumped out of the car and opened the door for me. He took my hand and looked deep into my eyes.

'Don't settle for anything less than the best in your life, Madison. Don't look back and have regrets. I had a good life, don't get me wrong, and Jean was a lovely woman, but she wasn't the person I fell madly in love with and wanted to be with. It makes me so sad that I missed everything about your life, but I swear that I will spend the rest of mine, until my dying day, making it up to you. But for you I want the very best; I'd hate you to settle for something less than you deserve. And you deserve the world.'

An image of Alex flashed into my head and I pushed it away. I tried to picture Jamie instead, but I couldn't visualise what he looked like right at that very moment.

'I'm sorry that I'm a bit of a mess right now, Theo. This redundancy business has hit me harder than I ever thought it would. I have to be honest with you; I've gone through my life, pushing myself as hard as I could. I never thought for one minute really that I'd ever meet you, but I wanted to make sure that if I did, I'd be a successful businesswoman that you'd be impressed by and want to know. It was really important to me and I think somewhere along the way, I forgot to be myself.'

'But look at you, darling. You are beautiful, you are bright, you are kind, and you are everything I could ever want a daughter to be. I never thought I'd get the opportunity to meet you either. I felt like I gave up the right to meet you when I decided to stay with Jean, but when she died, she told me that I had to make my peace with you and try my hardest to find you if it was the last thing I did.

'I wish you could see what I see. I see a person who is beautiful inside and out, someone who is kind and generous and who is helping out her best friend, and who wants her mum to be happy. Someone who is good and genuine and has a huge heart and someone who is giving a silly old man like me a chance to get to know her and to maybe have a second chance in her life.

'Life isn't about what you have, Madison; it's about who you are. And I couldn't wish for a more wonderful daughter than you and I am so incredibly grateful that you have allowed me to be a part of your life. I couldn't be more proud of the person that you are.'

I kissed his cheek, hugged him and told him that I'd see him very soon. He waited to make sure I'd got in through my front door before he walked back to his car. As I went to shut the door, I hesitated. I opened the door and shouted after him.

My voice wobbled. 'Wait!'

He turned towards me.

'Goodnight, *Dad*.'

He beamed at me.

'Goodnight, *daughter*.'

He blew a kiss and smiled. I beamed right back and closed the door.

* * *

So, that was Mum sorted. She and Theo were free to make a go of their relationship in any way they wanted. They had my blessing and they had to find their way forward the same way that Dad and I did. It still felt a bit strange to call him 'Dad', but it was good strange.

Now, it was my time.

Holding my breath, I dropped a text to Jamie, first thing the next morning, telling him that I'd like to see him that evening if possible so we could talk. Despite me asking him not to contact me until I'd made a decision and would get back to him, he'd been texting me on and off, asking me if I'd thought about his proposition. So I was quite surprised that it took him a while to text back, but when he did say he could be free, I asked him for his new address and said that I'd be there at 7 p.m. tonight after I'd had my dinner. I didn't want it to be any more than a chat at this point and I wanted to drive because I didn't want to end up drinking and be persuaded to spend the night. I wasn't ready to slip back into that just yet.

When I arrived, he buzzed me into the apartment, which was on the top floor of a four-storey block on a marina complex. He answered the door when I reached the top looking his usual dashing self, in a pair of beige linen trousers and a plain white t-shirt, designer of course. When he asked what I wanted to drink, I chose coffee; I wanted some time to look around this place while he made it and to get a feel for Jamie and his home. I wandered over to the window and the view was breathtakingly pretty over the marina, the canal boats gently swaying on the water.

The apartment was all black and cream, and it felt clinical. I thought about the muddy footprints that Baxter could have fun making on that carpet and smiled. I'd have to talk to Jamie about Baxter and see what he said. I couldn't give him up now. He was my friend, furry or not.

Jamie returned and we sat facing each other across the coffee table.

'Have you reached a decision, Maddy?'

'I have, and yes, I'd love to come back and work for you, Jamie.'

He stood and punched the air. 'Yes! Oh, Maddy, I'm over the moon. When do you want to start? I'm so excited that you've said yes.'

'And us, Jamie?'

'Oh, yes, and us too. I presumed that the two things went side by side.'

'Well, perhaps they might one day. But I want to take things very slowly and see where it takes us. Is that OK with you?'

'Of course, but please say that you'll start your job anyway. I have so many ideas that we can work on together.'

'Yes, I'll sort out when Beth is going to be able to get back to work and we can firm up a date to suit us both. Hope that's OK.'

'Of course, I'm so excited that we'll be working together, Maddy.'

His enthusiasm was infectious and he came around to my side of the table and took me in his arms. It felt a little forced, but I was sure I'd soon get used to it again before long. He went into the kitchen and I heard the fridge door open. He returned with a bottle of champagne and two flutes and popped the cork. 'We must celebrate!'

'Not too much for me, please, I'm driving.'

'You don't have to, Madison. You could stay.'

'That's not really taking it slow, is it, Jamie? I'm sorry but I'm not ready for that yet. And I have to get back to Baxter too.'

'Oh yes. Baxter.'

He handed me a glass which was full even though I'd asked for a small one. 'I'm so happy, darling, I really am.'

I realised that if we were to end up living together again at some point, we'd have to have a conversation about Baxter pretty soon. We came as a package these days and I wasn't sure how Jamie would feel about that, but now didn't feel like the right time to bring it up.

As I sipped the champagne (I think I actually preferred G&Ts these days, even though we used to drink champagne all the time) I wondered whether Jamie was as happy at the fact that we were going to try again with our relationship as he seemed to be about me being back in his business, but then I batted away that thought as we started to make plans about our future together.

20

After a few weeks of physio for Beth saw her returning to work, and as the seasons changed, it was soon well into autumn, and after plenty of days of me walking Baxter in the forest and watching the trees shed their leaves, it was time for me to start my new job.

Alex very kindly offered to take me to pick up my new company car so I didn't have to use public transport to get to my new office. It was only ten minutes in the car and as always when I was in close proximity to him, my heart rate increased and I got a little tongue-tied.

We chit-chatted about life and I tried to inject some enthusiasm into taking over in my new job, but to be totally honest, I was struggling.

Stopping at a service station along the way, Alex filled the car up with fuel and as he went in to pay, I watched him walk away from me. I felt like he'd spent my whole life walking away from me.

As he got back into the car and switched the ignition on, his car system told him that he'd missed a call and that his voicemail was calling him. Sophie's voice rang out from every speaker in the car.

> 'Hi, Alex it's me. I hope you have found Madison and told her how you really feel.'

Alex looked absolutely mortified and desperately started pressing every button he could to stop the call, but it wouldn't stop playing.

> 'I can see it in your eyes every time her name is mentioned. I can see it more than ever when you are in the same room. You can't take your eyes off her. I know that you've tried to fight it and to just be friends, and I know that in your own way you've tried to make our relationship work, but if there are three people when there should only be two, it can never work.'

Alex was frantically swatting at every button to turn it off but still her voice went on.

> 'Thank you for letting me go to make a new life for myself. I will always love you, Alex, but it was never quite enough and your heart never fully belonged to me. Go get your girl, my love. Life is too short to have regrets. Be happy and take care.'

I could not believe what I had just heard. That wasn't right! Alex had never been interested in me in that way – he'd proved that by going off to America to be with Sophie. I looked up at him and he was staring ahead in horror. His face was bright red and he was sweating.

'God it's hot in here,' he said and put all the windows down. 'We'd better get you to your new job.'

'But Alex—'

'Just leave it, Mad. Please.'

We spent the rest of the journey in total silence, Alex continuously taking one hand off the steering wheel, rubbing his hand across the back of his neck. I kept sneaking glances at him, willing him to look across at me, but he just stared ahead. A few times, I went to speak but thought better of it.

My head was in a total spin when I got to the office. When I got out of the car, Alex said he'd hang around for a bit until he knew everything was sorted out and to make sure that everything was OK with the company car before he drove off.

When I arrived, Jamie was waiting for me in reception and led me up a flight of stairs and through into a main boardroom which was full of around fifteen people. There was a bottle of champagne on the table and I walked in to a round of applause. Jamie tapped the side of his glass with a spoon.

'Can I have your attention please, ladies and gents. I'd like to officially welcome Madison Young into our company today. I can't tell you how delighted I was when she agreed to be on the board of directors here with me. And I can't tell you now how delighted I am to ask Maddy to make me the happiest man in the world and agree to be not just my business partner, but also my wife.'

Shock and horror were my very first emotions as he made his announcement. Embarrassment came next as he went down on one knee and produced a black velvet box from his jacket pocket and opened it. There was the most exquisite diamond ring I had ever seen. I looked around the room and all these faces were staring back at me in anticipation. I couldn't speak. I couldn't get my breath. A whoosh of air hit me and my head started to spin. That was when I passed out.

I came round to hushed whispers and found I was sitting on a seat next to an open window with people fussing around me. I asked someone to get my handbag and I rummaged around inside for some tissues. My hand touched something plastic and I smiled as I took a poo bag from my handbag. Oh how my life had changed over the last three months. Where I was once happy in Louboutins, I was now so much happier in wellies. Where I was once so taken with Mulberry handbags, I was now happier to see poo bags. And even though I was back in the world of work of PR where I once felt I belonged, I still felt like there was something missing.

I turned to the window and took some big gasping breaths and that was when I saw him.

Alex was still standing, leaning with his back against his car, smouldering and tapping away on his phone. He'd been a big brother figure all my life and I'd always looked up to him. But that message from Sophie blew my mind. What if he really did love me? What if she had spoken the truth?

Jamie coughed and broke the spell. 'How are you feeling, darling? I'm sorry I shocked you. I think we're all still waiting for your answer though.'

A pressure was crushing against my chest and I turned to the window once more. Alex looked up. We locked eyes. For a moment, time stopped. I grinned at him. He grinned back.

My tummy did that very jittery thing that it did every time he looked at me in that way. It was like a rocket had just launched in my heart. And I realised exactly what was missing from my life: him.

'I'm so sorry, Jamie, but I just can't do this. Any of this. I really am sorry.'

I picked up my things and walked out of the boardroom past enquiring faces and practically ran down the stairs, feeling so much better as I walked out of the reception doors towards Alex, taking in once more just how totally unaware of exactly how handsome he was. He held his hand out to me and I took it. Our fingers linked and intertwined. Our hands fit together perfectly.

I moved nearer and grabbed him by the lapels, pulling him close until there was no space between us, and reached up on tiptoe. This was the moment I had dreamed of so many times. My lips brushed softly against his. A shiver ran down my spine as the bristles of his stubble gently scratched against my chin and his arms wrapped around my back. Our lips moulded together in perfect sync. We kissed, soft and slow. A low moan escaped from him and I pulled away and looked deep into his eyes.

Alex pulled the clip from my hair and ran his fingers through it, shaking it loose. 'That's better.'

'I love you, Alex Millington. I always have and I always will. Why didn't I just marry you and have your babies twenty years ago?'

He took my face in his hands and his thumbs caressed my cheeks, this man that I had loved for the whole of my life. He kissed me back tenderly at first, but then more passionately. I was sure he was totally oblivious to the fact that a billion and one fireworks were exploding in my heart when he replied, 'It's never too late!'

EPILOGUE

THREE MONTHS LATER

Beth turns to me and I hand her the angel. The last two hours have been spent decorating the seven-foot-high Christmas tree, which I have to say is looking absolutely stunning in the corner of the lounge in the farmhouse. Flames flicker in the open fire, and a garland entwined with fairy lights adorns the huge wooden mantelpiece. Beth kisses the angel, stands on the stepladder and reaches to place her on the top of the tree.

'Merry Christmas, Mum,' she whispers.

I offer her my hand and she very carefully lowers herself to the ground. She's doing really well but I know she's still got some way to go. She's so happy in her new relationship with Dan and he's helping her massively with her recuperation. Once they'd got round the ethical issue of him having a relationship with a patient, and his boss had suggested that he passed her on to another physio, they'd been inseparable.

'Go on then, turn on the lights,' I say.

The tree lights up beautifully, twinkling brightly, and the glass baubles hanging off the tree create sparkly patterns on the ceiling.

A sudden loud bang makes us both jump, as we're plunged into darkness, the only light coming from the fire.

'What the bloody hell...?'

Uncle Tom and Alex fling open the door and barge into the lounge where Beth and I are giggling.

'It's only a fuse, I'm sure. I'll go and check.' Beth opens the bureau door and grabs a candle, going over to the fire to light it, and walks into the hallway to find the fuse box.

Hands caress my back and work their way down to my bottom.

'I do hope that's you, Alex Millington, and not your father.'

His breath is hot against my ear. 'I could do anything I want to you now and no one apart from you and I would ever know.' A moan escapes his lips and I can feel that's he's turned on.

We spring apart like two teenagers being caught out as the lights come back on and we notice that a bulb in one of the side lamps is not on. Alex adjusts his trousers and it makes me smile.

'Just a faulty bulb then,' Uncle Tom explains. 'Good job it was nothing more serious; I don't know how we'd cook that massive turkey in the morning otherwise.'

Tomorrow is a big day and now that the tree is done, and the vegetables all prepped, we can go to bed.

* * *

'Happy Christmas, gorgeous,' he whispers into my ear as he presses up against my back.

'Is that a pistol?' I laugh at him and he flips me over and grins as he pins me underneath him. He kisses me tenderly and then more passionately. God, I love this man. The last three months have been the most incredible time of my life. My body tingles as he gently nudges my knees apart with his and I glance over at the bedside clock.

'Shit!' I push him off me and jump out of bed. 'Alex, it's 7 a.m. I needed to get the turkey in at five! I must have slept through the alarm. If I don't go and do it now, we won't be eating Christmas dinner until ten o'clock tonight!'

'Come back to bed babe, I've done it.'

I am confused, so he explains that he heard the alarm go off and because I looked so comfortable, he turned it off, left me sleeping, and followed the instructions I'd written on a note propped up on the kitchen table. He'd put bacon over the top of the turkey, seasoned it and stuffed it and had put it in the Aga.

'Oooh, you are wonderful.'

'I know! And I'm so glad I did because now we can get back to what we started a minute ago.' He grins at me. I love that grin, full of mischievousness and sexy as hell. I get back into bed and he kisses me. I forget all about the turkey.

There's a knock at the bedroom door and it bursts open as Beth shouts, 'Coming in!' and walks straight in with a tea tray, and Baxter leaps onto the bed. Once more, Alex and I spring apart.

'Oops, sorry! Hope I'm not stopping you getting some Christmas action there, bro, but I've brought you both a cuppa. Couldn't sleep!'

'Seriously, Beth. You did that to us once before at Mad's eighteenth birthday party when I was just about to snog her. You were such an annoying little sister then, and some things never change, do they?'

'Oh, you love me really! And you know it.'

I gaze at Alex. It's the first time in nearly twenty years that he's ever spoken of that night. So he does remember, after all.

'Oh how our lives may have been different if you hadn't interrupted us that night, sis. We might have been celebrating our china anniversary soon.'

'Shove over!' she says as she wriggles her way into bed with us, grinning inanely. This double bed was made for two, not three and a medium-sized dog who is now sprawled out upside down, letting it all hang out.

Mum and Theo stayed at the barn last night so that we could all be together on Christmas morning, so Alex and I spent the night in his old room at the farm. Our first Christmas together as one big happy family.

We drink our tea and Alex tells Beth to bugger off back to her own room, while we get dressed. She does make me laugh. I'm so glad that she's nearly made a full recovery from her operation. She's very lucky, and we're so very lucky to have her in our lives.

'Don't think that I've forgotten what we were just about to do, young lady, I'll be calling in my debts later!' Alex winks at me suggestively as he leaves the room. The smell of smoky bacon wafts up the stairs through the open door and my stomach rumbles.

I grab a quick shower, pull my hair into a ponytail and head on down to the kitchen where Uncle Tom is standing at the cooker in a pinny, making a huge pile of bacon sandwiches. I grab one from the plate as I sweep pass him and kiss his cheek, wishing him a Merry Christmas.

'I'm just going to go into the office and Skype Alice, will you all pop by and say hi? Come on, Bax. She'll be dying to see you.'

Morning for us is Alice's evening, so it's a perfect time to call her. She answers immediately, her sister sitting beside her. She looks wonderful; a healthy tan and fresh air seem to be doing her the world of good.

'Come here, Bax. Merry Christmas, ladies.' He jumps up onto my lap and Alice laughs at the fact that he is dressed as a little Christmas elf.

'Oh Baxter, my darling, how are you? How is he, Madison? And how are you all? Did the presents arrive?' Alice has very kindly sent a parcel over with presents for us all, but the biggest presents are for her fur baby.

Half an hour later, we've caught up on all of the news from this side of the world and theirs. Mum and Uncle Tom have popped in to say hello and Alex finally joins me. It is so lovely to see Alice so well and enjoying herself, and we leave the call saying that we'll catch up again on New Year's Eve.

Alex turns and kisses me tenderly.

'Alex, I have something to tell you. I'm glad you're here, I wanted a quiet moment. Sit down. It's important.'

'Bucks Fizz anyone?' shouts Beth as she bursts into the room. She's done it again. It's a good job I love the bones of her.

'Alex? Can you come and give me a hand please?' yells Uncle Tom from the kitchen. Alex looks at me and grimaces.

'It's OK, babe, it can wait. We'll talk later.'

* * *

A glance at the clock as I wander up the hall tells me that if we want to get dinner at a respectable time, we all need to get a move on. I pause at the door of the dining room. It's a stunning room, ornate yet cosy with a huge oak table in the centre of the room surrounded by eleven chairs. Beth and I laid the table last night before we sorted the tree and it looks beautiful.

As I look around at the table, at the nameplates and the table presents, I think about how much my life has changed over the last year. In spring, I was made redundant and I was devastated. It felt like my life would never be the same. It wasn't, but Beth's operation, while painful and inconvenient, meant that I could use my time doing the things that she did. All those things that I'd always thought were dull and boring were actually the most fulfilling things that I've ever done. They filled my heart and my soul with joy in a way that I'd never experienced before. I've learned over the past few months that things are not important, but time is; that we should educate our future generations not to be rich, but to be happy. These days, I don't count the things I have, but the memories I make and the people I meet along the way.

The kitchen is chaos as there are definitely too many cooks, and all of them are trying to be in charge. I shout at everyone to go and sit down so that I can serve lunch.

As I stand at the dining room door, a hush falls across the room. I look around the table. Uncle Tom sits at the head of the table, with Mum and Theo giggling like teenagers to his left and Rebecca and her younger two children and Russell to his right. He smiles at her tenderly and as he pats her hand, I see a special look pass between them and my heart lifts. Uncle Tom deserves love and so does Rebecca after everything she has gone through.

Beth sits next to the children and she smiles lovingly at Dan, who has just arrived after spending the morning with his sister and their children.

Alex bowls into the room and takes his seat. He's just popped two plated up Christmas dinners over to the Darbys' house. They couldn't get out to join us for Christmas so we've taken it to them.

Between my dad and Alex there is an empty chair, which I slide into, between a man who I didn't even know six months ago, and another who I have loved all my life and never knew had always loved me right back.

Under the table, hoping that some food might fall onto the floor, or that if he nudges people's legs enough, they might just feed him some titbits, is my furry friend, Baxter. He was in disgrace for about five minutes earlier because when we weren't looking, he jumped up to the kitchen table and nicked some pigs in blankets off a plate. The poor dog was tantalised by the smell of the turkey cooking and obviously thought he'd treat himself, so we hadn't the heart to let him sulk for too long after being told off.

I'm so glad that Dad is in our lives. He really is a lovely man, and he makes Mum really happy. The past is in the past. We are all really enjoying getting to know him better. Her hand is under the table and he's holding it.

'Tell them!' I can hear him whispering to her. Something sparkles under the table and my heart feels like it could burst right open.

'Mum, show me your hand!'

'Erm, what did you say, Madison?'

'Don't play for time, Mum. I know your game. Put your hand on the table.'

She laughs, takes her hand from her lap and places it in front of her. On the third finger of her left hand, a huge diamond solitaire ring catches the light and sparkles away. A collective intake of breath comes from the table and I get up and hug them both and tell them how happy I am for them.

'I didn't know a thing about it, Madison, until I opened the present this morning. I hope you don't mind.' She looks at me nervously.

'Of course I don't mind, Mum. And I hope you like it. It took Theo and me a while to choose the right one.' I hug her tightly to me. 'I'm so happy for you, Mum. I really am.'

'You knew! You little madam. I can't believe it.'

'You don't think I'd have done it without checking with Maddy first, do you, Josie?' Theo asks. 'Can you imagine what a hard time she'd have given me?'

I grin at my dad and squeeze his hand.

On the mantelpiece is a photograph of a smiling Aunty Jen. She appears to be watching over the table and I know that she'd approve of all the changes that have happened over this year.

She'd want her children to be happy, and her husband to find love again.

I look around at my family. Family comes in all shapes and sizes, but they are still a family in every way. Family isn't always blood, it's the people in your life who accept you and love you for what you are and not for what you have; the people who would do anything to make you happy and who love you unconditionally.

I stare at the photograph, and she looks like she's staring straight back into my eyes. Putting my hand on my stomach protectively, I raise my glass of orange juice and make a silent toast to her. My news can wait until later; I don't want to rain on Mum's parade right now.

When I break my news this time, no one is going to interrupt me. After all, there's plenty of time before two become three in our little part of this dysfunctional, amazing and wonderful family that I love with all my heart.

A LETTER FROM KIM

Thanks so much for reading *Escape to the Country*.

I do hope you enjoyed it. If you did, I would be eternally grateful if you might leave a short review. I'd love to hear what you think and it's super helpful for new readers to discover my books.

You can also contact me via my Facebook page, through Twitter or my website.

http://www.facebook.com/KimTheBookWorm

@KimTheBookworm

https://www.kimthebookworm.co.uk/

Thanks

Kim

Xxx

ACKNOWLEDGMENTS

Once again, there are so many people to acknowledge when writing a book and firstly my thanks from the bottom of my heart go out to every single person who has read *Escape to the Country* and to those who have left a review or got in touch with me to tell me how much they loved it. It really is very much appreciated.

The support that I have received from the world of books and the friends that I've made along the way has been fantastic. In a world where everyone is competing for the same reading space, the author community is such a great place to be, with kindness, wisdom and inspiration being passed on. It's an amazing industry and I'm so very grateful to be part of it. I really do value every single DM, PM, tweet, retweet, blog post, Facebook post, comment and your general support. The book blogging community that I mix in is truly marvellous and your passion for books and helping authors just like me every single day is mind-blowing! Don't let anyone ever dull your blogging sparkle!

Thank you to Keshini and Lindsey at Hera Books for giving me the opportunity and for making my dreams of becoming a published author come true. Also huge thanks to Emily Yau and Boldwood Books for re-launching them into the book world.

To Rachel Gilbey, who has once again arranged another staggering blog tour to launch my second book into the world. You are amazing, lady! Thank you!

To my Bookworms United book club buddies! You rock girls! Love you all! Here's to making many more fabulous memories.

To my Bookouture work family, you are so awesome, gifted and encouraging. An absolute pleasure to work with every single day!

And to the Bookouture Author Lounge. Your wit, talent, generosity and advice are beyond awesome and so much appreciated. You are all so inspirational and I love you all!

To my sister Lisa, thank you for embarrassing me by telling everyone that your little sister is now an author! Thanks for being my cheerleader and for sending me the most hilarious text messages, which you don't intend to send. Love you!

To my oldest friend Bev. Thanks so much for being my friend when we were in Girls' Brigade and for still being my bestie today! Thanks for the get-togethers we still have, which always make me smile! Love you!

And finally to Ollie and Roni, for putting up with me writing, editing, talking about writing and editing, moaning about writing and editing and then listening to me loving writing and editing! I love you both so much.

Ollie, you've had a huge summer while I've been writing *Escape to the Country*. I'm so proud of how you have taken everything in your stride. You make me laugh every single day and I adore you.

Roni, thank you for trusting Ollie and me to rescue you and for making our home an even better place to be.

ABOUT THE AUTHOR

Kim Nash is the author of uplifting, romantic fiction and an energetic blogger alongside her day job as Digital Publicity Director at Bookouture.

Sign up to Kim Nash's mailing list for news, competitions and updates on future books.

Visit Kim's website: https://www.kimthebookworm.co.uk/

Follow Kim on social media here:

facebook.com/KimTheBookWorm
x.com/KimTheBookworm
instagram.com/kim_the_bookworm
bookbub.com/authors/kim-nash

ALSO BY KIM NASH

The Cornish Cove Series

Hopeful Hearts at the Cornish Cove

Finding Family at the Cornish Cove

Making Memories at the Cornish Cove

Standalone

Amazing Grace

Escape to the Country

Printed in Great Britain
by Amazon

44196105R00156